CASTLE CORVINUS WAS UNDER SIEGE

A mob surrounded the castle, yelling furiously and shaking their fists at the mammoth stone fortress. From their crude attire, Lucian judged the men to be primarily peasants and villagers from the surrounding countryside. Pitchforks, scythes, and flesh-hooks waved above the crowd, along with a surfeit of crosses and wooden stakes.

"Death to the demons!" a strident male voice called out, and dozens of other throats took up the cry.

"Death to the demons!"

Lucian cursed under his breath. It was just as Lady Ilona had feared; the marauding lycans had driven the victimized mortals to rise up against the immortals in their midst. . . .

UNDERWORLD
BLOOD ENEMY

A NOVEL BY GREG COX

BASED ON THE CHARACTERS CREATED BY
KEVIN GREVIOUX AND
LEN WISEMAN & DANNY McBRIDE

POCKET STAR BOOKS
New York London Toronto Sydney

An *Original* Publication of POCKET BOOKS

 A Pocket Star Book published by
POCKET BOOKS, a division of Simon & Schuster, Inc.
1230 Avenue of the Americas, New York, NY 10020

This book is a work of fiction. Names, characters, places and
incidents are products of the author's imagination or are used
fictitiously. Any resemblance to actual events or locales or persons, living or dead, is entirely coincidental.

ISBN: 0-7434-8072-4

First Pocket Books paperback edition December 2004

10 9 8 7 6 5 4 3 2 1

POCKET STAR BOOKS and colophon are registered
trademarks of Simon & Schuster, Inc.

Manufactured in the United States of America

For information regarding special discounts for bulk
purchases, please contact Simon & Schuster Special Sales at
1-800-456-6798 or business@simonandschuster.com.

Now

A.D. 2002

Chapter One

BUDAPEST

A full moon shone down on the graveyard of history.

Statue Park—or Szoborpark, as it was known to locals—was a repository for all the immense Communist monuments that had once dominated the Hungarian capital during the long years of Soviet oppression. After the Communists were finally ousted, their imposing statuary was removed from perches throughout the city and exiled to this desolate field on the outskirts of Budapest, surrounded by red brick walls and industrial-strength power lines. Now towering figures of Marx, Lenin, Engels, and other heroes of revolution, arranged in overlapping rings, stared silently at one another, condemned to eternal obsolescence and irrelevance.

By day, Statue Park was a popular tourist attraction, luring curious hordes to gawk at the outmoded monuments. But tonight, only a few minutes short of midnight, the park was totally deserted.

Or, at least, it appeared to be.

Selene hid behind a huge bronze portrait of a flag-waving revolutionary. Her dark brown hair and glossy black trench coat blended with the shadows cast by the lambent moon as she kept careful watch over the park below. A pair of matching Berettas were holstered beneath her coat, and her slender fingers gripped an expensive night-vision camera. She waited impatiently for an opportunity to use both the camera and the guns.

Especially the guns.

She paid no heed to the monuments looming around her, whose historical significance meant little to her. The Cold War may have ended, but her own war continued, just as it had for the better part of a thousand years. A shadow war fought by immortal creatures of the night, vampires versus werewolves.

Soon, she thought. Tonight's prey had not yet arrived, but if her informants were to be believed, it would not be much longer now. *Let's hope our intel is correct.* She ran her tongue over her fangs in anticipation of the hunt to come. Beneath her oiled black leathers, her lithe body was tensed for action. *I haven't killed a lycan in weeks. . . .*

As a Death Dealer, a member of an elite corps of vampire warriors, Selene was sworn to the destruction of her people's ancient foes. For centuries, she had known no other calling—nor had she desired any.

She glanced across the empty park, checking to see if her partner was in place. Directly opposite her, on the other side of the park, a large granite bust of a forgotten Communist leader looked out over the gravel pathways winding around the collected monuments. Selene could not see Diego lurking behind the mammoth bust, so she raised her hand to signal him. Her smooth white fingers glowed like polished ivory in the moonlight.

An answering wave greeted her from across the way.

Good, she thought, lowering her hand. Everything was in order. A cool summer breeze blew toward the rear of the park, carrying the scent of the two Death Dealers away from the front gate. With luck, the lycans would never know she and Diego were there, until it was too late. *As long as the wind doesn't shift, that is.*

The sound of an approaching car sent her pulse racing. She ducked behind the bronze revolutionary, pressing her face and body against the cold metal as though to merge completely with the shadows draping the sheltering statue. Her own Jaguar was discreetly parked several blocks away in the adjacent housing complex.

A mud-spattered gray van stopped in front of the park, which was marked by a classical brick façade. Selene watched as the van disgorged a trio of shadowy figures, who furtively entered the park by means of an inconspicuous side door next to the main gate.

The trio consisted of two men and one woman, with feral eyes and sullen expressions. Their shabby brown leather jackets looked cheaper and grungier than Selene's own sleek black leathers. *Typical lycan scum,* she thought, studying the three intruders through the high-powered lens of her camera. Their human appearance did not deceive her. She knew lycanthropes when she saw them.

The mere sight of the creatures enraged her, and she had to fight the temptation to draw her Berettas and start filling the unsuspecting lycans with red-hot silver. Even after hundreds of years, her hatred of the loathsome beasts burned as fiercely as ever. The sooner they were all exterminated, the better.

But not just yet, she reminded herself. Tonight's primary objective was reconnaissance: to find out what the lycans were up to and perhaps even trail them back to their secret lair. Once she and Diego discovered where the entire pack was hiding, they could lead a squadron of Death Dealers in to clean out the den completely—but only if she could be patient. *I have to let these three live—for now—if I want to kill them all later on.*

That didn't make holding her fire any easier.

The three lycans reached the center of the park, a small island of grass surrounded by gravel, and looked around suspiciously. "Where is he?" the woman asked. Her greasy blond hair looked as if it hadn't seen a comb in weeks.

"He'll be here," one of the men said gruffly. From his tone and posture, Selene guessed he was the alpha male. A muscular black man with a shaven skull, he had possibly the deepest voice she had ever heard. His right hand gripped the handle of a scuffed leather briefcase. "Just be ready."

"You bet," the second male said. Spiky black hair, Caucasian features, and a slighter build distinguished him from his leader. A gold tooth glittered in the moonlight.

He and the female drew automatic pistols from beneath their jackets, while the bald lycan rested his briefcase on the ground beside his boots. Wary eyes scanned the moonlit park, forcing Selene to retreat farther behind the tarnished bronze proletarian.

The female Death Dealer silently cursed the glowing orb overhead. The full moon posed a double threat to her; not only did it increase her risk of exposure, but it also meant that her lycan targets were at their most dangerous. It was surely no coincidence that the lycans had chosen tonight of all nights to venture out into the open.

If the wind shifted, Selene understood, things could get hairy, in more ways than one.

The sound of a second vehicle approaching distracted

the lycans from their relentless scrutiny of their surroundings, much to Selene's relief. She swung her camera toward the parking lot, where a gleaming black limousine had pulled up in front of the gate. Four passengers emerged from the limo.

The new arrivals turned out to be a middle-aged human male accompanied by three thuggish bodyguards. Selene recognized the older man as Leonid Florescu, a well-known arms dealer. A stout man in an expensive silk suit, Florescu had ruddy skin and slicked-back silver hair. His well-groomed appearance stood in marked contrast to the scruffy attire of the waiting lycans, not to mention that of his own hulking bodyguards.

Leonid himself, right on schedule, Selene thought with satisfaction. She made sure to get a good shot of the mortal's florid countenance. *Seems my informant knew what she was talking about. . . .*

Florescu and his goons joined the three lycans at the center of the park. Facing off in the moonlight, the two parties exchanged intimidating glares and scowls. Florescu's men drew their own guns in imitation of the armed lycans.

The alpha-male lycan did not waste time with small talk. "Do you have the sample?" he demanded. His basso profundo voice echoed in the stillness of the night.

"Of course," Florescu replied. Despite his confident tone, Selene detected a note of trepidation in his voice. She didn't blame him; bodyguards or not, any one of the lycans could easily reduce him to a midnight snack. "I'm a professional."

He snapped his fingers and one of his men stepped forward, bearing a large metal case. Florescu opened the case and removed an Uzi submachine gun.

The lycan leader eagerly snatched the weapon from Florescu's hands. He examined the Uzi carefully, testing its weight and heft. His dark eyes peered down the gun sight, taking aim on the various bronze and granite figures surrounding him.

Ever the salesman, Florescu rattled off specs while his potential customer inspected the merchandise. "Muzzle velocity four hundred meters per second; effective range two hundred meters; rate of fire six hundred rpm." He glanced nervously at his watch, as though anxious to conclude the encounter. "Strictly top-of-the-line quality. Only the best, I assure you."

Lowering the weapon, the lycan leader grunted in satisfaction. "We'll take fifty," he announced, handing the Uzi off to one of his scruffy associates, "plus a thousand rounds of ammo." He lifted the briefcase from the ground and opened it in front of Florescu. Selene glimpsed stacks of multicolored bills, mostly euros and American dollars. "A down payment," the lycan said, "as discussed."

To Selene's surprise, Florescu didn't even bother to count the cash. "Excellent," he declared, hastily accepting the briefcase. His gaze darted toward his waiting limo. "As always, a pleasure doing business with you."

So that's where the lycans have been getting their ordnance, Selene thought, feeling a surge of vindication. She had long suspected Florescu of supplying the lycans, but now she had definitive proof to present to Kraven back at the mansion. *There's no way he can dismiss my evidence this time.*

Ironically, Florescu was also the primary source for most of the coven's weapons and ammunition. In other words, he'd been providing firepower for both sides in the war. *I think someone's going to have to have a firm talk with Mr. Florescu,* Selene thought coldly. *If not Kraven, then maybe me.*

For now, however, she was content to let the greedy arms dealer depart with his ill-gotten lucre. The lycans were her chosen prey tonight. Now that they had concluded their business with Florescu, perhaps they would lead her back to their lair. Selene waited expectantly to see what the three lycans would do next.

Then, just as Florescu and his guards pulled away in their limo, the breeze shifted direction, leaving Diego upwind of the lycans. They immediately reacted to his scent. Eyes wide, they lifted their chins and sniffed the air. Three deceptively human-looking heads turned toward the massive granite bust hiding Diego. "I smell a blood!" the darkskinned lycan snarled.

Damn! Selene thought, only half disappointed that their cover had been blown. She thrust her camera into the pocket of her jacket and reached for her Berettas. *Looks like I get to slaughter some lycans tonight after all.*

Before she could draw her weapons, however, a shiny metal object came flying through the air from the rear of the park. The lemon-shaped projectile caught a glint of moonlight before plummeting to the ground right where the three lycans were standing. It exploded on impact, unleashing a sudden blast of heat and noise.

Selene dived behind the concrete base of the statue. Her ears rang from the explosion, and the smell of gunpowder filled her nostrils. A grenade, she realized instantly. *But who . . . ?* The bomb had not come from either her or Diego, that was for certain. One of Florescu's people, doubling back behind the park?

Lifting her head, she peered over the top of the concrete base at the aftermath of the explosion. Smoke and dust clouded the air, but she could see the three lycans lying sprawled on the ground around a smoking crater. Their blood, foul and toxic, stained the gravel pathway, while they groaned and whimpered in pain, not yet dead but clearly injured.

Jagged shards of shrapnel jutted from their bleeding bodies. Steam rose where the metal fragments pierced their flesh. Selene recognized the characteristic gleam of silver.

Good, she thought. As long as the silver fragments remained embedded in their flesh, the lycans were trapped in their human guise, leaving them all the more vulnerable to Selene, Diego, and whoever had hurled the grenade in the first place.

Tearing her gaze away from the intoxicating sight of the wounded lycans, Selene turned her eyes toward the rear of the park, searching for the origin of the mysterious grenade. A flicker of movement caused her to zero in on an impressive sculpture depicting a couple of dozen life-sized Soviet soldiers charging triumphantly into the future, rifles and bayonets at the ready.

Before Selene's startled eyes, one of the uniformed figures detached itself from its fellows and hopped onto the ground in front of the sculpture. *That's no statue,* she grasped. *That's a person in a spray-painted mask and uniform.* She couldn't help admiring the ingenuity; chances were, the camouflaged stranger had been hiding in plain sight all this time.

Who in the world . . . ?

Selene was reluctant to expose herself before determining the stranger's intentions. Just because the grenade thrower had attacked the lycans didn't necessarily mean that he or she was an ally. As far as Selene knew, there were only two sides in this war, but what if she were mistaken?

She started to signal Diego to stay down, only to see the masked stranger produce another grenade from beneath its painted uniform. At first, she thought the assailant intended to finish the writhing lycans off, but, to her horror, the anonymous figure hurled the grenade directly at Diego.

No! Selene thought, her brown eyes wide with shock.

The second grenade blew the massive bust apart. Broken chunks of granite went flying into the air, along with the flailing body of Diego. Her fellow Death Dealer, his face and leathers scorched by the heat of the explosion, crashed to earth only a few feet away from his lycan enemies.

Was he still alive? Selene had no time to find out, as a third grenade came flying straight toward her hiding place. She threw herself away from the doomed sculpture, somersaulting across the ground before rolling back onto her feet again several meters away.

The grenade went off right behind her, the shock wave propelling her through the smoky air. She fired wildly in the direction of the masked stranger before plunging face-first into the gravel.

The crash landing left Selene stunned and breathless. Her face stung from numerous small cuts and abrasions. She tasted blood on her lips and realized it was her own. The metallic tang made her mouth water. Her chestnut-colored eyes turned a luminous blue, revealing her immortal nature.

A stabbing pain in her right side caused her to hiss in agony. Blinking the grit from her eyes, she discovered a razor-sharp piece of silver embedded in her hip. Cool undead blood streamed from the wound, pooling on the gravel beneath her. "Dammit," she cursed at the sight of the injury. The silver was not poison to her, as it was to the lycans, but it still hurt like hell.

Looking up from the ground, she saw the intruder shed its faux-sculpted army jacket, revealing a suit of Kevlar body armor and a flamethrower strapped to its back. Selene stared in shock as a stream of incandescent fire was unleashed and swept the area before the stranger, igniting everything in its path. The bright orange flames lit up the night.

Selene could feel the heat of the flames upon her skin as the intruder marched toward her. Scrambling to her feet, she darted behind the nearest convenient monument, which consisted of two enormous bronze hands cupped around a polished marble globe that presumably symbolized the world or something like that. Selene was less concerned with deciphering the sculpture's meaning than with putting something large and heavy between her and the advancing flamethrower.

There weren't a lot of things in the world that could kill a vampire for good, but fire was one of them.

Striding across the park, the murderous attacker turned the flamethrower on its previous victims. The blond lycan female went first, her fallen body igniting into a living bonfire. A howl of pain—half human, half wolfen—erupted from the burning lycan, who thrashed wildly on the ground as the flames consumed her. Melted silver flowed across her body like molten lava.

Selene almost felt sorry for the lycan bitch.

The spiky-haired male was next, his anguished howls supplanting the female's as her blazing form fell still and silent, except for the crackling flames. The nauseating stench of burning flesh suffused the warm night air. A single gold tooth shone brightly amid the flames.

The intruder then turned toward Diego, and Selene realized that her fallen comrade was next in line to be cremated. "Leave him alone!" she shouted angrily. Peering out between the upraised palms of the giant metal hands, she fired at the stranger in a desperate attempt to keep the flame-throwing killer away from Diego. Pain and blood loss left her dizzy, however, while the spreading smoke and flames interfered with her aim. A few lucky shots bounced off the mysterious assailant's Kevlar body armor, but most of her frantic shots went wild. Crouched behind the cupped steel hands, the blood-slick shard of silver jabbing into her side, she could only watch in dismay as the flamethrower's blazing spray found Diego.

It happened in a heartbeat, as though the stricken Death Dealer had been caught in the noonday sun. Selene had known and fought beside Diego for more than one hundred seventy years, but his screams were unrecognizable. Immortal flesh burned like kindling.

"Bastard!" Selene yelled at the masked stranger, firing away with her Beretta despite the shakiness of her aim. Even though she knew it was too late to save Diego, she couldn't stop squeezing the trigger. She didn't care if the killer were human or lycan; she wanted him or her dead.

The screams and gunshots roused the last surviving lycan, the black male with the shaved head. His dark eyes quickly taking in the situation, he stumbled to his feet and began loping toward the exit and his waiting van. He grunted through clenched teeth as he staggered across the park, leaving a trail of sticky red blood.

The intruder hurried after the fleeing lycan, swinging the flamethrower toward him, only to be distracted by a hail of gunfire from Selene. Silver bullets sparked where they glanced off the aggressor's armor, and the killer, perhaps realizing that Selene posed the greater threat, switched gears and came after the gun-wielding female vampire instead.

The armored assailant advanced toward the huge upraised hands, preceded by a voracious tongue of flames. Selene felt the searing heat on her face, even as, out of the corner of her eye, she spotted the surviving lycan hightailing it out of the park.

As much as Selene hated to admit it, the injured alpha male had the right idea. *Time to get out of here,* she concluded, realizing there was nothing more she could do for Diego. *I have to let Kahn and the others know what happened here.*

But how to get away from the oncoming assassin? Her guns were barely slowing the killer down. She swiftly examined her surroundings, her gaze coming to rest on the huge marble sphere, about the size of a large boulder, poised between the gargantuan bronze hands. A crazy idea occurred to her.

Ignoring the excruciating pain in her side, Selene stood and reached for the little fingers of both giant hands. Grabbing hold of the colossal digits, she pulled herself upward until she hung suspended directly behind the polished stone globe. She swung backward, gathering momentum as she got ready to put every bit of her remaining strength into one last, desperate kick.

The tip of the fiery tongue was less than a meter away when she came swinging back toward the globe, both of her legs extended before her. *Here goes nothing.*

The soles of her boots collided with the marble sphere. More than mortal strength knocked the globe loose from its pedestal, sending it rolling toward the flame-throwing assassin like an oversized bowling ball. The masked killer was forced to dive madly to one side in order to avoid being flattened.

Nice to have the world on my side for once, Selene thought.

She took advantage of her opponent's momentary confoundment to make a break for the wire fence surrounding the park. The shrapnel in her hip sent a fresh jolt of agony through her body with every step, and her head was spinning from lack of blood, but still she bolted for the fence, quite literally like a bat out of hell. The tail of her trench coat flapped in the breeze as she hurdled the wires in one bound and kept on running until she had left Statue Park well behind her.

Her adrenaline exhausted, Selene collapsed against the side of her silver Jaguar XJR. She glanced anxiously behind her but was relieved to see no flame-throwing killers in pursuit.

Praise the Elders, she thought. *That was a close one.*

An emergency packet of freshly cloned blood waited in the glove compartment of the Jag. The blood would restore her, but Selene needed a few minutes to recover before she had the strength to go looking for it. Resting her weight against the car, she let her ragged breathing stabilize and her heartbeat slow down. Her vampiric blue eyes turned brown once more.

She peeked at her wristwatch: 12:28 A.M. Dawn was still hours away. She had plenty of time to get back to the mansion before the sun rose.

This realization brought little comfort. Diego was dead, his immortal existence brought to a fiery conclusion, and for what? She had confirmed the connection between the lycans and Florescu, only to find herself confronted with an even more urgent mystery.

Who else has entered our war?

Then

A.D. *1201*

Chapter Two

CARPATHIAN MOUNTAINS

*S*tars glittered like silver in the cold night sky, but the moon was nowhere to be seen.

A perfect night for a hunt, Lucian thought, peering up at the sky through an opening in the treetops. He crouched in the underbrush, beneath the towering pines and firs, inspecting the foliage for broken branches. Low-hanging fog swirled around his bended knees. A cold wind rustled his flowing black hair and neatly trimmed black beard. His sable locks were combed back from his brow, exposing a prominent widow's peak. Coarse woolen clothing protected him from the chill, although his every breath fogged the air before him. *Ideal for hunting those of my kind.*

"Well, Lucian?" an imperious voice demanded from above. "Have you caught wind of our quarry?"

Lucian looked up into the aristocratic features of Lady Ilona, the mistress of tonight's hunt. The pure-blooded vampire noblewoman sat astride Lucifer, her magnificent black charger, gripping the reins with one hand and a ready crossbow with the other. A suit of intricate silver chain mail covered her molded leather armor, while a crested steel war helm crowned her skull.

The lady and her steed tarried at the forefront of the hunt. Behind her, a full contingent of Death Dealers awaited her command. Armed with swords, pikes, crossbows, and nets, the vampire warriors were visibly eager to catch up with their prey. As silver chain mail was a rarity reserved for only the most exalted of vampires, the other Death Dealers made do with iron mail over their oiled leather armor. Frothing mastiffs strained at their leashes, held back only by the preternatural strength of Soren, Viktor's handpicked overseer. The brawny Irishman, who had been inducted into the coven four centuries earlier, wore an iron helmet and a bearskin cloak over his armor. His fierce hounds pawed the ground, eager to be set loose.

Lucian was the only lycan trusted to take part in the hunt, a distinction that filled him with pride. A pewter badge, bearing the Corvinus coat of arms, was pinned to his jacket, testifying to his elevated rank among the servants, that of reeve. "Almost, milady," he assured her. "Permit me merely another moment or two."

"Very well," the lady consented, "but be quick about it. I promised Marcus that I would see to this matter in his absence."

Lucian recalled that the Elder was presently in Buda, preparing for the upcoming Awakening. Lady Ilona had been left in charge of the castle until the time came for her and the other vampire nobles to join Marcus at Viktor's estate outside the city. Lucian hoped to make the pilgrimage himself, as part of the Elder's household.

Perhaps if I prove myself invaluable tonight!

"I will not fail you, milady," he vowed. Returning his attention to the forest floor, he devoted every effort to tracking his quarry. His keen senses searched the night, quickly detecting the spoor of both wild stags and boar, but those game, although tempting, were not what he sought. Frustrated, he sniffed the air once more.

Hold! What's that? A sickly odor, both familiar and disturbing, reached his nostrils. Lucian smiled to himself, nodding as he grew more confident that his nose was not deceiving him. He rose excitedly to his feet. "This way," he informed Lady Ilona. "Follow me!"

He ran stealthily through the woods, dodging thick tree trunks and bounding over fungi-encrusted logs. The dense pine canopy overhead blocked out most of the starlight, casting the forest floor into darkness, but his lycan eyes penetrated the shadows as easily as any vampire's. The undeniable exhilaration of the hunt sent his blood racing; he almost wished the moon *were* full, so that he could savor the moment in his most primal form.

Then again, he hardly desired to flaunt his bestial origins in such highborn company. *Bad enough to be a mere lycan among the elite of the immortals,* he lamented. *Let me not become a slavering animal in their presence.*

Lady Ilona and the other Death Dealers followed closely behind him, making as little noise as possible. Like Lucian, they needed no torches to navigate the murky woods at this late hour; even more so than their lycan tracker, they were fundamentally creatures of the night.

Lucian's nose led him to a narrow mountain pass, where a rocky dirt trail, only infrequently traversed by the occasional peddler or wandering minstrel, led between craggy stone cliffs too steep for any mortal soul to scale. It was, Lucian immediately noted, an excellent spot for an ambush.

Or a massacre.

Evidence of the latter littered the road. Human bones, stripped clean of flesh, were strewn upon the earth. Arm and leg bones had been cracked open to get at the marrow, while shattered skulls had been emptied of their brains. Splashes of dried blood stained the granite walls of the pass, in addition to the trampled ground around the bones. Most of the clothing was missing as well, but from the profusion of religious artifacts scattered amid the debris—Bibles, crosses, rosaries, saints' medals, and such—Lucian guessed that the unlucky mortals had been pilgrims en route to a holy shrine on the other side of the mountains.

Alas, their piety had proven no protection against the ruthless predators who had devoured them. Despite his finer instincts, Lucian's mouth watered at the thought of the carnage that had clearly taken place there.

No doubt, the pilgrims had been delicious.

"Revolting," Lady Ilona declared, arriving on the scene. She shook her head in disapproval. "Atrocities like this stir up the mortals, increasing the danger to us all." A determined look settled on her elegant features. "We must put an end to these outrages at once."

Shame stabbed Lucian. Lady Ilona was quite right; there was nothing at all appetizing or appropriate about what had transpired there. The Elders had expressly forbidden feeding upon mortals, and for good reason; in their numbers, the humans posed a significant threat to lycans and vampires alike. Better to leave them alone than to risk inciting a vendetta that could consume them all. Immortals had been captured and burned at the stake for less.

This atrocity was only the most recent of a string of attacks on the mortals of this realm. Isolated farms and villages had fallen prey to the same ravening beasts, thus necessitating tonight's hunt. Tracking down the killers was more than mere sport; it was essential to the safety of the castle and all who dwelled there.

A Death Dealer named Casmir bent to inspect the grisly scene. He lifted a hard-carved wooden crucifix from the dirt. Contrary to the mortals' ridiculous superstitions, the cross did not sear his flesh. "Milady?" he inquired respectfully. "What would you have us do with these mortals' remains?"

Lady Ilona sighed impatiently. "I suppose we shall have to dispose of this mess eventually and hide the bones where they will not be found." Her voice held no sympathy for the unfortunate pilgrims, only concern that their gruesome fate might incite their fellow humans. "But not this very moment. First, we must attend to the perpetrators of this butchery." She turned her steely gaze toward Lucian. "Lead us to your savage brethren, lycan."

He winced to be linked in the same breath with the barbaric monsters responsible for this unlawful slaughter. He felt a surge of volcanic anger at the renegades; it was creatures like these that made the vampires think that all lycans were without breeding and self-restraint, much to Lucian's eternal chagrin.

"With pleasure, milady!" he told her.

Although the massacre obviously had taken place several days ago, beneath the light of a full moon, it was child's play to follow the scent of the bloodstained lycans back into the woods on the opposite side of the pass. Lucian raced through the nocturnal wilderness until the smell of smoke and the din of raucous voices caused him to slow his pace and advance more warily through the brush and bracken. He crept furtively toward the noise and smoke, taking care to stay downwind of whatever lay ahead. He gestured for the vampires to move quietly as well, so that the hunting party passed through the night like specters, barely disturbing a single twig.

The flickering glow of a roaring campfire could be seen through the tree trunks as Lucian and the vampires drew nearer. He glimpsed humanlike figures around the fire and smiled in silent triumph. Try as they might, the rogues could not hide from one of their own.

Just ahead, the forest gave way to an open clearing surrounded on all sides by dense pine woods. Lucian snuck up to the very edge of the meadow and peered around the trunk of a venerable old fir. He stared, with a mixture of victory and disgust, at the quarry he had gone to such lengths to locate.

A pack of wild lycans cavorted around the fire, which Lucian knew had been kindled merely to dispel the cold; lycans preferred their meat raw. More than a dozen men, women, and children were present, each, to Lucian's eyes, more barbaric than the one before. Although trapped in human guise until the moon waxed full once more, the debased lycans looked almost as bestial as their wolfen alter egos. Their greasy hair was matted and uncombed. Their nails were as long as talons. Dirt and sweat caked their unwashed faces. Yellow teeth, with notably pointed canines, gleamed behind the tangled beards of the adult males. Lucian could smell the stench of the renegades' fetid bodies from halfway across the clearing. He suspected even a mortal could.

The lycans' clothing, such as it was, obviously had been ripped from the bodies of their victims and donned without any sense of style or propriety. Lucian recognized the tattered remnants of the dead pilgrims' long woolen tunics, still rent where a werewolf's claws had slashed them and soiled with their original owners' blood. Other lycans wore a mismatched assortment of garments plundered from who knew how many unfortunate mortals: a monk's black robe, a jester's motley, a noblewoman's brocade gown, hats of straw or felt, ill-fitting hose and doublets, miscellaneous boots, sandals, and stockings. All were uniformly filthy and in need of repair.

The renegades' behavior was even more appalling. Males and females rutted openly around the fire, while their neighbors laughed and egged them on. Others engaged in wrestling matches of uncommon viciousness, biting and clawing each other in sport, or anger, or both. Hungry lycans gnawed on the bloody bones of a disemboweled deer until their faces were liberally smeared with gore. Naked children ran amok, unheeded by the carousing adults. Grunts, groans, screams, snarls, and howls assaulted the ears.

Lucian blushed with shame, humiliated to the depths of his soul by his kinship to these noisome brutes. *They're animals,* he thought bitterly. *Nothing but animals!*

Not for the first time, he wished with all his heart that he had been born a vampire instead.

"Well done," Lady Ilona whispered to him from her horse. Moving like shadows, the Death Dealers spread out around the clearing. Soren tugged on the leashes of his hounds, urging them to follow him as he vanished into the woods to the east on his way to the opposite side of the meadow. Expertly trained, the hunting dogs would keep silent until Soren set them loose.

The lady waited until all the beaters had sufficient time to get into position before raising an ivory hunting horn to her immaculate lips. Behind her, grim-faced Death Dealers readied nets of iron mesh. Silver links were interspersed through the netting, adding to its potency. Lucian stepped to one side, to avoid getting in the way of the restless vampire warriors.

He had done his part tonight. The rest was up to his undying masters.

The horn sounded and was immediately answered by fearsome war cries and the baying of the hounds. Startled lycans, caught unaware amid their crude revelry, looked up in alarm as Soren and his dogs burst from the woods on the far side of the clearing, accompanied by vampiric pikesmen whose silver spearheads pierced the flesh of the nearest lycans, regardless of age or gender. The frenzied dogs fell upon unarmed savages, tearing out their throats in exquisitely poetic justice for the marauders' own depredations. Letting go of the hounds' leashes, Soren threw back his bearskin cloak, revealing a pair of silver whips wound around his shoulders. He uncoiled the whips, which were composed of sculpted silver vertebrae, and cracked them against the exposed flesh of a naked male. The twin lashes left steaming welts on the cur's body.

As anticipated, the other lycans ran frantically away from Soren and the other beaters—straight toward Lady Ilona and her Death Dealers. "In the Elders' name!" she shouted boldly as, astride Lucifer, she charged into the throng of fleeing savages. Her crossbow released its deadly bolt, the silver-tipped missile lodging right between the bloodshot eyes of a shaggy male lycan. Lucifer reared up his hind legs, then brought his silver-shod hooves crashing down on lycan skulls. "Let none escape!" the lady commanded. "Not a single bitch or whelp!"

Panicked renegades, evading Lucifer's thunderous hooves, attempted to dart around the lady and her steed, only to run directly into the upraised nets of the Death Dealers behind her. The metal webbing descended upon the hapless lycans, weighing them down to the grassy floor of the meadow. They thrashed wildly within the nets, unable to break free, and howled in agony every time one of the intermittent silver links brushed against their skin. Straining Death Dealers held the nets in place, while their brothers in arms bludgeoned the trapped fugitives with silver-plated maces, knocking the fight out of them.

It was less of a battle than a rout. Deprived of the full moon's transforming light, the outmatched lycans were unable to unleash the mighty beasts within them. Accustomed to tearing mortal prey apart with nothing but their own teeth and claws, they were pitifully equipped with weaponry, having only a few crude knives and axes among them. Lucian watched from the edge of the clearing as a hulking barbarian, his hairy frame naked from the waist up, tried to fight his way past an armor-clad Death Dealer a few feet away.

The lycan brandished a blazing torch, snatched up from the campfire, in one hand and a rusty iron dagger in the other. Matted brown hair fell past his shoulders, and a voluminous beard obscured his features. Crazed blue eyes glowed with feral rage as he bared his fangs at the sneering vampire standing between him and freedom. "Out of my way, blood!" the savage roared.

The Death Dealer, whom Lucian recognized as Janos, merely drew his sword from its scabbard. Silver gleamed in the starlight, hurting Lucian's eyes. An icy smile lifted the corners of the vampire's lips as his free hand tauntingly invited the lycan to advance.

Bellowing like a rabid animal, the barbarian charged forward. His dagger was raised high above his head, and his torch produced a trail of fiery sparks as he waved the burning brand before him. "Burn in hell, blood!" he growled as he swung the torch at Janos, who evaded the flames with effortless grace. "Burn, damn you!"

The silver blade flashed in the night, and the lycan's torch went flying, as did the hand that was holding it. The dumbstruck brute froze in shock, staring aghast at the gushing stump at the end of his arm. He stabbed clumsily at Janos with his dagger, but the Death Dealer easily blocked the blow with the hilt of his sword, then rammed a spiked gauntlet into the man's exposed belly.

The silver spikes tore through the lycan's guts, as Janos's armored hand plunged elbow-deep into his enemy's abdomen. A heartbeat later, the hand emerged again, clutching a foot-long segment of the man's spine. Gore dripped from the dangling vertebrae, which Janos casually tossed aside. He stepped backward and watched with amusement as the lycan's burly frame scissored in half, then toppled to the ground.

Lucian shook his head at the uneven contest. The lycan's attack had relied entirely on raw strength and ferocity, lacking any trace of finesse or strategy. No doubt, that was enough, even in his human form, to overcome the strongest mortal easily, but against an experienced Death Dealer, the blustering savage hadn't had a prayer.

If I had been in charge of this pack, Lucian reflected, *I would have seen to it that the camp was better defended.* There would have been guards posted throughout the night, well armed and trained in the use of their weapons. There would have been an evacuation plan in place, in anticipation of a raid such as this, and a commander who knew better than to cavort in the open on a moonless night when vampires might be abroad. *Yes, there is much that I would do otherwise—were I ever insane enough to side with such rabble against the coven!*

His musings were interrupted by a lycan female, who

came rushing toward the woods where he stood. A bawling infant was clutched to the woman's breast, and her glowing cobalt eyes were wide with fright. The tattered remnants of a nun's black habit barely covered her lean, sinewy form. A mass of unkempt red hair fell past her waist.

Her headlong flight came to an abrupt halt as she spotted Lucian blocking her path. Drawing an iron knife from his belt, he displayed it before her. "Come no farther," he warned.

The woman's eyes looked about anxiously, seeing only chaos and bloodshed in every direction. "Please!" she pleaded. Beneath the grime, desperation contorted her features. Flared nostrils sniffed the air between them. "You're one of us, I can tell. Please, for mercy's sake, let me go!"

The fervency of her plea touched Lucian's heart. "Very well," he declared. "You shall have mercy."

Rotating his wrist, he turned his knife around and struck her skull with the hilt of the blade rather than the point. The woman dropped like a stone toward the ground, but Lucian managed to snatch the baby from her limp fingers before it crashed to the earth as well. He held the yowling whelp at arm's length from his body, wrinkling his nose at the reek of the infant's soiled flesh.

He stared down at the woman's insensate form. An ugly bruise already marked her temple, but Lucian knew that she would soon recover from his blow. *I did not lie*, he informed her silently. *I have shown you mercy.*

You and your child shall live to serve the vampires, as I have always done.

The raid was over almost as soon as it had begun. Dead lycans were strewn across the blood-soaked floor of the clearing, their unclean bodies left to rot where they fell,

while the surviving pack members—mostly women and
children—were chained together by links of forged iron too
dense to be broken by any immortal short of an Elder. Metal
collars were fastened around their necks, holding them in
place. Heavy manacles locked their wrists together.

Lady Ilona kept her distance from the foul-smelling captives, letting Soren take charge of the prisoners. He wielded
his silver whips freely, dealing out painful lashes at the
slightest hint of defiance. He took obvious pleasure in his
work. Castle gossip had it that while still mortal, the dour
Irishman had been stolen away from his homeland by
Vikings and forced into slavery himself. Four centuries later,
he clearly enjoyed being at the other end of the whip.

Dawn was still hours away, so there was time enough to
introduce the defeated rogues to the realities of their new
existence. Soren lined the captives up before the fire, which
had been stoked to a blazing intensity by the vampires. All
resistance whipped out of them, the pathetic lycans miser-
ably awaited their fate. Shaggy heads drooped over their
iron collars. Their arms hung limply before them, weighed
down by their shackles. Strapping Death Dealers gripped
the chain at both ends, holding it taut. Sobs and whimpers
were all that escaped the line of prisoners.

Several yards away, Lucian watched the proceedings from
beside Lady Ilona's black steed. Seated above him, the pure-
blooded vampiress casually fed bits of lycan flesh to her
mount. To his considerable relief, she did not offer any such
morsels to Lucian himself. *I may be no more than a lycan,* he
thought, *but I am no cannibal.*

Soren handed off his whips to an assistant, then pulled a
heavy leather glove over his right hand. He reached into the
fire and drew out a silver-plated branding iron that he had
placed in the blaze several moments before. The heated end

of the iron glowed in the night, as bright and red as the fires of perdition.

A rare smile lightened his usually stoic features. He had removed his war helmet earlier, revealing a thick black beard and a mane of long black hair. Iron in hand, he approached the front of the line and a slender lycan youth, who appeared to be roughly fourteen years in age, although looks could be deceptive where immortals were concerned.

Most immortals, vampires and lycans alike, were originally mortals, transformed by the bite of either a vampire or a werewolf. And only the most fortunate of humans survived the process; an immortal's bite proved fatal in the vast majority of instances. Rarer still were purebloods, such as Lucian himself, who had been born immortal, conceived by the union of two immortals. Both of Lucian's parents had been lycans, so he had never known any other life.

He wondered idly what this particular lad's story was. Had he been human once, or had he always run with the pack, wild and undisciplined? Lucian hoped for the former; the boy might be easier to train if he had once lived a semi-civilized existence as a mortal.

At the moment, however, the youth's eyes grew wild with terror as he watched Soren approach with the red-hot branding iron. "No!" he cried out, thrashing violently within his bonds. "You can't! Stay away from me!" His bare feet clawed at the grass beneath him as he tried unsuccessfully to get away from the steaming iron. "Mercy! Mercy!"

Soren paid little heed to the young lycan's hysterics; he was used to such displays. He nodded at a pair of nearby Death Dealers, who stepped forward to subdue the thrashing youth. The first guard calmly kneed the lycan in his privates, leaving him stunned and breathless, while the second guard wrapped an arm around the boy's arms and chest to keep him from waving them about. "Stay still," the second Death Dealer barked, "or we'll break every bone in your body, one by one!"

Despite the threats and abuse, the quaking lycan flinched as Soren ripped off the sleeve of the youth's greasy tunic, exposing his right arm. Held back by his steel collar and chains, the lycan snapped impotently at Soren and the guards with his fangs. Spittle sprayed from his lips—until Soren calmly pressed the glowing end of the branding iron against the youth's bicep.

An inhuman howl erupted from the young lycan's throat. Smoke rose from his arm where the heated silver seared his skin. The smell of burning flesh turned Lucian's stomach.

In a heartbeat, it was over. Soren drew back the iron, revealing the mark now branded onto the lycan's arm for all time, an ornate letter M.

For *Marcus*.

Lucian caught himself rubbing his own right arm, where a similar brand adorned his own bicep, except that Lucian bore a V upon his flesh instead, testifying that he had begun his service during one of Viktor's reigns. Mercifully, he had little memory of the branding itself, which had taken place when he was but a young pup; unlike these prisoners, he had been born in servitude.

Soren worked his way along the line of prisoners, branding each in turn. The excruciating procedure yielded a succession of anguished shrieks and howls, but when at last the dire business was complete, he signaled Lady Ilona that the captives were ready to be escorted back to the castle.

The highborn vampiress wasted no time turning her horse around and leading the procession back the way they had come. Although the starry sky remained as black as pitch, Lucian knew the vampires would be anxious to return to their stronghold before dawn. Sunlight posed a more lethal threat to their kind than any rampaging werewolf.

He contemplated the dispirited prisoners as they stumbled past him, whimpering in pain and distress. As the highest-ranking lycan at the castle, it would be his responsibility, in part, to turn these trembling vermin into decent servants. Looking over the unsightly throng, he feared he had his work cut out for him.

No matter, he thought. *They will learn to obey the vampires—or suffer the consequences.*

His gaze fell upon the scarlet-haired lycan female he had personally subdued earlier. Separated from her child, who was now in a canvas bag slung over the shoulder of a marching Death Dealer, she trudged sullenly after the prisoner in front of her, tugged along by the chain affixed to her neck. The right shoulder of her stolen habit had been torn asunder, laying bare her arm and breast. The freshly burned M on the former showed blood-red against her dirty brown flesh.

The woman lifted her head, and her eyes met his. He offered her an encouraging smile, to assure her that her future was not nearly so dismal as she might imagine. In truth, he had rescued her from a life of barbarism. *She will thank me someday,* he thought.

Tonight, however, hatred blazed in the woman's blue eyes. She spat at him as she passed, the gobbet of saliva striking Lucian on the cheek.

Her defiant gesture was swiftly rewarded with a lash from Soren's whip. The silver vertebrae snapped against her bare shoulder, and steam rose from a crimson welt. The woman's fangs snapped shut, biting back a scream.

Lucian wiped the spit from his cheek as he watched the woman stagger away, her chastened form receding into the shadowy woods. Soren's whip cracked overhead, spurring the lycans behind her to pick up the pace of their forced march.

Lucian had no regrets.

At least, he thought, *her child will grow up civilized.*

Chapter Three

CASTLE CORVINUS

Castle Corvinus loomed before them, its familiar turrets and battlements thrusting upward at the night sky. An imposing stone fortress, the castle was built atop a rocky crag overlooking the forest below. The light of myriad torches and lamps shone through the castle's lancet windows, making the stronghold appear to glow from within. Crimson pennants, the color of freshly spilled blood, streamed above the watchtowers.

Home at last, Lucian thought as the hunting party marched up the well-trod road toward the castle's front gate. The ground sloped away steeply from the path on both sides, permitting only a single avenue of approach to the castle. Dense woods surrounded the forbidding granite peak on all sides.

Sentries posted outside the gatehouse and upon the crenellated battlements overhead cheered at the return of Lady Ilona and her troops. Their welcoming cries grew louder and more exuberant as they spied the long line of lycan prisoners shambling between the triumphant Death Dealers.

A deep chasm, one that descended farther than any human being could fall and live, was surmounted by a drawbridge that led straight into the fortified stone gatehouse. A raised portcullis hung over the entrance, its iron fangs guarding the mouth of the castle.

Weary from the night's strenuous activities, Lucian was looking forward to a warm meal, followed by several hours of sleep on his humble mattress in the servants' quarters. It was the lycans' responsibility to guard the fortress during the daylight hours, but under the circumstances, he doubted that anyone would object if he slept late that morning.

Lucifer's hooves clattered on the wooden drawbridge as Lady Ilona led the procession into the castle proper. Beyond the gatehouse, the way opened onto a spacious courtyard paved with weathered clay bricks. High limestone walls looked down on the courtyard, which faced the great hall of the vampires themselves. The heraldic symbol of the Corvinus family—a raven gripping a ring in its beak—was emblazoned above the main entrance of the hall. A wooden belfry rose from the slate-covered roof.

A lycan stableboy, clad in simple woolen attire, hurried forward to assist Lady Ilona, who dismounted gracefully and handed Lucifer's reins to the servant. "See to it that he is properly fed and groomed without delay," she instructed.

"Yes, milady," the stableboy replied, keeping his gaze respectfully fixed on the ground. He led the steed away toward the nearby stables, which were built against the inner walls.

Chimes rang out from the bell tower atop the great hall, warning that dawn was but an hour away. A flock of bats flapped overhead as the squeaking night flyers began to return to their roosts in the belfry.

"Well, a good night's work," the lady pronounced with satisfaction. She turned toward one of her lieutenants, a Death Dealer named Istvan. "Send word to Marcus that the lycan renegades have been dealt with severely. With the Awakening drawing nigh, I would not have his mind troubled by such petty annoyances."

"As you wish, milady," Istvan said, departing instantly to carry out her wishes. A carrier pigeon would convey the lady's message to the Elder ere long.

Before Lady Ilona could issue another command, the door of the great hall swung open, and a vision of surpassing loveliness came running out into the courtyard. Lucian's eyes widened, and his heart leaped at the sight of a beautiful vampire maiden clad in a flowing damask gown.

Shimmering golden hair tumbled down onto her shoulders like the sunshine she had never known, and a gilt circlet rested gently on her head. Chestnut eyes gazed from a snow-white face that surely rivaled the greatest beauties of myth and history. A crest-shaped pendant, centered around a polished turquoise gemstone, dangled from a chain around her swanlike throat. The precious ornament bounced atop the ivory slopes of her bosom as she scampered across the torchlit courtyard toward Lady Ilona.

In all his immortal existence, Lucian had never seen anything to compare with the unearthly radiance of this enchanting vampire princess. Not even the moon at its fullest could ever outshine such perfection.

"Mother!" she cried out, her musical voice ringing out over the courtyard as she embraced Lady Ilona. "You've returned!"

The lady laughed as she held her daughter in her arms. "Did you doubt it?" she teased. "Really, Sonja, you don't truly believe that your mother could be undone by a pack of unruly lycans? Don't be absurd!"

"Then the hunt went well?" Sonja inquired.

"But of course," Lady Ilona declared. Keeping her arm around her daughter's shoulder, she turned Sonja so that the flaxen-haired maiden could behold the captives in their chains. "These wretched beasts will not be dining on our mortal neighbors any longer."

Behind the prisoners, the heavy portcullis descended, cutting off the feral lycans from the lives they had known. Heavy cables drew up the drawbridge, sealing the castle in preparation for the dawn. Double doors of thick oak reinforced with iron provided a third and final barrier against intruders. Many of the captives gasped out loud as the mighty doors were bolted shut, blocking their last glimpse of the outside world.

Lucian scarcely noticed the renegades' despairing moans. Sonja filled his vision, to the exclusion of all else. *She grows more lovely each time I see her,* he thought ardently. *Like the very embodiment of all that is pure and unblemished.*

Soren strode up to Lady Ilona and Sonja. The tips of his silver lashes were red with lycan blood. "Shall I escort these animals to the dungeons, milady?"

"By all means," the lady replied. Many weeks of discipline and captivity would be required before the rogue lycans could be integrated into the servant population. Invariably, a few of the more stubborn prisoners would have to be tortured to death first, as examples to the others. "And have those filthy rags they're wearing burned." She placed a silk handkerchief over her nose. "They stink abominably."

Soren nodded dutifully. "As you command." He cracked his bloody whips over the heads of the trembling lycans, who flinched in anticipation of yet more painful lashes.

"Move, you mongrels!" he snarled at the captives. "Move before I flay your flea-ridden hides!"

"Poor things!" Sonja exclaimed as the renegades were dragged away. Compassion shone in her eyes, enhancing the delicate grace of her angelic countenance. "They look so lost and forlorn!"

Her mother frowned. "Your sympathy is wasted on such creatures," she informed Sonja sternly, eyeing the departing lycans with contempt. "Your father would not approve."

Sonja's father was none other than Viktor himself. Although he was then hibernating in his crypt in Buda, the legendary Elder was due to be Awakened in a little more than three weeks.

Lady Ilona noted Lucian standing by, enthralled by Sonja's captivating allure. "That will be all, Lucian," she said, dismissing him. "You may go now."

Lucian realized with embarrassment that he had been staring openly at the elegant princess, a grossly presumptuous act for one such as he. Tearing his gaze away from Sonja, he ducked his head and backed quickly away from the vampiric noblewomen. "Yes, milady," he murmured as he turned away and scurried toward the servants' quarters, all thought of food and sleep forgotten.

Fool! he chastised himself, as he always did whenever Sonja's presence stirred up impossible yearnings within him. *She's a vampire—and the only daughter of an Elder, no less! How can I possibly dream of loving her? It's more than just insane. It's forbidden!*

In his mind's eye, however, he could still see her wondrous face, shining brighter than the moon.

"Lucian!"

An insistent hand tugged at his shoulder, rousing him

from dreams of Sonja. Blinking in confusion, he lifted his head from his straw pallet to find Nasir, another household servant, shaking him frantically. Consternation marked the other lycan's features. Lucian knew at once that something was very wrong.

"What is it?" he demanded.

"Mortals!" Nasir gasped, his cobalt eyes wide with alarm. A swarthy complexion betrayed his Turkish ancestry. "The mortals are attacking the castle!"

What?

Lucian leaped to his feet, instantly alert. He hastily pulled on his boots, then threw a woolen jacket over his plain brown doublet. He thrust an iron dagger into his belt. "Show me!" he commanded Nasir.

Already, his keen ears caught the unmistakable sound of combat. Angry shouting and screams of pain penetrated the cold stone walls of the castle. He smelled fire and blood. Alarms rang out from the bell tower, calling every able-bodied lycan to action.

Following Nasir, Lucian rushed out of the servants' quarters into the great hall. Brightly colored tapestries adorned the walls, while shuttered windows kept out the sunlight. Dried rushes carpeted the floor. The undead masters of the castle were nowhere to be seen, having retired to their private chambers at dawn, leaving the protection of the fortress to their faithful lycan guardians.

Lucian and Nasir ran up a spiral staircase, taking the steps two or three at a time, until they reached an arched doorway that led to the battlements overlooking the front of the castle. Throwing open the door, the pair bolted out onto the ramparts, which were already occupied by a throng of lycan defenders, engaged in battle against a foe Lucian had yet to behold.

Sunshine poured from a blue and cloudless sky, momentarily blinding him. It took a moment for his eyes to adjust to the sudden glare, but when his vision cleared, he found that Nasir had spoken truly.

Castle Corvinus was under siege.

A mob of enraged humans assailed the castle, yelling furiously and shaking their weapons at the mammoth stone fortress. From their crude attire, Lucian judged the men to be primarily peasants and villagers from the surrounding countryside. Pitchforks, scythes, and flesh hooks waved above the crowd, along with a surfeit of crosses and wooden stakes.

"Death to the demons!" a strident male voice called out, and dozens of other throats took up the cry.

"Death to the demons!"

Lucian cursed under his breath. It was just as Lady Ilona had feared; the marauding lycans had driven the victimized mortals to rise up against the immortals in their midst. *Damn those savages! Their unchecked appetite for human flesh has brought this calamity upon us.*

Even as he looked on, taking stock of the crisis, longbowmen below unleashed a volley of flaming arrows that came hissing through the air like a swarm of irate hornets, forcing the lycans on the ramparts to duck behind the rectangular stone merlons jutting up from the battlements like a bottom row of teeth. Nasir tugged on Lucian's arm, yanking him behind the safety of one of the merlons before a lucky arrow strike could deprive the lycans of their leader. Unlike the sleeping Death Dealers, the lycan sentries wore no armor.

"Take care, Lucian!" Nasir warned. Fear showed on his swarthy features. "The mortals mean to kill us all!"

So it seems, Lucian admitted. Peering around the side of

the hefty stone block, he watched the determined humans press their attack against the fortress. Under the cover of the archers' fire, more peasants poured from the woods surrounding the castle, carrying scaling ladders long enough to reach to the very top of the battlements. Bracing the wooden frameworks upon the rocky hillside at the base of the castle, they angled the ladders against the sturdy ashlar walls. Shield bearers positioned themselves around the foot of the frameworks, protecting the stalwart men charged with holding them in place. Lucian watched with dismay as armed humans began scaling the castle walls.

"Death to the demons!"

Lycan eyes turned to him for guidance. "Deploy the forks!" he called out resolutely. The safety of every vampire and lycan within the castle, he knew, depended on their swift action. He thanked the Elders that silver weapons, at least, appeared to be beyond the economies of this peasant rabble. "Bring those ladders down!"

The other lycans hastened to obey. Crouching low in order to present smaller targets to the archers below, they took up long poles with forked metal ends and used them to push the tops of the enemy ladders away from the battlements. Lycan strength overcame the weight of the climbing mortals, and Lucian smiled as first one, then another ladder toppled over backward, sending shrieking humans crashing to the ground.

His gaze swiftly turned to a large copper vat sitting above a quantity of dry kindling. The vat rested on a wooden hoarding draped in wet animal skins. Stepping out from behind the protective merlon, he snatched a flaming arrow out of the air and hurled it into the kindling, igniting a fire under the vat. "See to the pitch!" he ordered Nasir. "I want it hot as hell!"

Another fiery missile thudded into the northwest turret, only a few yards away, setting a pair of sealed wooden shutters ablaze. "Someone put that out!" he shouted. Buckets of water were fetched and hurled against the crackling flames. "Make certain every fire is doused!" he bade his lycan brothers. The last thing he needed was for a conflagration to spread out of control. "Water! We need more water!"

The sun's rays beat down on him, making him sweat beneath his doublet and hose. Lucian cursed the radiant solar orb for emboldening the mortals—and trapping the Death Dealers indoors, where they could be of little assistance. If only he could somehow transform the infernal sun into a full moon instead; a battalion of werewolves would make short work of these bloodthirsty varlets!

Still, even by day, each lycan possessed the strength of many mortal men. Under Lucian's direction, they now hefted goodly chunks of broken masonry, stockpiled for just such an occasion, and hurled them at the besiegers. As though propelled by catapults, boulder-sized fragments of limestone arced through the air before crashing down on the screaming humans.

Wooden shields provided no protection against the rain of masonry. Lucian watched with satisfaction as a weighty stone block flattened a cross-waving villager. Blood spurted from beneath the rubble like juice from a winepress.

For a moment, he dared to hope that the devastating bombardment might break the spirit of the attackers, sending them back from whence they came. But an impassioned voice boomed out from the rear of the mob, urging the mortals to press on.

"Do not lose faith!" the zealous voice exhorted. "Remember your wives and children! Do not suffer these spawns of Satan to contaminate our land one day more, endangering the lives and souls of all you hold dear! God commands that we rid the earth of the Devil's obscene progeny—and he will lead us to victory in His holy name!"

The incendiary words bolstered the spirits of the teeming mortals, who came at the castle with renewed fervor. A barrage of flaming arrows came soaring over the battlements, driving the lycan defenders back. A blazing shaft struck Imre, the carpenter's apprentice, just as he was lifting a ponderous stone fragment above his head. Imre lost his grip on the heavy block, which crashed down on himself, shattering his skull and spine. Hot lycan blood gushed across the wall walk, splashing against Lucian's boots.

A tremendous crash seized Lucian's attention, yanking it away from the mangled apprentice to the gatehouse below. To his dismay, he saw that a horde of straining humans, wielding ropes and hooks, had successfully pulled the drawbridge back down over the defensive chasm, despite the best efforts of the lycan guards stationed above the gate, who found themselves sorely beset by an onslaught of spears and flaming arrows.

Now a colossal battering ram came charging at the gate, driven by a gang of sweaty humans. Dozens of boots pounded over the drawbridge, which groaned beneath the combined weight of the ram and its crew. The mighty timber, which was at least three feet in diameter, slammed into the iron portcullis and the great double doors beyond, producing an earth-shaking clamor loud enough to wake every slumbering vampire in the castle. Lucian imagined Sonja in her bedchamber, trembling beneath the covers at the fearful din, knowing that something was terribly amiss yet unable to venture out into the sunlight to find out what was happening.

No! Lucian thought, the image fueling his anger against

the ruffians. *Nothing ill shall befall you, my princess,* he vowed passionately. *Not while I live!*

He turned toward the vat, whose burnished steel reflected the dancing flames beneath the cauldron. "How fares the pitch?" he demanded impatiently.

"It boils, Lucian!" Nasir called out to him. The Turk stood behind the copper kettle, stirring its contents with a long metal rod. He withdrew the rod; thick black tar dripped from the further end of the stick. Lucian could hear the hot pitch bubbling within the vat. The smell of brimstone filled his nostrils.

Excellent, he thought.

Peering out over the battlements, he saw the scaling ladders swing back against the castle walls once more. "Hold one minute more," he instructed Nasir, holding up his hand to forestall the other lycan. Lucian waited until a new wave of besiegers was halfway up the high ladders before stepping safely to one side of the steaming vat. "Now!" he shouted.

Nasir used his metal rod to tip the cauldron toward the battlements. A flood of viscous black pitch poured from the vat onto the floor of the rampart, where it swiftly flowed into the gutters, which led to holes in the protruding stone machicolations, from whence the tar spilled out onto the men below. The boiling goo splattered the unlucky mortals scaling the walls before inundating the shield bearers and ladder holders at the base of the castle. Agonized screams rose toward the sky as the scalding tar clung to the mortals' bodies. Blackened figures ran about frantically, clawing fruitlessly at the molten pitch, before dropping to the earth, where their tortured forms spasmed briefly before falling still. Tar-coated peasants stumbled headlong into the gaping chasm, impaling themselves on the spikes waiting at the bottom of the abyss. Scaling ladders, abandoned by the men who had held them secure, teetered precariously before toppling over once again. The shrieks of falling men joined the high-pitched wails of those burned by the oozing tar. A sulfurous stench rose from their blistered flesh.

Lucian felt a flicker of pity for the suffering mortals, which was speedily dispelled by the mere thought of his beloved Sonja falling into the hands of these varlets. He imagined brutal hands driving a stake through Sonja's gentle heart. He saw her lovely head severed from her body, her delicate mouth stuffed with garlic by ignorant humans who had no understanding of how truly precious she was.

Never! he thought, clenching his fists at his sides. Fury turned his brown eyes an unearthly blue, and a low growl emanated from the back of his throat. He would gladly tear out the throats of the entire mortal world to protect his princess, even though he knew in his heart that she could never truly be his. *I shall not fail you, fair maiden.*

"Did it work?" Nasir asked eagerly, his eyes agleam. "Did the tar succeed?" He rushed over to the battlements, keen to witness firsthand the damaged inflicted by the boiling pitch. "Hah!" he laughed, peering through the gap between two merlons. "They look like bacon frying on the hearth!"

An arrow came from out of nowhere, spearing Nasir through the throat. The Saracen clutched at his neck as hot blood sprayed from his jugular. His mouth gaped wide, revealing wolf-like fangs, before he tumbled forward over the battlements. Lucian watched in horror as his fellow servant disappeared into the chasm, joining the bodies of various ill-fated mortals.

Yet there was no time to mourn his fallen comrade, not while the relentless battering ram continued to pound against the castle gates. Again and again, the prodigious timber collided with the portcullis, so that the iron framework resounded like an enormous drum. Each powerful blow reverberated throughout the castle, shaking the entire stone edifice. *How many such strokes,* Lucian wondered, *could the portcullis and the oaken doors withstand?*

That same rancorous voice called out again, urging the ramming crew to greater efforts. "That's the spirit, men! Keep pounding away at the demons' defenses! The good Lord will grant you the strength to prevail against our satanic foes!"

Who is that miscreant? Lucian reacted angrily. Peering out over the battlements, his eyes finally located the source of the hateful rants: a portly monk lurking at the back of the mob. His black robe proclaimed his calling, while his tonsured skull shone like an egg beneath the glaring sun. A gilded crucifix rested on his chest, and his florid complexion grew ever more scarlet as he endlessly spewed his venom.

"Take heart and fear not, brave souls! The foul masters of this palace of sin dare not brave the cleansing light of day. 'Tis only their inhuman vassals that oppose us now. Break down the demons' door and slay the undead monsters while they lie helplessly within their unhallowed tombs!"

In fact, the castle's vampiric inhabitants preferred comfortable beds and mattresses to coffins, but the daylight left them vulnerable nonetheless. Determined to silence the rabble-rousing monk, Lucian snatched up a cracked paving stone and flung it with all his strength at the black-robed figure standing at the bottom of the winding road leading up to the castle.

Alas, the deadly missile fell short of its target, striking instead an anonymous peasant, whose skull was instantly pulped by the descending brick. Lucian drew little consolation from this incidental kill; it was clear that the nameless monk was the true provocateur of this dire emergency.

The gates trembled beneath the repeated strokes of the battering ram. Driven by the force of two score men, the wooden juggernaut was dashed against the iron portcullis, which began to buckle before the persistent assault. Oak splintered, and wooden chips flew from the bolted doors behind the portcullis. Mortal varlets cheered in anticipation of the inevitable blow that would reduce the gates to pieces, breaching the fortress's defenses.

Atop the gatehouse, only partially protected by their own row of battlements, lycan sentries struggled in vain to fend off the besiegers. Lucian watched as his embattled comrades jabbed at the ramming crew with their forked poles, only to be driven back behind the battlements by the never-ending hail of flaming arrows. A club-footed lycan retainer retreated too slowly and was skewered by a blazing shaft that set his coarse garments ablaze. He thrashed wildly, howling in pain, while his brothers in arms batted at the flames with wet blankets.

"Well done, my children!" the red-faced monk crowed. He turned a sizable tree stump into a podium upon which to preach his noxious obloquies. "Give the godless fiends a taste of what awaits them in hell!"

Tortured metal screamed in protest as the portcullis came apart at its hinges. Now only the stout double doors stood between the besiegers and the interior of the castle. Once they were inside, Lucian realized, there would be no stopping the invading horde from setting the keep's many tapestries and furnishings afire, igniting an unquenchable blaze that would engulf the entire castle, burning the trapped vampires alive or else driving them out into the daylight where the sun's deadly rays would consume them just as surely as the devouring flames.

By the Elders, no! Lucian thought vehemently. *Not on my watch!* He could not imagine a greater nightmare than seeing Sonja's flawless skin reduced to ash before his very eyes. *I will die before I will permit such an obscenity to occur!*

The great doors shuddered before the unceasing battering ram, and the timber walkway beneath Lucian's feet shook as though rocked by an earthquake. Knowing that time was of the essence, he eschewed the stairs and climbed up between two large gray merlons. Fiery arrows whizzed past his head and shoulders, but Lucian paid them no heed. A full three stories below, the gatehouse projected beyond the castle proper.

Without hesitation, Lucian leaped from the battlements to the roof of the gatehouse. The vertiginous drop, some one hundred feet, would have killed a mortal man, yet he landed as nimbly as a panther on the flat stone roof. The soles of his boots had scarcely touched down before he hurried over to the lower battlements to take charge of the gates' defense.

"You!" he shouted to one of the lycans still on his feet, a stablehand named Pyotr. "Get down to the courtyard and round up every lycan you can. Pile whatever you can find against the door. Kegs, hogsheads, mattresses, benches . . . the heavier the better! And put your own shoulders to the door as well. We have to keep these murderous varlets out of the castle!"

"Yes, Lucian!" The other lycan hurried to implement Lucian's instructions, disappearing down a stairway at the back of the roof. Lucian could not help noticing that Pyotr limped as he departed, the result of a bloody puncture wound in one leg.

He was hardly the only casualty; dead and wounded ly-cans were strewn atop the gatehouse, their maimed bodies riddled with arrows and scarred by burns. Pitiful moans escaped a huddled figure whose body was hidden beneath a heap of soggy blankets. Fresh blood painted the ancient stones.

Lucian snarled at the carnage. "Man the murder holes!" he barked, referring to a number of vertical slits in the rooftop that exposed the paved gateway below to attacks from above. At his command, each surviving lycan positioned himself above a hole, armed with sharpened poles and buckets of boiling water. Once the besiegers breached the doors, as they seemed destined to do, they would find death and injury waiting for them as they passed beneath the gates.

But would that be enough? Lucian feared that such tactics would only delay the mob's entrance into the castle. The humans were too many, their will to murder stoked to a feverish pitch. Even now, he could hear the crazed monk inciting the ruffians with his bellicose rantings.

"Lay on, men, lay on! Bring down this sanctuary of Satan, and reap your reward in heaven! Yea, even though you may fall in battle against the Evil Ones, know that an eternity of bliss awaits those who do battle in the Lord's almighty name!"

Lucian had had enough of the monk's insane jeremiads. Drawing his dagger from his belt, he took aim at the distant cleric and let fly the blade, which went straight and true toward the choleric human. *If I can just slay the monk,* the lycan hoped, *perhaps the other mortals will abandon this demented crusade!*

Avid blue eyes tracked the speeding dagger, which looked to strike the nameless monk squarely in the chest.

Lucian held his breath while fierce glee surged within his heart. *Yes!* he thought expectantly. *Taste my steel, monk!*

His only regret was that he couldn't rip the man to shreds with his own teeth and fangs.

At the last minute, however, an unwary peasant stepped between the monk and the zooming knife. The dagger caught the luckless mortal totally by surprise, sinking deep into his chest. "Brother Ambrose!" the man cried out, perhaps not even realizing that he had just saved the monk's life. "Bless my poor soul!"

Lucian roared in frustration as the peasant fell dead at the monk's sandaled feet. Taken aback by his close brush with death, Brother Ambrose crossed himself hurriedly and hopped off his stump, retreating to a safer distance while continuing to hurl imprecations at the castle and its immortal denizens.

"Fiends! Abominations! You cannot frighten the pure of spirit. The vengeance of heaven is upon you, and all your unholy powers will not save you from the final reckoning. Your dread dominion ends today in righteous fire and blood!"

Lucian looked about for something else to fling at the mad monk, only to feel a sudden searing pain in his left shoulder. His eyes widened at the sight of a smoking arrow jutting from his person.

He had been hit!

Flames licked at his jacket, and he smothered the fire with his bare palms, wincing in pain. He dropped behind a defensive merlon and took hold of the shaft with his right hand. Gnashing his fangs, he yanked the arrow from his shoulder, producing a spurt of dark red blood.

He inspected the smoldering tip of the arrow, thankful to see that the point was made of sharpened wood, not silver.

Miniature crosses, however, had been etched into the sides of the shaft, no doubt to increase its potency against the vampires and their "demonic" ilk. *Superstitious peasants!* Lucian thought contemptuously.

But wait! Was there perhaps some way to turn the mortals' ridiculous misconceptions against them? An outlandish idea occurred to Lucian, bringing with it a flicker of renewed hope. *It's insane, but what other option do I have?*

Only a few feet below, the reinforced oak doors split apart before the indomitable battering ram. Lucian heard the lycans in the courtyard grunting and growling as they threw themselves against the sundered wooden planks, pushing against the great doors as they bulged inward toward the open courtyard. Each thunderous hammer blow from the battering ram echoed throughout the innermost chambers of the fortress, making the very walls groan.

Lucian realized there were only moments to spare. Scrambling away from the battlements, he called out to the gatehouse's remaining defenders as they squatted over their respective murder holes. "Hold fast!" he encouraged them. "Make the mortals pay dearly for every inch!" He grabbed an empty fire bucket and a pair of metal tongs and headed for the far end of the rooftop, where the back of the gatehouse met the outer wall of the castle. "I go in search of deliverance!"

It was a measure of his status among his brethren that none of the other lycans questioned his sudden departure. Thrusting the tongs into his belt and the handle of the bucket between his jaws, he dug his sharpened nails into the mortar of the limestone wall and began climbing up the side of the castle toward the belfry many dozens of feet above.

Please, he prayed to the unseen moon, *let this bizarre strategy prove more than a hopeless fancy—for Sonja's sake!*

Defying gravity, he scaled the wall within seconds and

clambered over the wooden balustrade into the bell tower itself, which was silent and deserted, the bell ringer having gone to join the defenders on the castle walls. Lucian found himself alone within the murky belfry, save for the multitude of slumbering bats hanging upside down from the rafters. Hundreds of furry bodies, their wings wrapped about them, clustered beneath the thick wooden beams like a bounty of quivering fruit.

Lucian stared at the bats with anxious eyes. His vampiric masters had a sentimental attachment to the nocturnal creatures, which legend held to be their kin. Contrary to mortal folklore, though, the vampires could not actually transform into bats.

But the besiegers didn't know that.

Taking hold of the tongs and the metal bucket, he banged the objects together loudly, producing an earsplitting din. He howled at the top on his lungs and stamped his feet upon the dusty floorboards. *Wake up, you wretched flying mice!* he beseeched them mentally. *Wake up, damn you!*

At first, the sleeping bats refused to stir. In desperation, Lucian hurled the bucket at the bats, followed shortly by the metal tongs, which smacked against the rafters, startling a cluster of bats which began to squeak and flap in protest.

That's more like it, Lucian thought, *but not nearly enough.*

Ignoring the massive bells, which he assumed the bats were inured to, he called upon his inner beast and unleashed a roar of unparalleled ferocity. Snatching up the fallen bucket and tongs, he tossed them again and again at the recalcitrant bats, all the while roaring and growling like the werewolf he truly was. He scrambled up the walls of the bell tower and chased the bats across the ceiling, snapping and frothing at the mouth.

The terrified bats reacted as though a ravening lion had invaded the belfry. Hundreds of tiny claws released their grip on the rafters as the entire colony took flight at once. The fluttering of countless leather wings filled the upper reaches of the tower as Lucian hung on all fours from the rafters. His frenzied roar echoed through the castle.

The bestial display had the desired effect. Despite the daylight shining outside, the teeming bats fled the belfry en masse in a panicked attempt to escape the monster in their midst. Within seconds, the airborne exodus emptied the tower.

So far, so good, Lucian appraised, but had his lunatic ploy yielded the results he craved? Dropping to the floor of the belfry, he dashed to the balustrade to observe his handiwork.

He was not disappointed.

A chorus of hysterical shrieks greeted the sudden appearance of the bats as they filled the sky above the besiegers, who broke and ran for the woods, shielding their heads with their arms. "Run!" one ashen mortal shouted in fright. "The thirsty dead have awakened! *Wampyr!*"

Lucian laughed triumphantly. *I knew it!* he exulted. The credulous peasants assumed the disoriented bats to be the vampires themselves, roused from their crypts in search of vengeance. He watched from the tower as the frantic humans dropped their weapons and raced for their homes as fast as their trembling legs would carry them. The mighty battering ram, abandoned by its bearers, lay impotently on the drawbridge like a fallen tree trunk.

Brother Ambrose tried futilely to halt the men's disorganized retreat. "Cowards! Apostates! Do not fall for the Devil's trickery. Hold true to your faith! Turn around and fight!"

But his words fell on ears made deaf by unreasoning terror. Pale-faced and gasping, the besiegers fled the battle in droves, forcing the ill-tempered monk to retreat as well, lest he be left behind to face the castle's defenders single-handed. Casting a backward glance at the unbreached castle, he shook his fist and clutched the golden crucifix on his chest. "Rejoice not, hellspawn! You have but delayed the inevitable day of your terrible downfall. The vengeance of our Lord cannot be denied, and His fearsome wrath shall surely cast you down into the fiery pit!"

But not today, Lucian thought. He watched with amusement as the fear-stricken rabble disappeared into the woods. *Hot pitch and falling rubble are one thing,* he concluded. *A plague of flying "vampires" is another.* The former, at least, were threats of an earthly nature, against which a mortal fighter could steel his nerves. But faced with the supernatural, apparently, even the most fanatical vampire slayer proved a coward at heart.

Who needs the full moon, he gloated, *when the mortals' own superstitions prove their greatest weakness?*

Exuberant whoops and howls rose from the ramparts and courtyard below, as his fellow lycans realized that the day was theirs. Upon the battle-scarred walls, victorious defenders embraced and waved their weapons in the air, before turning to see to the wounded and the dead. With time, all but the most severely burned would surely recover, thanks to their immortal blood and robust constitutions. Mercifully, no silver tainted the casualties' wounds, increasing their chances of survival.

Lucian savored his victory. The siege had been broken. Castle Corvinus was secure.

And Sonja—his beloved Sonja—was safe!

Chapter Four

CASTLE CORVINUS

$\mathcal{T}$he throne room was packed with vampires and lycans as the castle's inhabitants gave thanks for their triumph over the besiegers. Beeswax candles glowed from hanging copper lamps, casting flickering shadows on the rich tapestries adorning the walls. A roaring fire blazed within the hearth, dispelling the winter's chill. Colored tiles, bearing the Corvinus coat of arms, decorated the floor.

Presiding over the ceremony, Lady Ilona addressed the assembly from the raised dais in front of the hearth. The castle's vampires were seated, according to their rank, on rows of benches divided down the middle by a long aisle. Lycan servants, Lucian among them, stood at attention at the rear of the chamber, facing the dais.

An empty throne, carved from polished ebony, rested on a marble platform behind and above the platform upon which Lady Ilona stood. Only an Elder was entitled to sit on the regal seat; thus, its very presence served to remind those in attendance that the absent Marcus remained the ultimate ruler of the coven, at least until Viktor rose to reclaim the throne some three weeks hence.

"Friends, comrades, and faithful subjects," the lady orated, resplendent in a velvet surcoat trimmed with fur. A gold satin robe and jeweled girdle showed from beneath the crimson velvet, while the lady's hair was concealed beneath a padded roll studded with pearls. A crest-shaped pendant, similar to that worn by her daughter, hung from a golden chain around her neck. "We are met tonight in the wake of a grievous assault upon our domain and persons. Happily, the threat was rolled back thanks to the merciful dispensations of fate and the valiant efforts of our loyal lycan defenders, to whom I extend the sincere thanks of the entire coven. In reward for your service on our behalf, I hereby decree that tonight shall be a holiday, during which all lycans are excused from their accustomed duties."

Raucous cheers arose from the gathered lycans. Standing at the front of his fellow servants, Lucian regretted that Nasir, along with a number of others, had not lived to see their courage so honored. *I shall always remember their sacrifice,* he vowed, *even if our masters do not.*

Despite Lady Ilona's opulent attire, Lucian's own eyes were irresistibly drawn to the alluring figure of Sonja, who accompanied her mother before the vacant throne. The enchanting vampire princess was simply but elegantly clad in a trailing gown of pale blue silk. Her braided blond hair fell past her shoulders, and a delicate golden chain encircled her slender waist. Polished turquoise gleamed from the gilded pendant upon her bosom.

She's more than just a princess, Lucian thought. A pang of longing pierced his heart. *She's a veritable goddess.*

Lady Ilona waited until the lycans' cheers had subsided before continuing her speech. "We are most especially indebted to one among our servants, whose leadership and cunning were instrumental in the defeat of the mortal invaders. Let the lycan known as Lucian come forward to receive our gratitude."

Startled to hear his name called, Lucian froze momentarily, only to be shoved forward by the lycans standing behind him. He gulped nervously as he walked down the long aisle leading to the dais, feeling the scrutiny of four score eyes upon him. He was acutely aware of the contrast between his own threadbare garments and the sumptuous raiment of the vampires. The pewter badge on his doublet, which proclaimed his rank as reeve among the servants, was a pitiful thing compared with the gold and rubies adorning the seated courtiers and their ladies.

At length, after what felt like an interminable trek across the span of the throne room, he arrived before Lady Ilona and Sonja. Only with effort did he refrain from gawking at the princess, who now stood mere feet away from him. Instead, he kept his gaze fixed respectfully on the floor.

The lady looked down on him from the dais. "Lucian, sworn vassal of my own noble husband, Viktor, your brethren have testified to your quick thinking and resourcefulness during the recent strife. Therefore, in grateful appreciation of your valor, I am pleased to present you with a small token of our esteem."

She extended her open palm to Sonja, who dutifully placed a shining object in her mother's hand. Lady Ilona stepped forward and held out the token, which Lucian saw to be a burnished steel dagger with a polished ebony hilt whose pommel had been carved into the semblance of a wolf's head.

"To replace the blade you sacrificed in our defense," the lady explained, although the finely crafted knife was infinitely superior to the simple iron blade he had hurled unsuccessfully at Brother Ambrose. Lucian had never possessed an object so exquisite, nor had any other lycan he had ever known.

"Many thanks, milady," he said, reaching up to accept the dagger. "I am greatly honored."

"Indeed you are," Lady Ilona agreed readily, "but not without reason. Your conduct during the battle was remarkable, especially for a lycan. Would that the rest of your breed were half as trustworthy and intelligent."

Lucian bristled slightly at the lady's condescending tone, yet he held his tongue. After all, he was already being accorded greater respect than any lycan had reason to expect.

"Your kind words overwhelm me, milady. I only wish that I had succeeded in slaying the black-robed monk I believe to have incited the mortals." Having the lady's ear, if only for the moment, he chose to take advantage of the opportunity. "I must warn you, milady, that I fear we have not heard the last of this Brother Ambrose and his murderous designs. In truth, the danger may be far from past."

A derisive snort came from the front row of the seated vampires. Lucian turned to see Soren rise from his bench to approach the dais. The bearded overseer bore a scornful expression.

"Begging your pardon, Lady Ilona," Soren said gruffly. "I would not trouble yourself with the baseless worries of a mere lycan. By the sentries' own admission, the mob that attacked the castle was composed of peasants and shopkeepers, not actual warriors. Hell, they were scared away by a flock of harmless bats! I doubt they have spine enough to mount a second attack after being repelled so easily before."

Easily? Indignation flared within Lucian's breast. He had not seen Soren upon the battlements, risking life and limb in the Elders' names. *How dare he dismiss my comrades' heroism so cavalierly?*

Still, he knew better than to challenge a vampire directly, even if Soren had left his silver whips behind on this occasion. "But what of Brother Ambrose?" he asked, taking care to keep his tone suitably deferential. "The monk struck me as a true fanatic, whose zeal will surely compel him to continue his murderous crusade against our kind."

Soren sneered at the notion. "This Brother Ambrose is probably halfway to Cyprus by now. Still," he added with a shrug, "if you desire it, milady, I will post a reward for the monk's head."

That will not be enough, Lucian thought. He doubted that the humans would willingly turn over one of their holy men to the hated immortals, regardless of whatever bounty Soren offered. "If I may be so bold, milady, mayhap you should delay embarking for Buda until we can be certain the danger has passed."

He feared to think of Sonja traveling outside the castle while Brother Ambrose still lived to foment violence against the coven. The image of her lovely form transfixed by a bloody stake haunted his imagination.

"What danger?" Soren mocked. "I daresay the rabble was enough to frighten the servants, but we vampires have nothing to fear from such riffraff." He peered down his nose at Lucian. "As the trick with the bats attests, the mortal mob runs at even the illusion of our presence. The events of yesterday prove beyond a doubt that while the humans may dare to challenge mere lycans, they would never dream of confronting those of our blood."

Lady Ilona nodded. "Your point is well taken, Soren. It is hard to believe that any mortals would risk attacking a caravan guarded by none other than my fellow Death Dealers."

Her immaculate features appeared set in stone. "In any event, I have not laid eyes on my husband for well nigh two centuries, and I shall not be kept away from his Awakening by a throng of troublesome mortals. The pilgrimage to Buda will proceed as planned."

Her adamant tone closed the debate. Nevertheless, Lucian could not resist pressing his luck a bit further. "In that case, milady, may I humbly request to accompany the pilgrimage, so as to assure myself of your safety?"

In actuality, it was Sonja's safety that was of paramount importance to him.

"Ridiculous," Soren jeered. "What difference could a single lycan make?"

Lady Ilona looked as though she agreed. "It hardly seems necessary . . ."

Before she could render a final decision, however, Sonja surprised everyone by speaking up. "I would be most grateful for your protection on our journey," she declared, stepping forward to address Lucian directly. "Your courage and devotion to our court have not gone unnoticed."

Lucian could scarcely believe his ears. *I must be dreaming,* he thought. Emboldened by the princess's kind words, he lifted his eyes to find Sonja smiling down on him. Their eyes met, and it was as though their souls reached out to each other, recognizing kindred spirits. A faint blush appeared on her alabaster features, and Lucian felt his heart pound within his chest. *Can it be,* he wondered, *that she feels something for me as well?*

"Very well," Lady Ilona conceded, breaking the moment. "I suppose one more pair of eyes cannot hurt." She took Sonja's hand and gently led her back to her place before the throne. "And it's not as though I intended to make the trip without a decent retinue of servants!" The lady laughed, a sound as cold and crystalline as ice. "That is all, Lucian," she informed him. "You may return to your fellows."

"Yes, milady," he answered. Bowing low, he turned and walked back down the aisle toward the other servants. Soren glowered at him as he passed, but Lucian barely noticed the overseer's baleful glare; his heart and mind were still reeling from his brief communion with Sonja. Not even in his wildest dreams had he ever imagined sharing such a moment with the sublime vampiress, let alone basking so in the warmth of her regard. *Is this just a wild fancy,* he asked himself uncertainly, *or did something profound transpire between us?*

A sort of euphoria enveloped him as he returned to his place at the back of the throne room. His lycan brothers and sisters congratulated him heartily, slapping his back and oohing over the ornate knife in his hand, but Lucian accepted the accolades as though in a daze. In his mind, he was still back before the throne, hearing Sonja praise his courage and devotion, lost in the depths of her bottomless brown eyes.

"This concludes tonight's ceremonies," Lady Ilona announced from the dais. "So let the festivities begin. There is wine and freshly decanted steer blood in the great hall, as well as ale and raw venison for the servants. Let all make merry until the dawn!"

The other lycans howled in anticipation of the feast. Although eager to get to the banquet, the servants nonetheless stepped aside to let the vampires exit the throne room first. Not until the lowest-ranking of the undead filed out of the chamber did the excited lycans pour into the corridor outside, jostling one another in their haste to get to the great hall. Fresh meat was a rare treat for their kind, and they were already drooling at the prospect.

Lucian did not join the rush. In no hurry to witness his peers' uncouth table manners, he lingered in the throne room, clinging to the memory of Sonja's smile. His fingers toyed with the ebony-handled dagger, which only recently had rested within Sonja's tender grip. He envied the blade that it had known the princess's touch. That it came from her own hand only made the trophy all the more precious to him.

A throaty voice disturbed his reverie. "You must be very proud, Lucian, to be honored so!"

Lucian looked up to discover that he was not quite alone in the empty chamber. Leyba, a lycan scullery maid, had apparently stayed behind as well. *Naturally,* he thought, thrusting the dagger into his belt. *I should have seen this coming.*

Of Gypsy stock, Leyba was as dark as Sonja was light. Inky black hair tumbled past her shoulders, and her exotic features were not unattractive, in a crude and slatternly fashion. A coarse wool kirtle, rather tighter than modesty dictated, struggled to contain her voluptuous figure. Saucy black eyes examined Lucian with obvious interest.

In the past, if the truth be known, he had occasionally allowed himself to succumb to Leyba's seductive wiles. He had always rather suspected, however, that it was his elevated status that attracted the lowly servant wench, rather than any uniquely personal qualities of his own. *It is the reeve she craves, not Lucian.*

"Thank you," he said coolly. He had no intention of sullying tonight's transcendent events by rutting mindlessly with this lycan trollop. "I am quite unworthy, of course."

"You mustn't be so humble," Leyba insisted. She stepped closer to him, so that their bodies were less than a hand's breadth apart. Beneath the smoky kitchen odor clinging to her garment, Lucian scented a muskier aroma. "Everyone knows how bright and talented you are, even the vampires. Why, they practically treat you like one of their own."

Would that it were so! Lucian thought. His hopeless yearning for Sonja made it easier to ignore Leyba's all too obvious advances. "Shouldn't you be joining the others in the great hall?" he suggested. "Best to take full advantage of the lady's generosity."

Leyba declined to take the hint. "Maybe venison isn't the kind of meat I'm interested in tonight." Her fingers suggestively stroked the hilt of his dagger. "I was thinking that perhaps you and I could slip away for a little celebration of our own, just like we used to."

For a moment, Lucian was tempted. His blood was wolfen, after all. Why shouldn't he couple the night away with this lusty bitch?

Then Sonja's radiant visage bloomed in his memory, shining down on him once more, and he felt shame at the weakness of his base lycan flesh. *I love Sonja,* he thought, *if only from afar, and I will not betray that love by behaving like an animal.*

"No," he said firmly, removing Leyba's hand from his person. His tone was as adamant and unbending as any vampire's. He stepped away from her, placing three or four paces between them. "Leave me now. I would rather be alone with my thoughts."

Surprise, followed by a look of extreme vexation, contorted the spurned female's face. Her cheeks flushed crimson. "You don't know what you're missing!" she spat angrily as she stormed out of the throne room.

Yes, I do, Lucian lamented, thinking of Sonja.

He wanted to howl mournfully at the night sky, even though the full moon was still some fourteen nights away.

Chapter Five

CARPATHIAN MOUNTAINS

"*H*ow much farther to the keep?" Lady Ilona asked Soren impatiently. Astride Lucifer, she rode at the head of the procession as the caravan made its way through the wilderness along a bumpy dirt road. Her silver chain mail glittered in the moonlight, and the legs of her leather armor were splattered with mud from the journey. A worried frown marred her elegant features as she glanced upward at the night sky, where a gibbous moon shone amid the starry vault. "Dawn will be upon us soon."

"Not far, milady," Soren assured her from atop his own steed. A dozen mounted vampires, plus half as many lycan servants on foot, trailed behind him. Arriving at a crossroads, which was marked by a weathered roadside shrine, he pointed to the right. "That road leads to the monastery of Saint Walpurga, which means that the keep is straight ahead of us, only a short distance away. We should spy the tower anon."

Let us hope so, Lucian thought, eavesdropping on the conversation. The procession had been traveling since sunset, en route to Ordoghaz, Viktor's estate outside Buda, and his legs were weary from trying to keep up with the vampires' horses. Along with the other lycans, he plodded along at the rear of the procession, stepping carefully to avoid the steaming piles of dung left behind by the vampires' mounts. A rolled-up tapestry, intended as an Awakening gift for Viktor, was slung over his shoulder, and his back ached from toting the heavy fabric for mile after mile. He was more than ready to shed his burden and rest for a spell.

There was good reason for the vampires' haste, however. In less than three nights, with the coming of the new year, Viktor would be Awakened from two centuries of hibernation, and Lady Ilona was determined to attend the ceremony along with her daughter. A company of Death Dealers rode to protect the two noblewomen until they reached Viktor's estate, where Marcus, the reigning Elder, currently made ready to take Viktor's place beneath the earth, in accordance with the hallowed tradition of the coven, which dictated that only one Elder ruled over the other immortals during any given century.

Lucian could not blame the lady for her eagerness to be reunited with her husband. He tried to imagine what it would be like not to lay eyes on Sonja for two full centuries. *That would be purgatory itself,* he mused.

Despite his fatigue, Lucian was unable to keep from gazing furtively at the unknowing object of his affections. Sonja rode behind her mother and Soren on a roan-colored palfrey named Clio. A fur-trimmed indigo riding cloak concealed the princess's beauty, yet Lucian occasionally caught a glimpse of blowing blond tresses or a delicate ankle. He fantasized about walking alongside her horse, perhaps engaging Sonja in conversation, but, alas, he knew that to do so would be the height of impertinence. *Besides,* he rebuked himself, *what could such as I have to say to so cultured and highborn a maiden?*

When not staring longingly at the back of Sonja's cloak, Lucian's eyes searched the night-shrouded woods lining the road, on guard against any hate-crazed humans who might want to waylay the procession now that Lady Ilona and others had left the safety of the castle. Unlike Soren, he was not at all certain that the caravan was not in jeopardy. He could not help thinking that the procession of immortals presented an all too tempting target to the likes of Brother Ambrose and his followers.

So far, though, he had yet to detect any lurking peril. The winter night was broken only by the steady *clip-clop* of the horses and the usual forest noises: the hoot of an owl, the rustling of branches in the wind, the distant howl of a very ordinary wolf.

The rogue lycans are in custody, he reminded himself hopefully. Perhaps, now that the massacres had ceased, the murderous hatred fueled by the brigands' depredations had cooled somewhat, so that the frightened mortals were no longer quite so ready to take up arms against the "demons" of the castle. *It would be comforting to think so,* he thought. *Still, I will feel better when we have safely arrived at our final destination one night hence.*

Lucian had another reason for wishing the pilgrimage completed. He glanced upward at the gibbous moon; only a sliver of shadow kept the radiant lunar orb from waxing entirely full. Already, Lucian could feel the tidal pull of the moon on the beast within him. His blood surged through his veins, while his teeth and nails tugged on their roots, eager to extend outward until they were as long and as sharp as knives. The hair on his scalp and skin stood on end, thicker and coarser than before. Blue haloes outlined the dark brown irises of his eyes. Lucian knew he could not resist the Change for long, not once the full moon rose tomorrow night.

Please, he prayed, *do not let me transform in front of Sonja!* He could not bear the thought of her seeing him reduced to a slavering beast. *Give me the strength to hold back the Change until we reach Ordoghaz and can go our separate ways!*

"Behold!" Soren called out as the outline of a dark stone tower could be glimpsed through the overhanging tree branches ahead. The entire procession quickened the pace as they spied the keep: a single imposing tower surrounded by a high wooden palisade. Crimson pennants waved in the wind atop the tower. "As you see, I spoke truly."

Not nearly so grand as Castle Corvinus, the keep was a welcome sight nonetheless. As it was impossible to journey all the way to Ordoghaz in a single night, the tower had been erected centuries ago to provide a safe haven for the vampires during the day. This particular keep was just one of several such way stations established across the continent.

"At last," Lady Ilona declared. "And none too soon."

The sky was already growing noticeably lighter in the east by the time the procession arrived at the gates of the palisade. Vertical timbers, sharply pointed at their tops, loomed before them.

"Open up!" Soren bellowed at the heavy wooden doors. "The Lady Ilona and her party desire admittance."

Lucian knew that a small complement of lycans manned the keep at all times; it was a thankless and monotonous posting, often employed as a punishment. *I would not want to be banished to this place, far from the comforts and camaraderie of the castle.*

Not to mention Sonja.

The oaken doors swung inward, allowing the procession to pass through the gate into the bailey, a ring of cleared earth surrounding the tower. A fire pit burned inside the yard, filling the air with a smoky aroma.

Primitive, compared with the castle, Lucian judged, assessing their accommodations, *but serviceable enough.* Within the impervious walls of the tower, Lady Ilona, Sonja, and their vampiric entourage could rest securely until the sun set once more.

Or could they?

The bailey seemed strangely quiet and abandoned. No lycan retainers hurried to greet the new arrivals. A sense of unease came over Lucian, and he sniffed the air warily. Beneath the pervasive smell of the smoke, he scented something else, something that sent an unaccountable chill down his spine. At first, he couldn't place the troubling odor, but then it hit him.

Garlic.

What the devil? he thought. It was a myth that garlic repelled vampires, but foolish mortals still relied on the pungent herb to shield them from the immortals they so feared. *Why would the bailey reek of garlic, unless . . . ?*

"Beware!" Lucian called out in alarm. Hurling the furled tapestry to the ground, he drew his wolf's-head dagger. "It's a trap!"

His warning came seconds too late. The oaken doors slammed shut, trapping the party inside the bailey. Lucian heard the sound of rushing feet beyond the wooden fence and visualized scores of humans running out of the forest to barricade the gates from the outside.

"By the Elders!" Lady Ilona exclaimed. Lucifer reared up in surprise. "What is the meaning of this?"

A barrage of flaming arrows rained down on the yard from the walkway atop the palisade, where dozens of mortal longbowmen suddenly revealed themselves. At least five blazing shafts struck the lady, knocking her off her horse even as yet more humans came pouring out of the tower itself. Strings of garlic were draped around the attackers' necks, along with numerous rosaries and crucifixes. Burly peasants and villagers, armed with pitchforks, axes, and other weapons, charged the caravan, screaming in rage.

"Death to the demons!"

Flaming arrows jutted from the flailing bodies of vampires and lycans alike. Steam rose from the latters' wounds, proclaiming that the mortal horde had added silver to their arsenal as well. Outnumbered and caught unaware, the skewered Death Dealers tumbled from their horses in disarray. Soren's steed landed on top of him, trapping the overseer beneath the weight of the husky charger. Lucian felt a searing pain in his side, where a burning shaft jabbed between his ribs.

"Well done, lads!" a familiar voice called out from high above the bailey. Lucian looked up to see a black-robed figure standing on the roof of the tower. "You have my blessing—and the Church's holy silver. Suffer not a single demon to live!"

It is just as I feared! Lucian thought. He wished that his suspicions had not proven quite so well founded. *Apparently, Brother Ambrose has not fled the Continent after all . . .*

Fire scorched his palm as Lucian grabbed on to the arrow, breaking the shaft and hurling it away from him. The flames continued to lick at his clothing, however, and he tore off his jacket in a rush. Steam rose from the silver arrowhead lodged in his flesh, but Lucian ignored the pain. Looking for Sonja, he saw her struggle to control her frightened mount while calling out in fear.

"Mother, beware!"

The mob descended on Lady Ilona almost as soon as she hit the ground. A sharpened ashwood lance pinned the fallen noblewoman to the earth. A gleaming sickle flashed in the moonlight.

The lady's severed head rolled across the yard. Cold vampiric blood gushed from the stump between her shoulders, while her leather-clad arms and legs twitched spasmodically.

"Mother!" Sonja cried out. The hood of her cloak fell away from her face, exposing her horrified visage.

"Success!" Brother Ambrose crowed. "The she-devil is no more!"

An arrow pierced one of Clio's forelegs, and the horse collapsed to the ground. Sonja was thrown from her saddle, landing in the yard not far from her mother's decapitated corpse. She lay sprawled in the dirt, while Lady Ilona's blood turned the packed earth to mud beneath her. A piteous moan escaped Sonja's lips as she stared in shock at her mother's head, which lay faceup in the gory muck, only a few feet away.

"Get the *stregoica!*" a human ruffian snarled, using a crude mortal term for a vampiress. Rough hands seized hold of Sonja, who seemed too stunned by her mother's grisly demise to fight back. Blood-spattered peasants threw her onto her back, holding her spread-eagled upon the ground. Her cloak fanned out beneath her like the wings of a fallen angel. "Chop off her head!"

"No!" Lucian shouted from across the bailey. To his dismay, he saw that all of Sonja's Death Dealer bodyguards were either fallen or caught up in battle against multiple foes. Slashing madly with his dagger, he fought his way through the chaos toward Sonja, stepping over the bodies of wounded lycans and Death Dealers while tossing mortals

aside in his frantic attempt to get to Sonja in time. Even in his human form, he still possessed the strength and speed of several mortals, but for one of the few times in his immortal existence, he wished that he could transform into a werewolf at will, if only to be able to defend Sonja with bestial fangs and claws.

"You are all God's soldiers!" Brother Ambrose cried from the tower, egging the butchers on. "Send the wanton succubus to hell where she belongs!"

The deadly sickle was raised once more, ready to commence its fatal descent. Lucian threw himself at the would-be executioner, slamming into the human with the force of a battering ram. Landing atop the dazed peasant, Lucian tore out the man's throat with his teeth, then leaped to his feet, brandishing the sickle in one hand and his dagger in the other. A vicious growl emerged from his throat as he glared at the men holding Sonja down. His eyes blazed with cobalt fury. Blood dripped from his chin.

"Who's next?" he snarled.

All but one of the mortals fled before him, abandoning their grip on Sonja. The remaining villager was a hulking brute wearing a blacksmith's leather apron, now liberally bedecked with gore. Placing his foot on Sonja's throat, he raised an iron hammer above his head. "Get back," he warned Lucian, "or I'll smash her skull in!"

Lucian hesitated. The silver in his side burned like acid, slowing him down. Could he get to the blacksmith before the man could carry out his threat?

Maybe not.

His abrupt appearance, however, roused Sonja from her state of shock. "Murderer!" she gasped at the mortal standing over her. Chestnut eyes turned icy blue, and her hands grabbed the blacksmith's leg. "Get away from me!"

Bones shattered audibly as Sonja tossed the man into the air with all the unearthly power of a pure-blooded vampire. His hammer went flying from his grip, landing harmlessly in the mud several feet away, while the blacksmith himself rose nearly ten yards above the ground before crashing to earth at Lucian's feet.

The man grimaced in agony—until Lucian used the captured sickle to relieve him of his head.

A quicker death than he deserved, Lucian thought.

Rushing to Sonja's side, he helped her to her feet. "Lucian," she whispered hoarsely, her voice full of dread. Her indigo riding cloak was soaked with mud and blood. "What's happening? I don't understand!"

It was very clear to Lucian. Obviously, the humans had seized control of the keep before their arrival, presumably sometime after Marcus and his entourage had passed through. They must have tortured the lycan servants to find out when the next caravan from the castle was expected.

But there was no time to explain. "We must flee this place, milady!" he urged Sonja. He looked about them anxiously; all around the bailey, his fellow immortals were fighting for their lives against the mortal mob. Nearby, Soren heaved his dead horse off his body and lumbered to his feet. Throwing back his bearskin cloak, he unwound his silver whips, which he used to keep the bloodthirsty peasants at bay.

Soren looked anxiously to the east, where dawn's scarlet fingers streaked the sky above the jagged peaks of the palisade. Like Lucian, the overseer plainly understood that their true enemy was time. The sun was rising, bringing death to every vampire still standing.

Including Sonja.

An axe-wielding peasant, possessed of more zeal than

sense, charged Soren. The vampire's whips snaked out with lightning speed, the right lash yanking the man off his feet while the left wrapped itself around the haft of his axe. A second later, Soren retracted the latter whip, taking the axe with it.

"Soren!" Lucian called out. "Over here! The princess requires your aid!"

If the dour overseer heard Lucian's cry, he gave no sign of it. Wrapping his whips around his beefy shoulders, he took the axe in his hands and ran toward the closed oak gates. The swinging axe cut a gruesome swath through the mob, but Soren was intent more on escape than on inflicting mayhem upon their foes. Reaching the sealed gates, he chopped at the hardened wood with his axe. Splinters of oak flew with every thunderous blow, until he had hacked out a crack large enough for him to squeeze his meaty frame through.

Lucian watched intently as Soren disappeared through the gap in the wooden door. Taking Sonja by the arm, he moved to follow the escaping vampire, only to be daunted by the sight of yet more mortal berserkers rushing into the bailey through the open crack. The reinforcements came on in a seemingly inexhaustible torrent, cutting off Lucian and Sonja from the gates.

Had Soren been brought down by the forces outside the keep, or had he been able to hack his way clear of the mob? Lucian had no way of knowing and little time in which to care. His eyes searched for another avenue of escape, quickly lighting upon a set of wooden steps leading up to the walkway along the top of the palisade.

That's our only way out, he realized. *We have no choice but to risk it.*

But the sun's deadly rays were already beginning to shine down into the blood-soaked bailey. Agonized screams filled the yard as the sunbeams ignited the flesh of the wounded vampires unlucky enough to be lying in their path. Lucian wrapped Sonja's heavy cloak about her tightly but knew that the garment would not be enough to protect her for long.

"Lucian?" she asked uncertainly. Her arm trembled. "The sun . . . I can feel its heat upon me already . . ."

"Do not fear, milady," Lucian vowed. He would not see her sublime beauty reduced to ashes by the merciless sun, not while breath remained within his body. An idea occurred to him. "Come with me," he said, guiding her back to where he had been when the ambush commenced. "There may yet be a way to keep you safe."

"But what of the others?" she asked.

Lucian shook his head. Even as they spoke, he saw a lycan groomsman cut down by the mob, his body sliced to ribbons by scythes, hatchets, and meat cleavers. Elsewhere, a kneeling Death Dealer dropped her crossbow as a golden sunbeam set her face on fire. The vampire's skin blackened and crumbled. Her hair burst into flames. Her dying screams tore at Lucian's heart.

He looked away. *I can do nothing to halt this slaughter,* he thought. The odds against them were too great. *It will be a miracle if Sonja alone survives . . .*

"Kill them all!" Brother Ambrose commanded his rampaging acolytes. "See how the cleansing light destroys night's unholy creatures. Heaven itself fights at your side!"

The light was indeed the enemy; that much was certain. The rolled-up tapestry was lying right where Lucian had left it. He swiftly unfurled the woven fabric on the ground. Grasping his intention, Sonja lay down upon the tapestry and let Lucian roll it back up with her inside it. With luck, the thick layers of fabric would protect her from the daylight while Lucian tried to get them both to safety.

If safety was to be had.

Heedless of her added weight, he slung the bundle over his shoulder and made for the wooden stairway. Carrying Sonja forced him to discard the sickle, but he held on to his dagger with his free hand.

A homely peasant, a swollen goiter bulging from his throat, attempted to block Lucian's path by waving a crucifix in front of the fleeing lycan. "Stand back, ye creature of hell!" the man ranted. "The power of the holy rood defies you!"

Lucian stabbed the fool in the gut, then darted around the peasant while the man was still staring in disbelief at the blood gushing from his torso. The useless cross dropped onto the ground.

"Look sharp, brave souls!" Brother Ambrose shouted, taking notice of Lucian's flight. "Do not let the dark-haired devil escape! The blood of my martyred brothers cries out for holy vengeance!"

Martyrs? Brothers?

Lucian had no idea what the crazed monk was raving about. He raced up the stairway, taking the steps two at a time. A torch-wielding peasant met him midway up the stairs, swinging the blazing brand like a club. Lucian ducked beneath the torch, then rammed his head into the man's chest, knocking him backward onto the steps. He thrust out the torch in self-defense, but Lucian sliced off the peasant's hand with a single swipe of his dagger. Both torch and hand plummeted to the bailey below, trailing sparks like a shooting star. Bright arterial blood spewed from the man's truncated wrist.

"My hand!" the maimed peasant screamed, a moment before Lucian stampeded up the stairs on top of him, trampling the human's body beneath his boots.

"Hark! The beast makes for the fence!" Brother Ambrose shouted, managing to sound both indignant and agitated at the same time. "Someone stop him! Anyone!"

Curse you! Lucian raged. He wanted to rip out the monk's tongue with his bare hands. *You spew venom with every breath!*

Lucian bounded onto the upper walkway and peered over the edge of the palisade. A fifty-foot drop separated him and Sonja from the ground below. Nothing to worry about, he thought confidently; any immortal could make such a jump with ease. Before he could leap over the pointed tips of the fence, however, an arrow slammed into his back, barely missing his spine. Glancing back over his shoulder, he saw the birchwood shaft of a crossbow quarrel and guessed that one of the mortal varlets had claimed the weapon of a fallen Death Dealer, perhaps even Lady Ilona herself. The silver arrowhead burned like hellfire against his flesh, joining the constant stinging in his side. He grunted out loud, unable to hold the pain in.

No matter, he resolved. There would be time enough to see to his wounds later—if he and Sonja survived. Thrusting his dagger back into his belt, he cradled the swaddled princess in his arms and leaped over the top of the palisade.

The cool morning air rushed against his face as he dropped nimbly to the mossy ground below. His powerful legs absorbed much of the impact of his landing, cushioning Sonja against the jolt, but the bump still caused the hellish burning in his back and side to reach new peaks in torment. He gnashed his fangs, biting back the pain.

He found himself in an open field, within sight of the surrounding forest. The beckoning shelter of the woods called to him, and he dashed across the field, holding tightly onto the tapestry and its priceless contents.

The blazing sun grew ever higher in the sky. The screams of incinerated Death Dealers followed Lucian across the field, as did the reek of burning flesh. The vampires' dying screams drowned out even Brother Ambrose's rantings.

His boots pounded the forest floor as Lucian plunged into the woods, clinging to the sylvan shadows for Sonja's sake. Even still, a whimper of pain escaped the tapestry as the sun's relentless rays penetrated the protective layers of fabric through countless minute gaps in the weaving. Lucian knew he must find sanctuary for Sonja soon.

But where? Castle Corvinus was many miles away, and this foreign countryside was unfamiliar to Lucian. To find an abandoned hut or cave by chance would require more good fortune than fate seemed likely to bestow. Lucian scoured his memory, trying to remember a suitable haven they might have passed on their way to the keep.

A crude roadside shrine appeared before his mind's eye. Had not Soren said something about a monastery in this vicinity, somewhere to the northwest?

We must try for that, Lucian concluded, even though Brother Ambrose's hateful jeremiads still rang in his ears. A mortal monastery seemed an unlikely refuge for a fugitive vampire and lycan, but Lucian saw no better alternative. Daylight posed a greater menace to Sonja than any monk.

He heard a band of shouting humans enter the woods behind him. "He went this way!" a fervid voice hollered to his fellows. "Don't let him get away."

The daylight makes the mortals bold, he realized. *Bold enough to pursue us even into the depths of the forest.* Lucian kept on running, never slowing for a second, even though every step jarred the silver in his flesh, sending spasms of pain through his body. He longed to yank the protruding bolt from his back, but there was no time to do so; it was imperative that he stay ahead of the humans, try to lose them in the greenery.

The hunt was on, and he and Sonja were the prey, yet Lucian refused to surrender to the determined demon slayers.

I will find a sanctuary for my love, he vowed, *even if I have to kill every monk on the premises!*

Chapter Six

CARPATHIAN MOUNTAINS

*A*ngry voices echoed through the forest behind Lucian, accompanied by the clamor of heavy boots crashing through the underbrush, as he caught sight of the monastery of Saint Walpurga, an austere brick edifice distinguished by gabled roofs and an adjacent church. Stained-glass windows adorned the upper stories of the abbey, while a sculpted representation of the Madonna and Child looked down from a niche above the front entrance of the church. Silence emanated from the bell tower at the rear of the chapel.

Lucian paused to catch his breath. Between the precious burden in his arms and the quarrel jutting from his back, even his immortal stamina was nearing its limits. The silver arrowheads lodged in his flesh felt like hot coals beneath his skin, and he had to grit his teeth to keep from crying out in pain. The morning sun beat down on his head and shoulders, drenching him in sweat. Chirping birds, singing sweetly in the branches overhead, mocked his tribulations.

He approached the monastery warily. Tradition held that

even a murderer could find sanctuary on holy ground, yet Lucian rather doubted that the Church's mercy extended to vampires and lycans as well. Still, there seemed no other choice than to take their chances within the abbey, especially with Brother Ambrose's minions still hot on their trail. *Better to face a chapel full of unsuspecting monks,* Lucian reasoned, *than a hate-crazed mob armed with implements of death.*

As he approached the wide stone steps leading up to the church, however, he saw at once that something was amiss. The great oak doors guarding the entrance lay in pieces on the floor of the vestibule. Broken hinges dangled where once the doors had been affixed to the archway. Deep gouges showed in the splintered wood of the door, the solid oak scarred by jagged claw marks.

Perhaps, Lucian thought suspiciously, *I am not the first lycan to come this way. . . .*

Rats scurried away as, clutching Sonja's shrouded form, he passed through the vestibule into the vaulted chapel of the abbey. Evidence of ruin and abandonment presented itself wherever he gazed. Dark brown bloodstains discolored the tiled floor of the church, which smelled of dried blood and piss. The lectern lay on its side before a desecrated altar that some rough beast had clearly marked with its scent. The torn pages of shredded hymnals littered the floor and pews, along with overturned collection plates and reliquaries. Dust and cobwebs testified to weeks, if not months, of neglect. A bloody pawprint, stamped on the floor of the sanctuary, left no doubt in Lucian's mind about what had occurred here.

The renegades! he realized as the roots of Brother Ambrose's murderous crusade became clear. Clearly, the vulnerable monastery had fallen prey to the same marauding pack

of werewolves that had been wreaking havoc in this terri-
tory for months, explaining the monk's vengeful invocation
of his "martyred brothers." From the looks of things,
Brother Ambrose may well have been the only survivor of
this monastic bloodbath. *Small wonder that he craves our
death so avidly.*

Despite ample evidence of the carnage, no corpses remained for the rats to feast on. No doubt, Brother Ambrose
had seen to the proper Christian burial of whatever fleshless
bones the ravening werewolves had left behind.

Would that he had ceased his efforts there! Lucian brooded
darkly. *Then Sonja and I would not be in such grave peril.*

Sunlight streamed through stained-glass windows depicting the life of the saint. Many of the colored panels were
cracked and shattered, but enough glass remained to cast
rainbow-hued shadows on the wreckage. The tinted radiance made the church no place for a vampire, so Lucian was
compelled to search further for a sunless nook where Sonja
could reside in safety.

Perhaps the dormitories or refectory?

To his relief, he found an arched doorway at the far end
of the southern transept. Beyond the open portal, granite
steps led down into darkness. Lucian gratefully descended
the spiral stairs, leaving the light of the day behind. Cobwebs clung to his face and clothing as he pushed his way
through a dense accumulation of webbing. Rats and cockroaches skittered at the periphery of his vision.

By the time he reached the bottom of the stairwell, the
utter blackness challenged even his nocturnal senses. He
trod carefully, navigating by smell and sound as much as
sight, down a musty tunnel that smelled of damp and decay.
His elbow brushed against a niche in the wall, dislodging a
pile of dusty bones that clattered noisily onto the floor. A

skull rolled against his boots before coming to rest behind him.

His nose identified the skeletal remains as human. He realized then that he had stumbled upon the catacombs in which the brothers of Saint Walpurga buried their dead. Generations of monks surely occupied these subterranean tunnels, carved out of the chalky limestone through decades of hard labor. Lucian nodded in satisfaction; it seemed as safe a place as any to hide from their pursuers.

A muffled noise came from the curled tapestry in his arms. Judging the sunlight sufficiently distant, he laid the bundle gently on the floor and unfurled it as he would a carpet. The bulky tapestry spread out before him, revealing the supine form of Sonja in all her beauty, like Cleopatra before Caesar. Glowing azure eyes shone in the darkness.

He knelt beside her as she sat up on the tapestry, looking about her in confusion. "How fare you, milady?" he inquired anxiously. As his own eyes gradually adjusted to the stygian murk, he saw that Sonja seemed relatively unscathed by her ordeal. A few red patches, no worse than ordinary sunburns, marked her neck and brow, but such blemishes already appeared to be fading away. Lucian had every hope that these minor burns would heal quickly, provided Sonja had rest and blood enough.

He wished he could offer his own blood to restore her. *I would gladly surrender every drop in my veins for her sweet sake,* he thought passionately. Alas, such a sacrifice would be in vain; lycan blood was anathema to vampires, and vice versa. His blood would only sicken Sonja, not aid in her recovery. *Yet one more way in which I am unworthy of her. . . .*

She opened her mouth to reply to his query, but before she could utter a word, an alarming clamor came from the chapel above them. Sonja gasped out loud as they heard the boots and voices of at least a dozen men invading the sanctuary over their heads. "Keep your eyes peeled, lads!" one nameless mortal called out to his comrades. "They can't have gone far!"

Sonja shuddered, realizing that the mob had caught up with them . . . almost. She reached out for Lucian, who placed a comforting arm around her trembling shoulders. Despite the extreme precariousness of their situation, he could not help feeling a thrill of excitement at this unexpected intimacy. Beneath the blood and dirt soiling her garments, he scented lavender and balsam. Her body was cool against his, not hot and rough like a lycan's. Hair as soft as gossamer brushed against his cheek. His fingers yearned to caress her silken skin.

Fie on that! he chided himself. Not only were such desires grossly inappropriate, given their respective stations, but they distracted him from the danger at hand. *I need all my wits about me if we are to live to see another night.*

They huddled in the darkness, afraid to breathe, let alone speak. Above them, only a single flight of steps away, the bloodthirsty humans prowled the ruined church in search of their immortal quarries. Lucian feared it was only a matter of time before one of the braver souls ventured down the stairwell into the catacombs.

He quietly handed his dagger to Sonja, prepared to battle the hunters with tooth and claw if need be. *Here in the dark,* he thought grimly, *Sonja will at least have a chance to defend herself.*

"Enough of this!" a voice bellowed from above. "I will tarry no longer in this cursed spot. Let us be clear of this place!"

"But the holy brother urged us to search everywhere for the demons!" another mortal objected. To Lucian's dismay, the man sounded as though he was standing at the top of the spiral stairway leading to the catacombs. "Look, I've found some steps."

"That's the way to the catacombs, you dolt!" the first man mocked. His derisive tone failed to conceal the uneasiness in his voice. "I wouldn't set foot in those goddamn crypts if my soul's salvation depended on it!"

A chorus of voices chimed in, expressing the same sentiments. "If Brother Ambrose wants to go looking for vampires among the bones of the dead," a third voice declared, "let him do so himself. Me, I've got a wife and four small children to think about!"

Lucian listened with excitement, a renewed sense of hope surging within his breast. Apparently, the intrepid demon slayers lacked the courage to enter the gloomy catacombs in search of their prey. *Can it be,* he marveled, *that fate has come to our rescue at last?*

Holding a finger to his lips, he waited silently as the voices and footsteps receded into the distance. Not until the last echo of their departure faded did he risk speaking again. "Rejoice, milady," he whispered. "I daresay the mortal varlets are gone from this place."

"Thank the Elders!" she said in a hushed tone. "I thought us doomed for certain."

Free from jeopardy, if only for the nonce, Lucian found himself alone with Sonja in the cramped underground corridor. Under other circumstances, this would have been a dream come true; the freshly spilled blood soaking both their garments, however, served as a pungent reminder that their situation was far from idyllic. The desiccated remains of dead monks, resting in their humble stone niches, added to the macabre atmosphere of the moment.

Reluctantly removing his arm from the princess's shoulder, he found himself at a loss for words. "My apologies," he said finally, "for these morbid accommodations. 'Twas the best I could manage, given our present difficulties."

A faint smile appeared on Sonja's face. "You need not apologize for saving my life, Lucian. If not for you, I would be naught but ashes, like the rest of our unfortunate brethren."

Hearing his name upon her lips was like receiving a benediction from the Elders themselves. "I was but doing my duty, milady."

"Please, dear friend, call me Sonja." She laid a cool hand atop his. "I think you have earned that privilege—and more."

Lucian knew not whether to be delighted or appalled. "I—I am beneath you, good lady," he stammered. Beneath his sleeve, as he knew too well, his very flesh bore her father's brand, signifying that he was no more than a vassal.

"Let me be the judge of that," she stated. Her eyes widened as she spotted the smear of blood on his side. "You're hurt!"

"It is nothing," Lucian insisted, but his pained expression belied his words. It felt as though the silver arrowheads were branding his flesh from the inside out. Fresh blood continued to seep from the unhealed cuts. "You need not concern yourself with my injuries."

"Do not be absurd," Sonja said. "Let me look at you." Examining him more closely, she was shocked to discover, besides the grisly wound in his side, the crossbow bolt protruding from his back. "This must come out at once," she declared.

Lucian could not deny the wisdom of her words. He would be of little use to the princess unless his injuries were treated promptly; the pain and poison were sapping his strength at a steady rate. Throbbing pangs spread from each wound, pulsing with every beat of his heart. His skin felt hot and feverish, despite the chills that set his body quaking. Cramps and nausea gripped his innards, while his mouth was as dry as the fabled Sahara.

"Turn around," she instructed. Lucian presented his skewered back to her scrutiny. Blood plastered his linen tunic to his skin, forcing Sonja to peel it away inch by inch. The wolf's-head dagger cut through the cloth around the exposed crossbow bolt, but, although Sonja worked as gently as she could, he still winced as the shirt came away, exposing his bleeding torso. He knew also that the worst pain was yet to come.

"Take this," she said, offering him the arm bone of a deceased monk. He took the dusty bone between his jaws, biting down on it in anticipation of the agony ahead. "Are you ready?" she asked, taking firm hold of the feathered quarrel.

He nodded in assent. Sonja pulled on the blood-slick bolt, working it back and forth in order to extricate the silver head without snapping the wooden shaft. Lucian clenched his jaws as tightly as he could, stifling the anguished howl building at the back of his throat. His veins bulged, and his muscles tensed, and it took all his willpower not to turn and snap at Sonja like a maddened hound.

The stubborn arrowhead resisted her efforts, as though unwilling to surrender its purchase within his side. Finally, though, with one last forceful pull on its shaft, the bolt came loose. "There," Sonja announced. She snapped the quarrel in half and tossed the broken pieces back the way they had come.

Lucian's head and shoulders drooped forward. He panted raggedly, letting the arm bone drop from between his jaws.

Toothmarks showed in the surface of the abused humerus. Exhausted, his bare chest heaving, Lucian could not even muster breath enough to thank Sonja for tending to his injuries.

But his ordeal had not concluded; there remained the silver arrowhead buried in his side. Blood yet spilled from the narrow gash, which would not heal as long as the toxic metal stayed within the wound. Looking down, Lucian saw that the flesh around the cut had already begun to fester. Traceries of silver gray spread beneath the skin, radiating out from the wound like metallic cobwebs. The skin itself was inflamed and sore to the touch. Sonja's fingers but grazed the site, and Lucian yelped as though stabbed with a red-hot poker.

Heartfelt compassion and sympathy tinged her voice. "Forgive me, friend Lucian, for what I must do next." She laid him down on his side, so that the infected area faced the ceiling, and picked up the dagger once more. "The deadly silver must be removed before it is too late."

"Wait!" Lucian blurted. The thought occurred to him that the silver arrowhead would surely prevent him from transforming come nightfall, provided it didn't kill him first. He still dreaded the prospect of Changing in Sonja's presence, perhaps even more than he feared death itself. "Mayhap you should leave it be."

Incomprehension showed on her porcelain features. "I fear the fever has addled your wits, dear Lucian. The silver cannot be allowed to poison you further." She placed the monk's arm bone between his jaws once more. "Hush now, I pray you, and be of stout heart. I promise that I shall be as swift as possible."

Brooking no further argument, she used the tip of the blade to open the gash in his side until it was large enough to accommodate her slender fingers. Lucian's body convulsed in torment as she thrust her thumb and forefingers into the wound, probing for the severed head of the crossbow bolt. She held him down with her free hand, exerting all her pureblood strength to hold him still upon the mud-encrusted tapestry.

The pain was unbearable. Lucian bit down so hard that the brittle humerus snapped apart between his jaws, sending splinters of bone flying from his lips. He howled in agony, unable to hold back the scream even if a thousand torch-wielding peasants stood at the top of the steps.

No more! he shrieked inwardly. Was this what every rogue lycan endured when pierced or branded by a Death Dealer's silver? Lucian felt an unprecedented stab of sympathy for his more bestial kinsmen. No one deserved to suffer such torture, not even a half-human savage.

In the Elders' name, no more!

Just when he thought he could not stand the pain any longer, Sonja's fingers retreated from the wound, holding a sharpened piece of blood-soaked silver. As she was a vampire and not a lycan, the hated metal had no effect on her delicate skin. She hurled it away into the darkness before wiping her gore-stained fingers on the hem of her cloak.

Lucian was impressed and surprised by her lack of squeamishness. Sonja was a lady of culture and learning, not a veteran Death Dealer like her mother. Then again, he recalled, her father, Viktor, was a warrior of great renown; it could well be that battle wounds were nothing new to her.

He moved to sit up, but Sonja pressed him back down onto his side. "Be still awhile longer," she entreated. "The worst is over, I assure you, but my work is not complete. The wound is badly infected, and the silver taint must be extracted before it can spread further." Unfastening the clasp beneath her chin, she shrugged off the fur-trimmed riding cloak. Her royal pendant rested on the bodice of a saffron-colored overtunic, beneath which lay a green damask gown. "Were I back at the castle, I would apply leeches to the site, but here we must resort to a more direct technique."

A pair of cool lips descended upon his exposed side and began sucking at the open wound. A jolt of surprise rocked Lucian from head to foot, dispelling all thought of danger and distress. The tips of her fangs indented his encrimsoned flesh, and he marveled at what was transpiring between them. Never in a thousand immortal lifetimes could he have imagined that such a moment could come to pass.

Sonja lifted her head to spit out a mouthful of contaminated blood, which she dared not swallow, then went back to sucking on the crimson gash. Lucian gasped at the touch of Sonja's mouth upon his naked skin; the mixture of pain and pleasure was intensely stimulating, and he struggled to conceal his growing arousal. It was just as well that Sonja's tender ministrations had rendered him speechless, for he knew not what to say to her.

Did the beautiful vampiress notice the effect she was having on him? If so, she betrayed no indication. Spitting out a second mouthful of lycan blood, she rolled Lucian face-forward onto the tapestry and moved on to the gash in his back. There, too, her supple lips drew the last traces of silver from the wound before spewing the tainted blood onto the dusty floor of the catacomb.

" 'Tis done," she announced, wiping her lips with the flowing sleeve of her yellow overtunic. "I believe the wound will heal now, but we must have your injuries attended to by an experienced physician at the first opportunity."

Lucian sat up beside her. Was it just his imagination, or was the princess's pale face slightly flushed? "Many thanks, milady . . . Sonja," he murmured hoarsely, unable at first to meet her eyes. "I am in your debt."

"No more than I to you," she insisted. Taking up the dagger, she cut strips of cloth from the hem of her gown, which she used to bandage the newly cleansed wounds. "We could very well spend the rest of eternity thanking each other, and not without reason."

Her eyes met his, and for one delirious moment, Lucian was tempted to confess his love, to reveal all that he had been feeling these many long months and years. Saner counsels prevailed, however, and he held his tongue. *By the Elders,* he reminded himself sternly, *this delicate maiden has just lost her mother. Now is no time to subject her to the unwanted advances of an overreaching servant.*

"I have been remiss," he said, assuming a more formal demeanor, "in offering my sympathies and condolences regarding the Lady Ilona."

A stricken look came over Sonja's face, and she threw her arm over her eyes, as though to blot out the memory of her mother's severed head rolling across the muddy yard. A sob escaped her lips, and she lowered her arm. A crimson tear trickled down her cheek. "Thank you, good Lucian," she replied. "So much has happened in these past hours, there has been no time to mourn for my poor mother, let alone all the others in our company who perished this awful morning." She looked over at him, a scarlet film glistening over her luminous blue eyes. "Were there no other survivors?"

Lucian gave Sonja an uncertain shrug. "I saw Soren make it through the gates of the keep. I cannot say if he eluded the rabble assembled outside." In truth, Lucian cared not whether the sadistic overseer had survived the massacre. "Take comfort at least that your father still lives and that, if fate is kind, you and your noble sire shall soon be reunited."

She looked over at him. Hope warred with despair in her eyes and voice. She fingered the pendant bearing her family crest. "Do you truly think that we will live to see our kinsmen again?"

"I swear it, milady . . . that is, Sonja."

I shall do everything in my power, he added silently, *to see to it that you make it safely to Ordoghaz in time for Viktor's Awakening, even if it means exposing my inner beast to your revolted gaze.*

His confident assertion seemed to ease her fears somewhat. "What of your parents?" she inquired pleasantly, as though eager to change the subject to less daunting matters. "Do I know them?"

"Not at all," Lucian admitted. Although deeply mortified by his bestial origins, he could not find it in his heart to lie to Sonja of all people. "My mother and father were feral lycans, living like animals in the forest. They were exterminated by your father centuries ago, when he first brought the pillaging lycan hordes under control." His words recalled a bygone era when fierce packs of werewolves terrorized the countryside, before Viktor and his original Death Dealers forced the unruly beasts into submission for the good of all. "I was captured as an infant during the same raid in which my parents were killed."

Sonja reacted with horror to his confession. "How terrible for you!"

"Do not injure your poor heart on my behalf," he said, dismissing his parents' fate with a wave of his hand. "If not for your father, I would have been reared as an ignorant savage, no better than my barbaric forebears."

Nor would I have ever met you, he added privately. The V-shaped brand on his bicep was a small price to pay for so transcendent a blessing.

"I cannot imagine you could ever be a renegade," Sonja stated. She laid a gentle hand upon his cheek. "You are too thoughtful, too noble of mind and spirit."

Her generous praise, which plainly came from her heart, unsettled Lucian, tempting him once more to declare his love. Instead, he rose from the tapestry and extended a hand to help Sonja to her feet. "Come," he said. "Let us find a less confining locale in which to wait out the day."

She eyed him worriedly. "Are you quite certain you are ready for such activity?" She gestured at the improvised bandages encircling his torso. "Better, perhaps, that you rest awhile longer?"

"That shall not be necessary," he assured her, not entirely without cause. Now that the silver had been purged from his body, its grievous effects were quickly fading away. He still felt weary enough to sleep like a hibernating Elder, but his wounds no longer throbbed quite so mercilessly. The chills and nausea had abated, the profuse bleeding had been stanched, and an itching sensation beneath his bandages indicated that his perforated skin had begun to reknit itself. "I am well enough to walk, thanks to your skillful nursing."

Sonja took him at his word, rising from the tapestry to stand beside him. An unlit torch rested in a sconce upon the wall, and Lucian wrested the brand from its perch, then lit the tallow-dipped fibers at the end of the torch with a flint he routinely carried in a bag on his belt. The sputtering flambeau cast flickering shadows on the crumbling walls of the catacomb, exposing the rotting monks in their dismal niches. Withered corpses, with empty sockets where their eyes had once been, stared blindly into eternity.

Hand in hand, they headed into the deeper recesses of the ancient catacombs, leaving behind a heap of bloody fabric composed of the cloak, the tunic, and the tapestry. In truth, Lucian was less concerned with comfort than with putting yet more distance between themselves and the steps leading back up into the monastery. The demon hunters seemed unlikely to return, thanks to their superstitious dread of the defiled monastery, but Lucian was not inclined to risk Sonja's immortality on that assumption.

Let us not tempt fate, he thought, *while daylight still favors our foes.*

He led the way, slashing through curtains of sticky cobwebs with the blade of his dagger. Nevertheless, tendrils of filmy webbing snatched onto them as they passed, streaking their hair and clothing. The air grew cooler and staler as they descended the winding tunnels. Their footsteps echoed in the lonely passages. Lucian took to scratching arrows into the limestone at every intersection to ensure that they would be able to find their way back to the surface come nightfall; he had no desire to become lost within this subterranean labyrinth.

"How far do you think these catacombs extend?" Sonja asked. Her blue eyes gazed in fascination at the endless succession of mummified monks. Lucian wondered if she was thinking of her own father, entombed beneath the earth at Ordoghaz. "How many years have these lifeless husks lain thus?"

"I know not," he admitted. "Mortal life spans are so brief, their dead surely outnumber the living."

"How strange," the immortal princess said, a pensive expression on her face. Barring accident or foul play, she could expect to live for all eternity. "And how very sad as well."

At length, the corridor they were following opened up to expose a larger chamber beyond. Lucian and Sonja stepped over the threshold, then gaped in wonder at what they beheld.

The light of Lucian's upraised torch revealed a spacious crypt grotesquely decorated with human bones. Skulls, vertebrae, ribs, scapulae, clavicles, and more were arranged on the walls and ceiling in intricate designs and patterns. Columns of craniums, all brown with age, reached to the vaulted ceiling, where the skeletal figure of the Grim Reaper was depicted entirely in artfully placed bones. More skulls formed graceful arches above the supine forms of mummified monks. Slender arm and leg bones, laid knob to knob, framed macabre rosettes composed of mounted ribs and vertebrae. Even the chandeliers hanging from the ceiling were made of dusty clavicles radiating outward from upside-down skulls.

Everywhere Lucian looked, he saw dried bones put to some bizarre use. He could not even begin to calculate how many human skeletons must have been required to create this charnel display or how many hours the holy brothers of Saint Walpurga must have spent to create this ghoulish celebration of mortality. "This is the work of madmen!" he exclaimed. "It's obscene!"

"It may seem so to us immortals," Sonja conceded in a much milder tone, "but we need not fear death as the mortals do." Compassion tinged her voice as she contemplated the morbid spectacle. "Poor, benighted creatures! I had never truly comprehended before how their inevitable extinction must prey upon their minds. They walk in death's bleak shadow every moment of their lives."

Lucian was astounded that Sonja could feel such sympathy for the humans, even after all she had just endured at their hands, including eternal separation from her butchered mother. Her outward beauty, he realized, gazing at the incandescent vampire princess in rapt admiration, was but a glimmer of her inner grace.

How could he *not* love such a woman?

He glanced around them with a more pragmatic eye. Grotesque as it was, the lonely ossuary struck him as a likely spot in which to take their rest. A mortal slayer would have to be courageous indeed to seek out immortal prey in so eerie a setting.

"This should do, milady." He used his fading torch to light the tallow candles suspended in the skeletal chandeliers. "Let us go no farther . . . with your leave," he amended hastily.

Sonja smiled at his embarrassment. "I defer to your judgment, Lucian," she said. "And please call me Sonja."

"I will try," he said sheepishly. In all honesty, he could not get used to addressing her so familiarly—except in his fantasies, of course—so he resolved to skirt the issue by avoiding all appellations and honorifics whatsoever.

He sat down between two towering columns of skulls, resting his back against the cold limestone. "Nightfall is many hours away," he observed. "You should try to sleep." He tucked his dagger back into his belt. "I will keep watch over you until it is safe to travel once more."

He glanced over at a horizontal niche occupied by a robe-clad skeleton. He briefly considered ousting the bones onto the floor to make room for Sonja, but the princess chose to lie down beside him instead, resting her head on his lap. "Would that you could guard me from troubled dreams as well," she murmured. "I fear the nightmares today's events must surely breed."

Lucian could not resist stroking her flowing hair in an effort to soothe her mind. The flaxen tresses felt like finely spun silk. "Perhaps sleep will grant you oblivion," he suggested softly, "and sweet relief from the woes of the day."

"Dear Lucian!" she breathed. He felt her tense shoulders

relax against his leg. "I can always count on you to champion me in my time of need."

He basked in her praise and affection, choosing to savor her warm regard while it lasted, which was unlikely to be much longer. Soon, he knew, the moon would rise, and Sonja would be forced to see him for what he truly was: a wolf in man's clothing, as hideous and repulsive as any other werewolf.

Sonja may have forgotten, for the moment, the vast divide between us, Lucian thought, *but I cannot. Only a few more hours of daylight stand between us and the dreadful truth, that she is beauty itself—and I am a beast.*

Chapter Seven

THE CATACOMBS

*L*ucian awoke with a start. Despite his best intentions, exhaustion had apparently gotten the better of him. The candles in the crypt had long since burned out, leaving him in utter blackness. He instantly reached for Sonja, only to discover that the princess's head no longer rested on his lap.

"Sonja!" he cried out in alarm. Panic gripped him as he sprang to his feet. "Sonja!"

"Be calm," a melodious voice addressed him. Azure eyes glowed in the darkness only a few feet away. "I am with you still."

Slowly adjusting to the gloom, his lycan eyes showed him Sonja's graceful silhouette standing in the murky crypt. Immense relief washed over him, accompanied by shame at having fallen asleep in the first place. "Forgive me, milady! I did not mean to shirk my duty so!"

"There is nothing to forgive," Sonja insisted. "After all your exertions on my behalf, it was only fair that I watch over you for a spell." Her gaze lifted toward the ceiling, and her voice struck a joyous note. "Can you not feel it, Lucian? The sun has gone down. Night is come again!"

Lucian shared her certainty. He did not need to see the sky to know that the full moon had risen. He felt energized and restored, as much by the fall of night as by his unplanned-for slumber. Unwrapping his bandages, he saw that his battle wounds were healed; only thin white scars revealed where the silver had pierced his flesh.

Moreover, his body trembled on the verge of the Change. His skin was drawn taut over his frame, as though his human epidermis were too small to contain the beast caged within him. Muscles rippled along his naked torso, while his remaining garments felt as tight and confining as his skin. If not for Sonja's presence, he would have stripped off his woolen leggings in a rush. Instead, he merely kicked off his boots, revealing sharpened yellow nails that were already coming to resemble the claws of an enormous wolf.

Even separated from the moon by several tons of solid limestone, he could still feel its irresistible effect. Tiny hairs bristled all over his body. Canine fangs slid from his gums. His fingers began to curl into paws. . . .

No! Lucian thought, determined to fight off the transformation for as long as lycanly possible. *Not now. Not yet.* He paced restlessly within the vault, unable to stand still. Snatching a fresh torch from a nearby sconce, he lit it with his flint, then headed toward the archway leading back to the surface. "We must make haste. Many miles lie between us and the safety of your father's estate."

"I am ready," Sonja answered bravely. The gleaming pendant on her bosom reflected the bright orange glow of the torch. Her glowing blue eyes took on their customary chestnut tint. "I know that I am safe in your hands."

That much was true, Lucian acknowledged, no matter

what the moon revealed. Sonja was in no danger from the beast he was doomed to become; as a werewolf, his strength and ferocity would be directed only against their human foes.

A thought occurred to him, and he handed Sonja his belt, bag, and dagger. "Take these," he told her, his voice already deeper and gruffer than before. "I . . . will soon have no need of them."

She accepted the items without argument. "I understand," she said simply, sparing Lucian any need to explain. She tied his belt around her own svelte waist. "I will keep them safe for you."

As if my lowly possessions are at all worth your concern, he thought disparagingly. Only the wolf's-head dagger possessed any modicum of value. *Sonja's safety is all that matters.*

Drawn by the ceaseless pull of the moon, he practically dragged her behind him as they hastily retraced their path through the underground labyrinth, using his scratch marks as a guide. After passing the blood-encrusted tapestry upon which Sonja had treated Lucian's injuries, they ascended the spiral steps back up to the ruined church. Lucian peered around the archway at the top of the stairs, searching the shadows for any hint of lurking demon slayers, but he saw no sign of danger. He sniffed the air; the only human smells he detected were several hours old.

The lack of adversaries did not surprise him. What mortal would be foolhardy enough to hunt vampires and werewolves after dark—and beneath a full moon, no less?

They emerged from the stairwell into the deserted abbey. Moonlight poured through the stained-glass windows, electrifying Lucian's senses. Bone and sinew crackled and twisted beneath his skin.

He tried to fight the Change, but it was like holding back

the tide. Claustrophobia gripped him, along with an over-whelming urge to flee Sonja's company, and he bolted down the nave like a lunatic, rushing out of the abbey into the churchyard. "Lucian! Wait!" Sonja called after him, but he could barely hear her over the roar of the blood pounding in his ears. His heart hammered like a drumming tabor, and his pupils shrank to pinpricks of black, surrounded by bright cobalt orbs.

The full moon shone brightly above the churchyard. No longer filtered through tinted glass, the potent lunar radiance fell directly on him, hastening the Change. With a sinking heart, Lucian realized that he could resist the transformation for not a moment more.

Sonja came rushing out of the abbey, her rumpled tunic and damask gown rustling about her. Her buckled leather shoes hurried down the steps toward him. "Lucian, please! You need not hide from me."

"Look away, milady! I beg you!" His guttural voice sounded scarcely human. He turned away from her, even as a violent tremor shook him from head to toe. He could feel his very entrails being wrenched into new shapes. "I would not have you see me thus!"

He threw back his head and shoulders, unable to resist basking in the moon's invigorating glow. His fair skin darkened, turning a mottled shade of gray. His widow's peak birthed a mane of coarse black fur that sprouted from his head and shoulders, then spread across his body and limbs, which themselves grew larger and heavier with every heartbeat. His spine lengthened painfully, as though stretched upon the rack, and his leggings came apart at their seams as he assumed the proportions of a giant. Jagged claws protruded from his fingers and toes.

A tortured moan was torn from his lips as his skull underwent a drastic metamorphosis. A canine snout protruded from his face. His brow sloped backward above fierce blue eyes. Tufted ears tapered to a point. Flattened nostrils flared above a mouthful of jagged incisors. Foam dripped from wolfen jaws.

His senses expanded, the night coming alive with a thousand new scents and sounds. As the transformation neared completion, the gut-wrenching convulsions gave way to an undeniable feeling of exhilaration. He stretched out his claws, reveling in his heightened strength and vitality. Succumbing to a primal impulse, he howled triumphantly at the moon.

Yes! the werewolf exulted. *I am free!*

"Lucian?"

Sonja's voice called him back to himself, reminding Lucian that he was not alone. The gigantic beast turned to face the princess, who was now at least three heads shorter than the two-legged monstrosity Lucian had become. Beneath his shaggy pelt, Lucian's heart dreaded the shock and revulsion that were bound to be written upon her face.

To his amazement, however, she gazed up at him just as warmly as before. He saw himself reflected in her eyes—a towering, subhuman brute—but she did not draw away from him. Rather, she stepped forward and laid her slender hand upon one of his hirsute paws.

"Foolish Lucian," she said with a smile. "Do not fear to show me this part of yourself. No aspect of you can be repellent to me." A gentle chuckle reached his ears. "Did you truly think that I had never seen a werewolf before?"

Lucian was overcome with emotion. The moment he had most dreaded had come and gone, proving all his fears unfounded. Sonja had seen past his bestial exterior to the thinking being within! Alas, his muzzle was no longer suited to human speech, so he could not reply to Sonja's sweet words in kind, but in his heart and eyes, her blessed visage outshone the moon.

He could conceive of only one way to repay her generosity. Scooping her up in his hairy arms, he set off toward Buda at a steady lope. She felt as light as a feather in his arms, and he knew that he could carry her all the way to Ordoghaz before the sun rose again. He raced into the surrounding forest, heading southwest by the stars.

Love, as well as the moon, lent him speed.

Dawn was lighting up the horizon as Lucian and Sonja drew near the high stone walls that guarded her father's estate. A heavy layer of fog hung over the land, and the ground was damp with dew beneath Lucian's paws. The mist obscured his vision, but he could dimly glimpse the enclosed guard stations flanking the gates of Ordoghaz.

Almost there, he thought with relief, *and with but moments to spare!* The dense fog provided Sonja with a degree of protection from the rising sun, but only for a few minutes more. He had to get her safely indoors before the daylight arrived in full force.

Sonja ran beside him, having insisted on completing the last leg of their journey under her own power to spare him the effort of carrying her any farther. In truth, his weary arms were grateful to be relieved of their lithesome burden; he had traveled hard and fast all through the night, sticking to the woods while skirting any mortal towns or villages. They had encountered no resistance. On this night of the full moon, it seemed, no mortal dared to venture into the untamed forest; they preferred to stay safe at home behind locked doors festooned with garlic and crosses.

The moon itself was sinking from view, and Lucian felt

his strength waning. Soon he would be compelled to shed his wolfen form, but not before he delivered Sonja unto the protection of the coven once more.

After that, what happened to him was of little account.

Two Death Dealers, armed with crossbows, emerged from their stations guarding the spiked gates. As Lucian lunged out of the fog, one of the sentries hastily raised his weapon and took aim at the charging werewolf. Without thinking, Lucian tried to address the guards, but all that emerged from his snout was an inarticulate yelp.

A silver-tipped bolt went whizzing past Lucian's head, missing his misshapen skull by mere inches. The werewolf froze in his tracks, uncertain whether to flee or advance. The bitter irony of being fired upon only yards away from their sought-after destination was not lost on him.

"Wait! Hold your fire!" Sonja called out frantically. She darted out of the fog and threw herself in front of Lucian, shielding the towering werewolf with her own willowy form. "We seek sanctuary—in the Elders' name!"

The trigger-happy guard looked unwilling to heed Sonja's desperate cries. Reloading his crossbow, he took aim once more and might have fired again, had not his comrade reached out and forced the point of the crossbow toward the ground. "Hold, Kraven!" the second Death Dealer barked. "Let's hear what the girl has to say!"

Sonja rushed forward while Lucian lingered behind, not wanting to provoke the first guard, whose name was apparently Kraven, into yet another rash attempt upon his life. The dark-haired Death Dealer eyed Sonja suspiciously as she approached the gates. "Careful, Vayer!" he sneered at his fellow guard. "I smell lycan trickery!"

Lucian had to admit that in her disheveled state, with her once fine garments now smeared with blood and muck,

Sonja looked more like a renegade lycan than a highborn vampire. Kraven kept his crossbow poised and ready as he sneered at the bedraggled princess.

"Bless you, kind sir!" Sonja said breathlessly to the more hospitable guard, Vayer. "We are sorely in need of the shelter of this, my father's house." She raised her crest-shaped pendant for the man's inspection. "I am indeed Sonja, daughter of Viktor."

Vayer's eyes widened in astonishment as he peered past the sweat and grime masking Sonja's beauty. "By the Elders, it *is* you, milady! We thought you dead!"

"Viktor's daughter?" Kraven blurted. His entire manner changed more rapidly than a lycan in the moonlight. "A thousand pardons, your ladyship. Kraven of Leicester at your service." He spoke Magyar with a recognizably English accent. "How may I assist you?"

"Assist *her*?" Vayer mocked. He tilted his head toward Lucian, who continued to keep his distance. "You nearly killed her servant, you fool!"

Kraven shrugged, as though Lucian's accidental demise would have been of little consequence. The werewolf's hackles rose, and he snarled beneath his breath, taking an instant dislike to the callow vampire, who had almost been the death of him. *I would not want to meet my end at the hands of a panicky vampire.*

"Come, your ladyship," Kraven said solicitously. "Let me personally escort you to the manor." Leading Sonja away, he glanced back at his fellow watchman. "Vayer, you stay here and see to the changing of the guard."

Lucian knew from experience that with dawn breaking, the vampiric sentries were due to be relieved by their lycan counterparts. Vayer looked taken aback by Kraven's presumptuousness but was apparently too level-headed to argue the point when an Elder's daughter was in urgent need of succor.

The spiked gates swung open, and Lucian followed Sonja and Kraven onto the grounds of the estate. Ordoghaz, known locally as Devil's House, was dominated by a sprawling stone mansion built by Viktor centuries ago while he was still but a mortal warlord. Jagged spires and battlements rose atop its looming stone walls, while majestic columns and pointed arches adorned its brooding façade. With sunrise nigh, the mansion's narrow lancet windows were tightly shuttered so that not a single candle could been seen from outside. Doubtless, most of the vampires had already retired for the day, leaving the household's lycan servants to tidy up after the night's activities.

A circular fountain, in the Roman style, was situated across the way from the mansion's front entrance. Lucian felt the spray of the fountain on his fur as they hurried up the marble steps toward the entrance. The warning pangs of another impending transformation gripped him, and he felt the bristling hairs begin to retract back into his skin.

A very human-sounding sigh of relief escaped his muzzle as Sonja slipped beneath the shade of an imposing portico. Kraven pounded with his fist on a pair of closed oak doors. "Open up!" he bellowed self-importantly. "The Lady Sonja desires admittance!"

A bewildered lycan retainer opened the doors, and Kraven barged into the foyer beyond. With a swooping bow, he graciously invited Sonja into her own ancestral manor. "Please, milady, enter freely and without fear." He barked orders at the hapless retainer. "Summon Marcus at once—and someone fetch Lady Sonja a flagon of warm blood!"

Sonja stepped inside, but Kraven balked when Lucian attempted to follow her. He regarded the werewolf's inhuman form with open disdain and wrinkled his nose at the pungent aroma of Lucian's damp and dirty fur. "Excuse me, milady, but this beast simply cannot enter the manor—like that."

"He goes where I go," Sonja stated firmly. She looked back at the werewolf without hesitation. "Please join us, Lucian."

Kraven was visibly appalled but was not about to contradict an Elder's daughter. Lucian enjoyed the Englishman's discomfort as he stepped inside the mansion. His height was such that he had to duck his wolfen head beneath the archway, but he could already feel his spine contracting along with the rest of him.

Indeed, he barely made it past the threshold before the Change came over him completely. He grunted out loud as his snout retracted and his hairy pelt receded. Claws shrank back into fingers. Canine fangs withdrew into gums. Mass and muscle evaporated into the ether. Cobalt eyes dimmed to brown.

Within moments, Lucian was a man once more. Panting with exhaustion, his body drenched in sweat, he stood naked in the spacious foyer, his pale white skin scratched and abraded from his rough trek through the countryside. His bare feet were dwarfed by the muddy pawprints beneath him.

I must look a very mess, he realized.

His scruffy, denuded appearance contrasted sharply with the refined elegance of the mansion's interior. Exquisite tapestries and paintings hung on lustrous, oak-paneled walls. Marble tiles, now tracked with mud, stretched across the floor to where the sweeping main stairway ascended toward the upper reaches of Ordoghaz. A hanging copper lamp supported the weight of a dozen beeswax candles.

"How fare you, Lucian?" Sonja asked. Brown eyes viewed him with concern, while demurely averting her eyes from his nakedness. Lucian felt a flush of embarrassment.

"Well enough, milady," he assured her. Now that she was back among her peers, he could not dream of addressing her by her first name. "Although I fear you find me not at my best."

His wry remark elicited a smile from her lips. "Likewise, to be sure," she replied.

Not surprisingly, their unexpected arrival generated much commotion. A hubbub of excited voices filled the foyer. Lucian looked up to see numerous pale faces staring down at them from atop the stairs and landing. More faces peered from the adjacent salon and antechambers. Vampiric gentlemen and ladies, many of them attired for bed, gazed at the newcomers with frank curiosity while chattering enthusiastically among themselves.

Lucian briefly worried that some unseemly gossip might attach itself to him and Sonja, only to realize the sheer preposterousness of the notion. Who save he could ever imagine a liaison between Sonja and himself? Never mind that such unions were forbidden by the Covenant on pain of death, the very prospect of a pureblood princess—the only daughter of an Elder—dallying with a lycan vassal was too manifestly absurd to be believed.

Or was it?

Despite everything, he could not forget the touch of Sonja's lips against his skin or the comforting feel of her beneath his arm. "Call me Sonja," she had insisted repeatedly. Could it be that she truly saw him as an equal—and perhaps as a man? It might be worth risking torture and execution to find out. . . .

A hush fell over the gawking vampires as the crowd upon

the stairs parted to make way for Marcus, the reigning Elder of the coven.

The powerful vampire looked deceptively youthful, appearing as a clean-shaven young man with slick black hair, but there was no mistaking the ancient wisdom in his dark eyes or the unquestioned authority in his stride. A black velvet gown, embroidered with golden trim, draped his regal frame as he marched down the stairs. A golden pendant, bearing ancient runes that differed somewhat from those on Sonja's own pendant, rested on his chest. Amazement transfigured his stern features as he spotted Sonja waiting in the foyer.

"Sonja! Dear maiden!" He took the last few steps in a rush and clasped Sonja's shoulders with obvious delight. "You are indeed restored to us, against all odds!" A more sober expression came over his unlined face. "The loss of your esteemed mother is a great tragedy to us all."

"Thank you, Lord Marcus," Sonja answered. "I can still scarcely believe she is no more." Fatigue and sorrow were evident in her voice. She swayed unsteadily on her feet.

"Poor child!" Marcus intoned, offering her the support of his arm. "A chair and sustenance for the lady!"

Kraven snatched a steaming goblet from the hand of a newly arrived servant. He proffered the cup to Marcus with much fanfare. "As you command, great Elder! I took the liberty of requesting this libation mere minutes ago."

Marcus accepted the goblet, then glanced at the eager Death Dealer without much interest. "And you are . . . ?"

"Kraven of Leicester, Elder, but lately arrived from Britain." He puffed out his chest. "I was standing guard at the gate when this precious lady came rushing out of the forest, in desperate need of deliverance."

"Well, now she has found it." Marcus gave the goblet of

heated blood, tapped from the ready veins of the estate's livestock, to Sonja. The smell of the blood made Lucian's own mouth water. "Drink deep, child. It will restore you."

Another servant managed to deliver a chair to the foyer without Kraven intercepting it first. Marcus helped Sonja onto the padded seat, then turned to find Kraven still standing at his elbow. "You may go, sentry," he said brusquely.

Kraven was unable to conceal a look of petulant disappointment. He stormed out of the foyer, unhappily thrust from the center of attention. *He's an ambitious one,* Lucian noted quietly, *with aspirations quite beyond his present station.*

The indignant Death Dealer passed from Lucian's mind, however, as none other than Soren suddenly burst onto the scene. The beefy overseer came pushing his way through the excited throng crowding the corridors. A look of surprise—and perhaps chagrin—came over Soren's bearded features as he spied first Sonja, then Lucian within the foyer.

So, Lucian thought coldly. *You made it past the mob after all.* He wondered where Soren had managed to hide away from the sun yesterday. A cave? A hollowed-out tree trunk? Another corner of the monastery? Wherever he had hidden, the Irish vampire had obviously made it to Ordoghaz before them.

Soren scowled at Lucian, who got the distinct impression that the undead overseer was not entirely pleased to see that he had survived the ambush at the keep. *Perhaps,* Lucian speculated, *because I proved all too correct concerning the threat posed by Brother Ambrose and his followers?*

Sonja, on the other hand, was too good-hearted not to be thrilled that another member of their party had escaped death. "Soren!" she exclaimed happily. "You're still alive!"

"Soren arrived on horseback several hours ago," Marcus explained calmly. He turned his forbidding gaze on the newly arrived overseer. "I am a trifle confused, Soren. You said you were the only survivor."

The Irishman placed a meaty hand over his heart. "Faith, Elder, I believed Lady Sonja killed along with her mother, else I would have never abandoned the fray!"

Lucian distinctly remembered calling out to Soren for assistance but held his tongue. As a lycan, he knew better than to challenge the veracity—or courage—of a vampire.

" 'Twas a scene of utter tumult," Sonja confirmed, quick to grant Soren the benefit of the doubt. "I can well believe that amid such bloody chaos, Soren thought himself the only survivor."

Marcus examined Soren through narrowed eyes. "Perhaps," the Elder said guardedly.

"Ho! What's all this commotion?" a sardonic voice interrupted. All heads turned to see Marcus's son, Nicolae, descending the stairs with a giggling doxy on one arm and a goblet of spiced blood in the opposite hand.

A cascade of curly blond hair crowned the head of the Elder's notoriously decadent heir. His ruddy complexion, quite literally flushed with blood, bespoke decades, if not centuries, of overindulgence. The sleeves of his plum-colored brocade tunic were fashionably slit, the better to display the expensive silk shirt underneath. His light purple hose was tucked into a pair of polished black boots. Sapphire and emerald rings glittered on his fingers.

His swooning companion, by contrast, wore little more than a skimpy linen shift, somewhat the worse for wear. She clung immodestly to Nicolae, as if too dissipated to stand without assistance. Her skin was pale, even by undead standards, and dark circles shadowed her glassy green eyes. Black hair fell in wanton abandon to her shoulders. A bawdy grin left little doubt about her virtue, or lack thereof.

Marcus regarded his heir without enthusiasm. "I should have known you would be the last to arrive," he observed icily. The Elder's disappointment with his wastrel son was common knowledge throughout the coven. "Behold your dear cousin, Sonja, whom we believed to have perished."

Nicolae arched an indolent eyebrow. "Risen from the dead, have we?" he addressed Sonja. "How terribly traditional of you. Small wonder the mortal riffraff insist on describing us as walking corpses."

The doxy on his arm guffawed at his jest. She threw back a tangle of unbound hair, revealing fresh bite marks on her bruised throat. Lucian caught a whiff of blood beneath too much perfume and was startled to realize that the pallid strumpet was human. Rumor had it, he recalled, that the Elder's jaded heir preferred the warm blood of willing mortals to the cooler blood and company of his own kind; apparently, gossip spoke truly in this instance.

Lucian could not help reflecting that such liaisons, although faintly scandalous, were not forbidden by the Covenant, provided the mortal was not taken unwillingly. For a lycan to love a vampire, on the other hand, was something else altogether; as far as Lucian knew, such a romance had never occurred in the entire history of their respective races.

'Tis not fair, he thought. *Why must the Covenant keep us apart?*

"Sonja's mother has but recently met her end," Marcus reminded Nicolae, clearly vexed by his offspring's cavalier attitude. Lucian, too, was offended by the prince's conspicuous lack of concern for Sonja's feelings.

"Quite unfortunate, to be sure," Nicolae conceded lightly before turning his attention to Lucian. Sweaty, bare naked, and unkempt, the exhausted lycan stood in stark contrast to the impeccably groomed heir. "And who might this sorry specimen be?"

Soren spoke up before Lucian could identify himself. "Merely one of the castle servants, nothing more."

"Nay, much more!" Sonja protested strenuously. "If not for this noble lycan, I would have most certainly never lived to enjoy your hospitality, Lord Marcus. It was Lucian who rescued me from the mob and brought me safely to Ordoghaz."

Nicolae chortled at her words. "A chivalrous wolf . . . how extraordinary! He should be pictured in a bestiary, alongside the phoenix and the unicorn!"

Marcus's response was considerably more restrained. "I see," he said flatly. "Very well. Escort him to the servants' quarters," he instructed Soren. "See to it that he is clothed and fed."

With that, the Elder dismissed Lucian from his mind. "Come, child," he said to Sonja in an avuncular tone that belied his apparent youth. "Let us see you to your chambers, where all your needs can be attended to. You must be exhausted from your ordeal, and I would not have my old comrade Viktor awaken to find you in such a state."

Marcus personally helped Sonja up from her chair and guided her toward the grand stairway. "Nicolae," he barked at his wayward son. "Make yourself useful for once and assist me. Your whores and debaucheries can wait."

"As you say, Father," Nicolae assented, sighing heavily. He lapped at the mortal wench's neck bites one last time before detaching his arm from her waist. The doxy tottered unsteadily, whether from inebriation or blood loss Lucian could not tell. Possibly both.

"Wait for me in my bedchamber," the prince directed her, not even bothering to lower his voice. "We'll continue our revels later."

"Aye, Nicky," the tart slurred saucily. She staggered out of the foyer, her bare feet sliding on the marble floor.

Lucian paid the mortal trull no heed. His eyes saw only Sonja as Marcus and Nicolae escorted her up the stairs, away from him. She looked back over her shoulder, and their eyes met briefly, before Soren took Lucian roughly by the arm and dragged him away from the foyer.

"Come along, cur!" the overseer snapped. "It's past time you got back to where you belong."

Chapter Eight

ORDOGHAZ

The crypt of the Elders hid deep beneath Ordoghaz, many feet below even the lowest dungeons and cellars of the ancient mansion. The vast chamber was dominated by an elaborate mosaic floor in which three large bronze disks were embedded. Each disk bore complex Celtic patterns surrounding one of three ornate capital letters:

A for *Amelia*.

M for *Marcus*.

V for *Viktor*.

Ordinarily, silence ruled over the somber crypt, which was seldom visited by the inhabitants of the manor, but tonight, on the occasion of Viktor's Awakening, the chamber held the entire Council along with various other dignitaries. These guests gathered just inside the entrance of the crypt, before the granite steps leading down to the bottommost floor, where Marcus himself waited at the center of the triangle of disks. Torches flickered in the arched alcoves lining the walls. A fourth bronze disk, bearing an intricate Celtic pattern, was mounted in the wall above the doorway.

Sonja stood at Marcus's right hand. In her mother's absence, she had been granted the honor of assisting the Elder in her father's Awakening, a grave responsibility that weighed heavily upon her mind. She shivered beneath her burgundy satin gown, both from the chill of the crypt and in anticipation of the momentous events ahead. Excitement at the prospect of seeing her father again, for the first time in two centuries, was leavened by the sobering realization that he must soon learn of his wife's untimely end.

Would that I could spare him so dreadful a revelation, she mused, *at least until he can recover fully from the Awakening.* Alas, as leader of the coven for the next hundred years, it was vital that he should know, as expeditiously as possible, all that had transpired during his long repose. *I should be thankful, I suppose, that it shall not fall upon me to inform Father of the tragic news.*

That burden rested with Marcus alone.

Sonja observed the distinguished company that had assembled to witness the Awakening. Clad in their finest robes, the Council members chatted softly among themselves as they waited for the ceremony to begin. Nicolae stood amid the other guests, a bored expression on his face.

The prince's blasé attitude insulted her. Although she had known Nicolae for many centuries, ever since they were both children, she had never liked him. Even as a toddler, he had cared for nothing except his own selfish desires.

Not for the first time, Sonja regretted that Lucian could not attend the Awakening. Certainly, he deserved the privilege more than the likes of Nicolae. She had even considered appealing to Marcus on Lucian's behalf but had ultimately thought better of it. She was not so idealistic as to think that Marcus, or any other Elder, would ever countenance the presence of a mere lycan at an Awakening.

Not even a lycan as dashing and heroic as Lucian.

Thoughts of Lucian dispelled some of the chill seeping into her bones. Never had she met his like, vampire or lycan. He had the high brow and sensitive features of a poet yet the heart of a warrior as well. As a scholar and historian, she could not help comparing him to the legendary heroes of the past, such as Perseus, Galahad, or even King David. And yet he was condemned to eternal servitude for no other reason than the accident of his birth.

The sheer injustice of it all appalled her. *Something is profoundly awry with this twilight world of ours,* she thought, *that so chivalrous a spirit cannot rise to the rank to which his considerable gifts and fortitude entitle him.* A passionate conviction filled her heart. *I, for one, will not be blinded to the true nobility of the man.*

Bells tolled high overhead, marking the midnight hour. A hush fell over the assembly as Marcus addressed all present. The raised collar of his dark robe fanned out behind his head. A golden dagger resided in his belt.

"Members of the Council, honored guests," he began. "Beyond these venerable walls, in the mortal world, petty despots constantly war for land and power. Kings and dynasties come and go in an endless and brutal cavalcade of conquest and usurpation. In contrast, we of the coven have known nothing but peace and stability for some five hundred years. Why is this?"

The other vampires, Sonja included, answered in unison: "Because of the Chain!"

Marcus nodded in acknowledgment. "We Elders—Viktor, Amelia, and myself—do not wage war against one another in pursuit of absolute power, nor do our differing views and instincts ever lead us into the conflict. Why?"

"Because of the Chain!" The ritual response echoed within the sepulchral confines of the crypt.

"Just so," Marcus confirmed. "The coven exists in harmony because we Elders have wisely agreed to divide eternity among us, a century at a time. One Elder above the earth, two below; that is the way of things, so that the coven has never more than a single ruler in any given century. Thus is order maintained, through an eternal cycle of rebirth and rejuvenation. And why?"

"Because of the Chain!" the guests chanted for the third and final time.

Sonja's gaze was irresistibly drawn to two of the three bronze disks on the floor. Beneath those circular markers, she knew, both her father and Amelia rested in their respective tombs. Marcus's own sarcophagus was empty, awaiting his imminent return to unbroken darkness and solitude.

"Now is the appointed hour," Marcus proclaimed. "Soon I will go into the earth again, confident that the destiny of our people will be safely guided by my fellow Elders for the next two hundred years—until I rise once more."

Nicolae scowled at his father's words. Sonja felt a twinge of sympathy for the frustrated prince; unlike any mortal heir, Nicolae could not look forward to *ever* inheriting his father's exalted position in the coven. Marcus was immortal, after all, and not even his coming internment could ever disguise that inconvenient fact. *Small wonder,* she reflected, *that Nicolae wastes his nights in vice and revelry. He's heir to a throne that shall never be his.*

"Let the Awakening begin," Marcus decreed. He nodded at Sonja and whispered, "You may proceed, child."

"Yes, Lord Marcus."

She knelt before the bronze disk that bore her father's initial. The stylized V, which resembled the upraised wings of a bat, reminded her of the identical mark branded on Lucian's upper arm, but she pushed the memory out of her mind; whatever her feelings for the handsome lycan, now was no time to be distracted by maidenly fancies.

Her fingers gripped the raised metal V, and she tried to rotate a circular segment of the disk, about ten inches in diameter. Untouched for precisely two centuries, the ancient hatch resisted her at first, but Sonja exerted her pureblood strength, and the miniature disk turned beneath her grasp, setting in motion a concealed clockwork mechanism. The intricate designs adorning the hatch shifted position as Sonja heard the muted rumble of long-dormant machinery awakening from slumber. The entire bronze disk sank into the floor, then split apart into four triangular segments that retracted from sight, exposing the top of the stone sarcophagus below. Another V, illuminated in lapis lazuli, identified the upright coffin as her father's.

The ponderous sound of stone sliding across stone resounded within the crypt. Propelled by hidden counterweights, the vertical sarcophagus rose from the floor like the Devil ascending from beneath the stage of a traveling mystery play. The coffin thrust upward until it towered above Sonja like a pagan monolith. She waited for it to come to a halt, then stepped forward and released a catch concealed in the sarcophagus's elaborately carved exterior. The coffin slowly pivoted on its axis, then snapped into place horizontal to the floor.

A supine figure was laid out within the sarcophagus, held in place by embossed metal bars. Sonja stepped toward the bier, then placed a hand over her mouth. Although she had been cautioned about what to expect, she still had to hold back a gasp at what she beheld.

After two hundred years of hibernation, her father bore scant resemblance to the regal monarch she recalled. The skeletal figure within the coffin looked more like an ancient Egyptian mummy than a vampire: dry, withered, and seemingly lifeless. Sere gray skin was stretched over his bony frame like age-old parchment. The bones of his rib cage jutted beneath his skin like the flying buttresses of an abandoned cathedral long since fallen into ruin.

Her father's pate was as bald as the skull his emaciated visage so resembled. Closed eyes rested at the bottom of sunken black sockets, while his desiccated lips had peeled away from his gums, revealing jagged fangs locked in a corpselike grimace.

A gilded pendant, akin to her own, rested on his still and silent chest. A jeweled belt and black satin leggings spared her the sight of his shriveled manhood.

Oh, Father! she lamented silently. *What has become of you?*

No sign of life, not a single breath or heartbeat, hinted that her sire yet lived. Any mortal observer would have readily believed her father's body to be long dead. Even Sonja, knowing better, found it hard to accept that the horrid corpse before her would soon be walking among them once more.

"Well done, child," Marcus said softly. "You may prepare for the transference."

A polished metal rod, containing a hollow glass ampule at its center, stretched across the top of the open sarcophagus. Sonja guided the rod along a built-in track until the empty ampule was positioned directly above her father's mouth. Then she stepped aside to allow Marcus to approach the bier.

"Now let the sacred rite proceed," he declared. Drawing a golden dagger from his belt, he extended his left arm and drew the tip of the blade across his wrist. A streak of crimson blossomed on Marcus's pale skin.

An audible gasp broke from the audience as the tangy scent of an Elder's blood filled the air. Nicolae licked his lips, and even Sonja's mouth watered as she lusted for a taste of the potent nectar.

Ignoring the crowd's visceral reaction, Marcus held his bleeding wrist above a series of shallow silver bowls embedded in the edge of the sarcophagus. Scarlet droplets fell into the first of the concave receptacles, beginning a gradual procession from bowl to bowl, where the spilled blood mixed with arcane catalytic residues to undergo a sublime alchemical transformation before flowing through the metal rod into the ampule above Viktor's petrified jaws. Slowly, meticulously, Marcus's blood dripped from the cavity into Viktor's mouth.

"My blood to thee, my thoughts to thee," Marcus chanted. "Partake of my memories, Viktor of Moldavia, and those of Amelia before me, so that the Chain shall not be broken."

Sonja held her breath in awe. Only an Elder possessed the knowledge and concentration to accomplish what Marcus was now doing: transferring a complete and coherent record of the last two centuries into her father's quiescent consciousness, so that Viktor would awaken with full knowledge of all that had taken place while he slumbered. Not only Marcus's memories but also Amelia's, passed on to Marcus at his own Awakening one hundred years prior, were being transmitted to Viktor by the absorption of Marcus's immortal blood.

The scarlet teardrops elicited an immediate response from the apparent corpse. Viktor's eyelids flickered as the blood trickled down his throat. A rattle escaped his withered lungs. Drawing away from the catalyst drip, Marcus placed his fingertips against Viktor's throat. He nodded with satisfaction as he detected the faint pulse therein.

"The Elder awakes!" Marcus announced. A few stray drops of blood fell onto Viktor's skin before Marcus's sliced wrist healed itself. Minute patches of healthy pink skin appeared wherever the scarlet droplets touched Viktor's epidermis. "The Chain endures!"

A full-throated cheer arose from the assembled vampires, albeit with a half-hearted huzzah from Nicolae. Sonja's throat tightened with emotion. She wiped a bloodred tear from her eye.

Her beloved father was not yet himself, of course, but Sonja knew that he would recover quickly, given sufficient time and blood. The latter was already waiting for him in the private infirmary at the rear of the crypt. By this time tomorrow, he would once more be the proud and majestic father of her memories.

"Many thanks for attending this hallowed event," Marcus informed the audience, "but now Viktor requires his privacy. You may all return to your various duties and diversions."

One by one, the Council members and their associates filed out of the crypt. Nicolae exited the chamber with unseemly haste, but the rest took their leave in a measured and dignified manner. Only Sonja lingered behind, to further assist Marcus with her father's restoration. Marcus waited until the last of the attendees had departed before beckoning to Sonja.

"So much for pomp and ceremony," he remarked. "Let us now see to your noble father's recovery."

The infirmary was hidden behind a pair of thick oak doors directly opposite the front entrance of the crypt. While Sonja hurried to draw open the doors, Marcus slid the massive sarcophagus upon a set of tracks laid into the tiled floor. Within minutes, the bier rested at the threshold of the infirmary, between two colossal stone pillars.

A Roman-style bath waited within the infirmary, the rectangular marble pool filled to the halfway point by a tremendous quantity of steaming red blood. A brace of healthy bulls had been sacrificed to replenish the bath, while a furnace beneath the tub kept its sanguinary contents as warm as though freshly spilled. An ingenious potion, extracted from the maws of leeches, prevented the crimson pool from coagulating.

The aroma of so much fresh blood was intoxicating. Sonja tried to imagine what it would be like to bathe in such a tub; her skin tingled beneath her gown. It was said that Amelia herself sometimes indulged in such luxurious ablutions in order to enhance her beauty.

The sarcophagus slid on its tracks into the bath, so that Viktor's body lay half submerged within the gore. His thirsty body absorbed the crimson fluid like a sponge, drawing new life from the abundant blood. Brilliant blue eyes snapped open, looking out at the world for the first time in two centuries. A hoarse whisper issued from his throat.

"Ilona . . . dead?"

Sonja fought back a sob. Marcus's blood had indeed conveyed the hideous truth to her father.

"Yes, my friend," Marcus said, leaning over the submerged bier. "I fear it is so."

The Elder turned toward Sonja, who stood nervously at the foot of the blood bath. "Leave us now, child. Your father and I have much to discuss."

Sonja paced back and forth within the frigid crypt. She gazed at the sealed doors of the infirmary, waiting for Marcus to emerge. Although anxious to converse with her father once more, she was apprehensive as well. Who knew how he was going to react to her mother's death? As far as she knew, they had been devoted to each other for almost six hundred years.

May fate grant that I someday know a love such as theirs, she thought wistfully. Beneath her feet, a bronze disk sealed her father's now-empty tomb. Sonja found herself alone in the silent crypt, save for the sleeping form of Amelia, still residing undisturbed beneath her bronze marker. The lonely sepulcher instilled a sort of melancholy in her, and she wished that Lucian were there to keep her company. *Was this how my mother felt,* she wondered, *whenever Father spent two centuries within his tomb?*

At last, the oak doors swung open, and Marcus exited the infirmary. "Your father will see you now," he informed her, heading for the arched doorway at the opposite end of the crypt. "I will leave you to your reunion, while I go to prepare for my own internment."

By tradition, Marcus's burial would take place the next night, after Viktor had a full day in which to recover his strength. During that time, Marcus would remain sequestered in his chambers unless an emergency arose, so as to provide for an orderly transition of power as laid out in the Covenant.

"Farewell, my lord," Sonja said dutifully. "May your meditations be fruitful."

Sonja watched the ageless Elder depart, then hurried toward the door to the infirmary. "Father?" she called out. "It is I, Sonja."

"Enter, daughter," a raspy voice croaked from the chamber beyond. Although rough from disuse, the voice was unmistakably her father's. "My thirsty eyes long to look upon your face once more."

Stepping inside, Sonja found her father seated on a marble throne at the opposite end of the pool of blood. His feet were still immersed in the crimson waters, like the roots of a mighty tree drawing strength from moist earth.

Although he remained as gray and wizened as a corpse, he had already regained much of his vitality. Azure eyes, alert and penetrating, stared out from sunken sockets. Strength and authority radiated from his commanding presence. Sonja detected no trace of infirmity in his manner, aside from his grotesque appearance.

"Greetings, Father," she said. "How fares your recovery?"

Viktor dismissed his emaciated state with a wave of his hand. "My vigor returns forthwith." He gazed at her, and a gentle smile softened his fearsome visage. "Ah, my beautiful Sonja . . . look at you! When I last went into the earth, you were but a mere slip of a girl. Now I find you transformed into a fetching young woman!"

His loving words brought joy to her heart, and she hurried around the edge of the blood bath to kneel beside his throne. She clasped her hand over his own skeletal claw. "Oh, Father!" she exclaimed. "I have missed you so!"

"You and your dear mother were ever in my dreams," he assured her. He stroked her flaxen hair with his free hand and looked down at her with great affection. "Imagine my dismay to discover what dreadful fate had befallen my beloved wife." He gnashed his fangs in frustration. "If only I had been there to defend you both from that mortal rabble, not buried impotently beneath the earth when you needed me most!"

"Please, sire, do not torment yourself thus!" Sonja

pleaded. "Who could have guessed what fate had in store for us?" Tearful eyes beseeched him. "Voice your grief as you surely must, but I beg of you, do not blame yourself for events no civilized being could have ever foreseen. We were taken unaware at dawn; there was naught you could have done!"

"We are not all quite as civilized as you," Viktor said ominously, "but you are correct. Now is not the time for recriminations." His rueful gaze drifted between their matching pendants. "I should be thankful that you at least survive, to continue our bloodline. You are my greatest treasure, Sonja. Never forget that."

"I shall not, Father." A look of relief came over her face. Guilt would only prolong her sire's suffering. "Nor shall I consider myself without family as long as I can call you Father."

"Which will be for all eternity," he assured her. "We shall always be together, no matter what fate has in store for us. Nothing will ever come between us."

A knock on the door disturbed their tender moment. Soren's gruff voice invaded the infirmary. "You asked to see me, Lord Viktor?"

The Elder's face hardened. Sonja rose from her father's side and stepped quietly behind his throne. "Enter," Viktor instructed.

The overseer came into the chamber. His dark eyes briefly registered Sonja's presence before turning their full attention to the seated Elder. He gave no reaction to Viktor's debilitated appearance, but Sonja sensed a degree of apprehension beneath Soren's stoic expression.

"Yes, milord?" he said.

"I understand that you were present when the Lady Ilona's procession was waylaid at the keep," Viktor said severely. "And yet you failed to prevent my lady wife's brutal murder and, furthermore, left my only daughter for dead." He shook his skull-like head in disappointment. "I am sorely disappointed in you, Soren."

The overseer's face blanched behind his beard. "Forgive me, milord! It will not happen again."

Viktor looked unconvinced. "Your repentance will not restore my lady wife to immortality. No amount of apology can ever atone for my loss."

"But I have served you faithfully for nearly four hundred years!" Soren protested, and Sonja thought she detected a tinge of resentment in his voice. "I have fought at your side!"

"True enough," Viktor admitted. "We have a long history, you and I."

"I beg of you, milord. Do not condemn me. 'Twas the wretched mortals who slew Lady Ilona, not I!" Soren fixed his gaze on Sonja as she stood silently behind her father's throne. "I swear that henceforth I will watch over your daughter with the greatest of care, so that nothing ill will ever befall her again!"

A shiver went through Sonja at the prospect of the brutal overseer serving as her self-appointed guardian. *I would have chosen another protector.*

Lucian, perhaps.

His fervent oath appeared to satisfy her father, though. "See that you do," Viktor charged him. The Elder's mummified face settled into a fearsome scowl. "You are correct in one respect. It is the mortals who are ultimately to blame for my poor wife's death." Bony fists clenched atop the marble arms of his throne. "But their treachery will not go unpunished. I swear upon my immortal blood that ere long, I shall wreak unholy vengeance upon all who are responsible."

The unalloyed hatred in his voice, so very different from the loving tones she was accustomed to, frightened Sonja. She had never seen her father so angry before . . . like a demon made flesh.

"They shall rue the day they dared to rise up against their betters—before I cast them screaming down to hell!"

Chapter Nine

STRASBA

Strasba wasn't much of a village. Nestled in a secluded valley, the tiny hamlet consisted of perhaps a dozen shops and a score of crude peasant huts. The two-story wooden shops occupied the head of the village, facing an unpaved road lined with thatch-roofed hovels. A modest stone church resided at the opposite end of the road, as though the town's founders had been determined to place as much distance as possible between God and Mammon.

The village slumbered beneath the light of a full moon, its narrow streets dark and deserted. Sunset had long since come and gone, so all of Strasba had retired for the night. Doors were bolted, windows shuttered, and every light extinguished. The hanging signs of the tradesmen blew in the cold winter wind. Only the faint glow of the night watchman's lantern disturbed the shadows draped over the unsuspecting hamlet.

They have no idea what awaits them, Lucian thought.

In wolfen form, he looked down upon Strasba from the

western slope of the valley. It was February, a full month since Marcus's internment, and the moon had once more liberated his bestial alter ego. Bristling black fur covered his towering form. Claws like daggers extended from his hands and feet.

A company of mounted Death Dealers, led by Viktor himself, also gazed down upon the village. The silver hooves of their mounts pawed the earth impatiently, and steam jetted from the chargers' nostrils, as the armored vampires awaited the Elder's command. Drawn swords and lances gleamed in the moonlight.

"Is that the place?" Nicolae asked archly. Like the other warriors, he wore a crimson surcoat over his chain mail. Unlike them, he wore rings of precious gemstones over his gloves. He drew his horse up beside Viktor's. "Why, it hardly seems worth sacking."

"My informants tell me otherwise," Viktor replied. Now fully restored to his prime, the regal Elder sat astride a coal-black charger named Hades. Fierce blue eyes glowed through the slits of his Corinthian-style helmet. Molded batwings formed a crest upon the helm. A heraldic dragon adorned the front of his surcoat. "The one we seek lies below."

He leaned in his saddle to address Lucian. "Stay close to me, werewolf. I shall need you anon."

Unable to do more than growl, Lucian nodded in assent. Once again, he was the only werewolf in the company, which also numbered Kraven among its warriors. Not Soren, though; he had been left behind to guard the castle and the princess, much to the overseer's obvious irritation—and Lucian's amusement. *It will do Soren good to be humbled,* he thought, *and it is no less than he deserves for leaving us behind at the keep.*

Viktor raised his mighty broadsword, easily holding it aloft with one hand. The sword's silver pommel bore the same capital *V* that marked the flesh beneath Lucian's fur. Celtic runes were inscribed on the blade's brightly polished guard. Viktor's imperious voice rang out in the night. "Death Dealers, ride now for vengeance!"

Racing hooves thundered down the slope into the muddy streets of Strasba. War cries trumpeted from the bloodthirsty throats of the vampires. Lucian loped alongside the horses, racing to keep up with the mounted Elder. His hot breath fogged the cold night air. Foam dripped from his panting jaws.

The nightmarish clamor woke Strasba from its peaceful repose. Candles flared to life behind the second-story windows of the shops, where the craftsmen and their families dwelt. Muffled voices cried out in alarm. Wooden shutters opened briefly, then slammed shut again as shocked villagers glimpsed the fearsome war party riding into their town. "God preserve us!" a frightened housewife exclaimed. "It is the undying ones!"

Viktor came to a halt in the market square before the row of shops. The upper stories of the wooden structures jutted out over the storefronts below, obscuring the sky. Cloves of garlic hung from the rough-hewn crosses nailed to every door.

As if that will save them, Lucian thought scornfully. It amazed him that the ignorant humans still placed their faith in such talismans. *Old myths die hard, it seems.*

"Who goes there?" A grizzled night watchman, possessing more duty than sense, came running toward them, raising his lantern before him. A kettle helmet surmounted his head, and he clutched a pike in one hand. Iron, not silver, tipped the point of the pike.

"I said, who goes—" The watchman's voice fell silent as he got a better look at the armored horsemen and the monstrous werewolf at their side. The color drained from his face as he squinted up at the pale faces of the riders, with their luminous blue eyes and flashing fangs. "Holy Mother of God!"

His pike and lantern crashed to the ground, sending up a geyser of sparks. Abandoning his post, the panicked watchman turned and ran for his life.

Nicolae laughed merrily. "Permit me, Lord Viktor," he volunteered, spurring his horse forward. He raised his lance and charged after the hapless mortal, who did not even make it to the end of the road before being impaled on the point of Nicolae's lance. The vampire prince tilted the lance upward, inspecting the skewered human as he might a morsel of meat at a banquet. "If this wretch is what passes for a soldier around here," Nicolae remarked, "then tonight's outing is going to be even more of a slaughter than I imagined."

He casually tossed the lance, along with its victim, into the dirt before him. Whimpers of pain reached Lucian's tufted ears, suggesting that the dying watchman still clung to life.

More fool he.

Nicolae was clearly having a grand time, but Viktor's voice was all seriousness as he addressed the company. "By their perfidy, the mortals of this village have forfeited their protection under the Covenant. Tonight—and only tonight—the prohibition on slaying humans is lifted. Feast as you will, Death Dealers. Slake your thirst with the lifeblood of these unworthy mortals. Only remember this: the monk is mine!"

With an enthusiastic cheer, the other vampires leaped from their mounts, handing over the reins to a lowly squire, only recently initiated into the coven. Swords drawn, the Death Dealers invaded the shops and residences, battering down doors and charging up stairs. Within moments, bloodcurdling screams erupted from behind the shuttered windows. Lucian heard the crash of toppled furniture and the sounds of short, unequal struggles. The high-pitched shrieks of men, women, and children blended into a cacophony of fear and torment.

A heavy body came smashing through the shutters above a bakery, as though flung by a catapult. The body, which belonged to that of a portly human roughly forty years of age, arced through the air before crashing to earth not far from Lucian. The man's heart was missing, and his lifeless face was frozen in a look of utter agony. Broken ribs protruded from the gaping hole in his chest.

A moment later, Nicolae appeared in the very window through which the dead baker had been propelled. The undead prince had discarded his helmet, revealing his flowing golden ringlets. Blood streaked his chin, spilling over onto his crimson surcoat. Unholy mirth set his azure eyes aglow as he effortlessly leaped from the upper story to the street below.

A trophy of sorts dangled from his grip: the severed head of a young woman, whose auburn locks were wrapped around Nicolae's fist. "Look what I found in the baker's bed," he quipped, holding up the head for all to see. "She's far too pretty, don't you think, for that fat bag of suet?" He kissed the maid's dead lips, then flung the head over his shoulder into the muck. "Hail and farewell, my sweet!"

Nicolae obviously regarded the raid as a rare lark. No doubt, Lucian surmised, the jaded prince saw massacring humans as merely another form of hedonistic indulgence, like hawking or whoring.

But he was hardly the only Death Dealer living up to the name tonight. More bodies came flying out of the windows above, raining down on the rutted dirt roads like slop from a chamber pot. "Gardy loo!" Vayer shouted from another window before hurling someone's elderly grandmother to her death. The old woman's dying wail terminated abruptly as she hit the ground headfirst. Lucian guessed that the crone's aged blood had been too thin and feeble to tempt Vayer, not when younger and more potent vintages were free for the taking.

Other mortals attempted to escape the invading vampires, fleeing out into the road in various states of dishabille. Frantic mothers clutched their babies to their chests, only to be ravished in the street by Kraven and his fellow soldiers. Lucian saw two vampires feast simultaneously on a single plump townswoman, their fangs embedded in her throat and breast, while a squalling infant flailed in the mud only a few feet away. A moment later, a third vampire snatched the babe up by its arm and crunched its tiny neck between her jaws. The thirsty Death Dealer sucked the blood from the infant's body in a single gulp, then tossed the lifeless body aside like an empty wineskin. Unsated, the vampire dashed into the nearest hut, looking for yet another unwilling donor.

Lucian watched the carnage from the Elder's side. Part of him was tempted to join in the bloodletting, tantalized by so much fresh human meat and marrow waiting to be devoured, but his more civilized instincts were troubled by the rampant butchery going on all around him. He thought he recognized a few faces and scents from the ambush at the keep, but it was difficult to be certain. Could any crime, no matter how heinous, justify such an atrocity?

Doubt plagued him, until he recalled more fully the recent attacks on both the castle and the caravan. He saw again Nasir's throat speared by a peasant's arrow, saw Lady Ilona dragged from her horse and beheaded by a mob of wild-eyed humans. He remembered Sonja spread-eagled upon the ground, only moments away from decapitation herself, and his pity for the terrified villagers evaporated completely.

These are but mortals after all, he thought. What did their mayfly existences matter compared with the security of the coven? The Elder knew what he was doing. *Sonja will never be truly safe unless this village is made an example of.*

"Goddamn monsters! You'll pay for your deviltry!"

Lucian turned to see a strapping male villager come charging out of the door of a butcher's shop. A bloodstained cleaver was clutched in his hand, and madness blazed in his eyes. "Demons!" he roared. "You slew my Anna!"

The werewolf knew not who Anna was, nor did he care. All that mattered to him was the memory of Sonja lying in her mother's blood, while humans like this one sought to sever her lovely head from her body. A snarl burst from Lucian's snout as he pounced forward to meet the oncoming butcher. His forepaws hit the villager head-on, knocking the brawny mortal onto his back. Lucian crouched atop the downed butcher. His claws raked the man's bare chest, digging bloody gashes in the fragile flesh of the human, who hacked at Lucian with his cleaver in desperation.

The edged steel bit into the werewolf's shoulder, but Lucian barely felt the pain. His powerful jaws chomped down on the butcher's wrist, and the cleaver went flying away, taking the man's right hand with it. An agonized scream tore itself free from the villager's lungs right before Lucian disemboweled him with a single swipe of his claws. The heap of steaming entrails was too savory to resist, and Lucian dug his snout into the spilled viscera, gulping down the man's organs with rapacious zeal. The hot, fresh, bloody meat was infinitely tastier than the cold, uncooked mutton that was his usual fare back at the castle. He could not help wondering if Brother Ambrose's fellow monks had tasted half so delectable.

Small wonder the renegades clung to their predatory habits with such fervor.

"That's enough, werewolf," Viktor commanded, calling Lucian back to his side. The Elder remained astride his horse, observing the slaughter with icy detachment. "You there," he called out to the nearest Death Dealer, whom Lucian recognized as Kraven. Blood trickled from the corners of the Englishman's mouth as he lapped at the neck of the half-dead maiden he was holding in his arms. "Attend me."

Kraven dropped the chalky white body onto the ground. "Yes, your lordship!" he said promptly, hurrying over to Viktor's side. His eagerness to curry the Elder's favor was almost comically obvious. "How might I serve you, Elder?"

"Fetch me a living tongue," Viktor instructed, "while there is still one to be had." Impatience colored his voice, as though the sacking of the village had not yet appeased him. "There are questions that require answers."

"At once, Lord Viktor!" Kraven exclaimed. All thought of his nubile prey forgotten, he darted into a nearby hovel, only to emerge moments later dragging a whimpering peasant by the collar. He threw the wretch onto the ground in front of Viktor's steed. "Kneel, varlet!"

Viktor nodded in approval. "Tell me, swine," he addressed the cowering mortal. "Where is the monk, Brother Ambrose?"

The peasant ignored the Elder's query. Clutching a string of rosary beads, he prayed frantically instead. "Holy Father, deliver me from the demons of darkness, deliver me, deliver me, deliver me . . . !"

"Answer the Elder, knave!" Kraven snapped at the man. He reached down and yanked a fistful of hair from the man's scalp. His nails dug painfully into the man's shoulder. "Answer the question, or I swear that hell will be a blessed relief by comparison!"

"The church!" the peasant blurted. Blood from his torn scalp dripped down his face. "God forgive me . . . the holy brother is in the church!"

"How predictable," Viktor observed. He nodded at Kraven. "Dispose of the blackguard."

Kraven obliged by twisting the mortal's head until his neck snapped. The dead peasant fell face-forward into the mud. "Done, your lordship," Kraven boasted as he blithely wiped the mortal's stink from his hands. "Your wish is my command!"

"As well it should be," Viktor replied drily.

He turned Hades toward the church at the other end of the village's main road. The horse reared up on his hind legs as the Elder exhorted the Death Dealers to continue their pillaging. "Kill them all!" he commanded. "Leave not a soul alive, not even a single babe!"

He galloped rapidly down the road with both Lucian and Kraven chasing behind him. Lucian kept one eye on the ambitious young Death Dealer, just in case Kraven got careless with his weapons again; he had not yet forgiven the English vampire for nearly sending a silver crossbow bolt through his skull.

The humble parish church was the only stone structure in Strasba. A single bell tower rose above the church's steeply gabled roof. A pair of oak doors barred the entrance, at least in theory. Here, too, garlic and hawthorn branches had been strung up in a pathetic attempt to keep out the Devil's minions.

Arriving at the front steps of the church, Viktor swiftly dismounted and strode up to the sealed double doors. He impatiently tore down the meaningless talismans and pounded on the heavy doors with his fist. "Open up!" he shouted. "I, Lord Viktor of Moldavia, demand it!"

When no one responded, he threw his shoulder against the doors, which went flying off their hinges to land with a crash in the church's vestibule. Viktor looked back over his shoulder to see if Lucian was still accompanying him. "Faster, wolf!" he beckoned. "With luck, I shall require your services posthaste."

Yes, Elder! Lucian thought. He bounded up the steps on all fours and followed Viktor into the murky interior of the church. Moonlight poured through stained-glass windows, much as it had at the ruined abbey a month ago. Kraven came rushing into the church after them, anxious to keep on demonstrating his worth to the Elder. He reminded Lucian of a jackal trailing a stalking lion.

They found Brother Ambrose kneeling before the altar at the far end of the nave. Hearing footsteps behind him, the hooded monk rose to his feet and turned to face the intruders. A simple wooden crucifix rested against the front of his thick black robe. He threw back his hood, revealing a round, red face topped by a tonsured dome.

"Get thee hence, creatures of hell!" If he was surprised to see two vampires and a werewolf striding down the middle of the church, he gave no sign of it. "You cannot set foot within the house of God."

"Your God cannot save you now, monk," Viktor declared. He turned toward Lucian, whose purpose on this raid was finally to be fulfilled. "Is this the mortal we seek?"

The werewolf nodded, confirming the monk's identity. There was no mistaking Brother Ambrose's florid features and strident voice. Here, Lucian knew, was the prime instigator of all the deadly assaults upon the coven and its members. His hackles rose as he fought an urge to tear the troublesome monk to pieces. It was not his place, however, to wreak vengeance upon Brother Ambrose; that privilege Viktor had reserved for himself.

The monk must have seen the murderous hatred in the werewolf's eyes—or perhaps he simply remembered the feral werewolves who had devoured his monastic brothers. "Hellhound!" he ranted. "Beast of the Pit . . . I know your weakness!"

Seizing a silver chalice from the altar, he hurled the vessel at Lucian. The chalice bounced off the werewolf's snout, leaving a bright red scorch mark behind. Lucian howled in pain and fury. It took all his self-restraint not to pounce on Brother Ambrose and rip out the human's throat with his teeth. He growled through clenched fangs.

"Hold, wolf!" Viktor commanded, fearing perhaps that Lucian had been provoked too far. Sword in hand, he marched down the aisle toward the altar. "Leave this deluded mortal to me."

Brother Ambrose thought himself prepared for the Elder as well. Lifting a silver basin from the altar, he flung the bowl's contents at the advancing vampire. Water splattered against Viktor's helmet and armor.

"Holy water, demon!" the monk crowed. He stared eagerly at Viktor, as if expecting the vampire to melt away before his very eyes. "Blessed in the name of our Lord!"

Viktor laughed for the first time since hearing of his wife's death. He lunged forward, knocking the basin from Brother Ambrose's hands with the flat of his blade. Then he grabbed the wooden crucifix around the monk's neck and yanked it free. "I'm afraid your scholarly pursuits have led you astray," he informed the startled monk as he tightened his grip on the useless crucifix, reducing it to splinters before the monk's eyes. "Silver, yes, at least as far as our brutish vassals are concerned, but the rest of this ridiculous folderol?" He shook his head dismissively. "I fear your faith was sorely misplaced."

"No . . . it cannot be," the shaken monk murmured in dismay. His bright red face went as pale as one of the blood-drained villagers, and he dropped to his knees before the altar. "Lord, though I walk through the valley of the shadow of death, I will fear no evil, for Thou art with me . . ."

Viktor sheathed his sword and peered down at Brother Ambrose. Removing his helmet, the Elder exposed his gaunt, clean-shaven features. Sandy blond hair, somewhat darker than his daughter's, receded from his lofty brow. An aquiline nose distinguished his patrician countenance, which was not nearly so young in appearance as those of Marcus or Amelia. Viktor looked to be roughly fifty years old by mortal standards, although his true age was measured in centuries.

". . . Thy rod and Thy staff, they comfort me. Thou preparest a table before me in the presence of my enemies . . ."

A cruel smile lifted the corners of Viktor's lips. "I am going to give you a chance for life, monk," he declared, interrupting the stricken mortal's feverish prayers, "which is more than your demented followers granted my late wife."

Grabbing Brother Ambrose by the collar of his robe, he lifted the monk from his kneeling position on the floor. Viktor's mouth opened wide, and he sank his gleaming fangs into Brother Ambrose's throat. The monk thrashed wildly, trying to tear himself away from the Elder's jaws, but Viktor held him fast, his blue eyes blazing as he drank deeply of Brother Ambrose's blood.

He did not drain the monk completely. After merely a moment, Viktor withdrew his fangs and let his victim collapse onto the floor of the sanctuary. Ashen-faced, Brother Ambrose clutched his throat, then pulled his hand away, visibly aghast at the sight of his own blood smeared over his shaking palm. "Sweet Jesus preserve me . . . the Devil's mark is upon me!"

"Let me explain the full implications of what has just transpired," Viktor said calmly, wiping the monk's blood from his lips. "For most, the bite of an immortal is fatal. Chances are, you shall die a painful death within the hour. But if you are truly fortunate—or unfortunate, depending on your perspective—you shall become a vampire like myself, in which instance you will serve as my slave for all eternity!"

"No!" Brother Ambrose gasped in horror. He turned his panic-stricken eyes heavenward. "Dear God, spare me from becoming the Devil's pawn! Let not my poor soul be damned forever!"

"Hah!" Kraven snorted at the monk. "An excellent jest, your lordship. A truly inspired revenge."

Viktor glanced at Kraven. He arched his eyebrow, as though just noticing that the fawning Death Dealer had followed him all the way to the church. "And you are . . . ?"

"Kraven of Leicester, Lord Viktor." He executed a sweeping bow. "Perhaps you've heard, I was instrumental in restoring your daughter to the safety of the coven. . . ."

A choking noise interrupted Kraven's self-aggrandizing recitation. All eyes turned to Brother Ambrose, who began to convulse violently on the floor. His eyes rolled upward until only the whites could be seen. A bloody froth bubbled past his lips. His spine buckled, so that his back arched above the floor, and his arms and legs jerked as though he were having an epileptic fit. Swollen veins bulged from his neck and forehead, while the bite mark on his throat turned black and gangrenous. His pallid face took on a bluish tint. Wet, gurgling sounds issued from his lungs. Groping fingers grabbed onto the cloth draped over the altar, yanking it from its place. Candlesticks and collection plates clattered to the floor.

Lucian recognized all the symptoms of a fatal vampire bite. Brother Ambrose must have been particularly sensitive to the venom in Viktor's fangs to have reacted so quickly. *No matter,* he thought. *The monk will be dead within seconds.*

Indeed, Brother Ambrose ceased his thrashing a few moments later. A final breath whistled from his throat. His entire body went slack. The whites of his eyes stared blankly at the arched ceiling of the church as the crazed monk joined his butchered brothers in the hereafter.

"It seems his prayers were answered," Viktor observed. He nudged the robed body with the toe of his boot, but Brother Ambrose remained limp and lifeless. "Just as well. I had no desire to look upon that porcine face for centuries to come."

"Nor did I," Kraven added obsequiously. He spat upon the monk's body for good riddance. "His death was more merciful than he deserved."

"Quite so," Viktor agreed. His keen eyes took the younger vampire's measure. "You seem a useful sort, Kraven. It may be that you shall have future opportunities to prove your worth to me."

Kraven beamed at the Elder's praise. "Whatever your lordship demands, you may rely on both my obedience and my discretion."

Provided neither judgment nor courage is required, Lucian thought, holding back a snarl. It vexed him to see the ambitious Englishman ingratiate himself with Viktor. Kraven had done little to endear himself to the lycans of the castle. *Still, these are matters quite above my station. The politics of the coven are the vampires' affair. Kraven is probably no worse than any of the other preening courtiers who flock around the Elders and Council members.*

Casting a final disparaging glance at Brother Ambrose's corpse, Viktor turned and headed toward the shattered front doors of the church. "Let us depart," he announced, leaving the monk's body splayed on the floor before the altar. Kraven and Lucian both followed in the Elder's wake.

They emerged from the building to find Strasba in flames. Bright orange tendrils of fire crawled up the wooden walls of the shops and turned the thatched roofs of the peasant huts into roaring bonfires. Billowing clouds of smoke filled the sky, hiding the moon. An occasional scream issued from the burning structures.

A blazing figure leaped from the top floor of an alehouse, crashing to the street below like a fallen star. The smell of burning flesh reached Lucian's nostrils. Saliva dripped from his snout as the tantalizing aroma made his mouth water. Flames continued to consume the roasting villager as he tossed and tumbled in the dirt, until Vayer silenced the mortal's screams with a well-placed sword thrust.

The smoldering corpse was but one of dozens of bodies lying strewn about the streets and square. Torn throats and pallid flesh testified to the final moments of many of the luckless townspeople. The Death Dealers had supped well tonight.

Viktor contemplated the flames and the mortal debris with obvious approval. By morning, Strasba would be nothing but burned-out ruins, populated only by carrion. "It is well," he pronounced. "It shall be a long time, mayhap many mortal lifetimes, before any human rabble dares to challenge us again." Putting his helmet back on, he remounted Hades and turned the horse around so that the church was at his back. "My dear wife has been avenged."

And Sonja, Lucian rejoiced within his wolfen breast, *is no longer in danger!*

Chapter Ten

CASTLE CORVINUS

*T*he feast began shortly after sundown, in celebration of Viktor's triumphant return to Castle Corvinus. Elegant vampires, bedecked in finery, crowded the great hall of the castle, which was a scene of most robust merriment. Crimson banners hung from the ceiling. Troubadours performed in the gallery, the sprightly music of their lutes and harps competing with the high-spirited laughter and chatter of the gossiping vampires. Blazing flambeaux lighted the hall, the better to show off the splendid raiment of the undying gentlemen and ladies.

Viktor presided over the high table, looking out over the assembly from his place on the dais. Sonja was seated to his right, while Nicolae occupied a position of honor at Viktor's left hand. August members of the Council occupied the remaining seats at the table, their relative proximity to the Elder reflecting their stature in the coven. Crisp white linen was draped over the table, while beeswax candles provided additional illumination by which the prominent vampires might see and be seen. Goblets and cutlery were made of gold or pewter, so as to avoid scalding the lycan servants whose duty it was to prepare and clean the table settings.

Below the dais, on the main floor of the hall, trestle tables and benches had been set up to accommodate the various courtiers, artisans, soldiers, and ladies-in-waiting in attendance. Fresh straw, cunningly scented with herbs, was spread upon the floor to soak up spilled sauces, wine, and blood. Lycan servers scurried back and forth between the hall and the kitchen (located a safe distance away, as a precaution against fire), toting a seemingly endless array of savory treats and dishes.

Although the vampires could live on blood alone, few were willing to deny themselves the epicurean pleasures of feasting on mortal food as well. They ate for the taste and sensation of doing so, rather than to sustain themselves. Eternity was too long a span not to require a bit of variety now and then.

Lucian observed the festivities from his post behind Viktor. Clad in his best wool tunic and hose, a new pewter badge gleaming on his chest, he stood at attention at the Elder's shoulder as he waited for the servers to deliver yet another fine repast for Viktor's enjoyment. It was Lucian's task to sample each course before the Elder, in order to ensure that the meal was not poisoned.

In truth, the risk was minimal, the practice more from tradition than necessity. Lucian had personally assigned himself the honor of tasting Viktor's food, mostly as an excuse to be close to Sonja. That the task also allowed him to sample the rich delicacies prepared for the high table was an added, and very welcome, benefit.

Already tonight Lucian had savored bites of roasted boar, starling, and peacock, along with exotically seasoned stews, tarts, and puddings. He had particularly enjoyed what he had tasted of a pastry "coffin" packed with dates, herbs, ginger, and eggs. Such rarefied cuisine was quite a change from the porridge and raw mutton he was accustomed to as a lycan. *Not quite as tasty as that butcher in the village,* he judged, *but delicious nonetheless.*

Yet, despite the gustatory splendors of the vampires' banquet, the greatest marvel at the high table remained Sonja herself. A gown of shimmering yellow samite graced her lovely form. Gold dust sparkled in her hair.

Lucian could not resist sneaking peeks at the ethereal princess, especially when her father was engrossed in conversation with his guests. Her delicate table manners were quite unlike the slovenly habits of his lycan peers. She did not gnaw savagely on the bones of her entrees or wipe greasy hands upon her clothing. Instead, she neatly picked apart her meal with her fingers and knife, making little or no mess. Lucian covertly admired her slender hands, remembering how gently they had once tended to his wounds. He watched dainty morsels of food pass through her lips, and his body stirred at the memory of those same soft lips pressing against his flesh.

"Keep your eyes to yourself, lycan," Viktor hissed in a low tone, and Lucian realized that he had been caught. He hastily looked away from Sonja, turning his gaze to the crowded hall before him.

Soren's hounds prowled among the lower tables, hunting for fallen food and handouts. The overseer himself, who had once enjoyed a place at the high table, was now relegated to one of the trestle tables on the main floor, a sign of Viktor's lingering disfavor. Soren glowered resentfully at the Elder and his honored guests, while snapping impatiently at the lycan server who was refilling his tankard. Lucian recognized the unlucky servant as the redheaded wench captured during Lady Ilona's hunt several weeks ago. The woman, who called herself Olga, shuddered at the overseer's wrath, perhaps envisioning a whipping later on. Soren's silver lashes were not presently in evidence, but that did not mean the brutal vampire could not resort to them after the feast.

Seated next to Soren, Kraven attempted to lift the overseer's spirits with some light remark. Lucian frowned at the sight of the two of them together; although he could not make out what they were saying over the general tumult, the prospect of Kraven and Soren getting to know each other troubled him. Neither vampire struck him as particularly trustworthy or well disposed toward him and his fellow lycans. Fate forbid that they should ever make common cause to advance their positions in the coven!

An outburst of cheers and applause heralded the arrival of the chef's masterwork: a spectacular subtlety of sugar, marzipan, and gelatinized blood, molded into a perfect recreation of the castle itself. A flourish of trumpets accompanied the sparkling scarlet dessert as a team of lycan bearers delivered the miniature castle to the Elder's table.

"Exquisite!" Viktor declared as the subtlety was placed before him. He used his own knife to cut a thin slice from the castle's outer walls, then nodded at Lucian, who broke off a piece of the slice with his fingers before popping it into his mouth. Viktor gave Lucian a baleful look, as though the Elder half hoped the dessert was poisoned after all.

When the sugary confection failed to strike Lucian dead, pieces of the subtlety were distributed to all present, with the diners on the dais receiving the lion's portion. Sonja herself was treated to a gelatinous red belfry, while Viktor devoured the better part of a turret. The taste of the dessert lingered on Lucian's tongue, the provocative tang of the congealed steer's blood recognizable beneath the sweetness.

After the subtlety had been consumed entirely, Viktor rose to address the assemblage. "Brothers and sisters of the blood, it pleases me greatly to see you all gathered together on this festive occasion. Our coven has known much sorrow in recent weeks, but I can assure you that our enemies have been harshly dealt with and will trouble us no more. Let tonight's feast mark the beginning of happier times for us all."

Jubilant cheers greeted the Elder's pronouncement. Viktor accepted the shouted accolades before speaking once more: "As a harbinger of that joyous future, it gives me great pleasure to announce the royal engagement of my own daughter, Sonja, to the crown prince Nicolae, son of Marcus. This superlative union, to be consecrated on the eve of Saint George's Feast, some three months hence, will strengthen the bonds between our two bloodlines and ensure that our coven stands united against whatever this new century holds!"

What? Lucian's heart plummeted. He could not believe what he was hearing. Nor, judging from the stricken look on her face, could Sonja. Her horrified expression suggested that this sudden engagement came as a total surprise to her.

And not a welcome one.

"But Father!" she softly protested. "You cannot be serious." She regarded Nicolae with open disgust. "I beg of you, please reconsider!"

Viktor silenced her with a look. "Not now, daughter," he whispered curtly. He raised a jeweled goblet filled with mulled blood. "To the happy couple," he toasted.

The entire assembly lifted their own cups. "To the happy couple!" they cheered in unison, their enthusiastic voices mocking Lucian's despair. Only Sonja declined to join in the toast.

"Drink deep, cousin!" Nicolae exhorted her. He leered at Sonja over the brim of his own overflowing goblet. His lascivious countenance was flushed with wine and blood. "It seems we are to become much more intimately acquainted."

The curly-haired prince seemed to be taking Viktor's unexpected announcement in stride. Was he aware of the Elder's intentions, or did he simply regard his coming marriage to Viktor's beautiful daughter as merely another amusing diversion? Lucian rather doubted that Nicolae would let anything as trifling as matrimony come between him and his notorious appetite for mortal women.

He does not deserve her! Lucian thought with fervor. *Never mind that I can never have her. Such a woman as Sonja is entitled to a husband worthy of her, not a heartless sybarite like Nicolae.*

For the first time in his life, Lucian truly hated a vampire.

Sonja obviously shared his distaste for her intended. Choking back a sob, she looked away from the smirking prince. For a second, her eyes met Lucian's, and he could see the scarlet tears brimming behind her lashes. In that moment, she seemed to look to him for comfort and deliverance.

If only they were his to offer!

"My mind is set, Sonja," Viktor declared. "I will not be dissuaded."

Her father's so-called solar was ironically named, given that not a glimmer of sunlight was ever allowed to penetrate its thick stone walls and heavy tapestries. Beeswax candles illuminated a cozy chamber generally reserved for the Elder's exclusive use. A flagon of chilled steer's blood rested on an intricately carved maple table, not far from a sloping pine desk that held a variety of parchments, inks, and quills. A roaring fire blazed within the hearth. A carved marble chess set rested on the mantel. The door was shut and all servants dismissed, so that father and daughter could speak freely to each other.

"But Father," she pleaded, "I do not wish to marry Nicolae! He is a vile reprobate, who cares only for his own filthy pleasures!" She wrung her hands in dismay. "He revolts me!"

Viktor scowled. "He is the son of an Elder and thus the only fit consort for you." He stood before the open hearth, warming his palms above the fire. "Marcus and I agreed to this union before he went into the earth, and I will not go back on my word."

Sonja remembered pacing back and forth in the crypt beneath Ordoghaz, while her father and Marcus conferred behind the closed doors of the infirmary. Could it be that her future had been decided then, while she waited unknowingly only a few yards away?

"But why now?" she beseeched him, stalling for time. Perhaps her father would relent if she could only delay the marriage long enough. "Why must we wed so soon? The fourth of May—Saint George's Eve—is only months away!"

Viktor's tone remained adamant. "You are no longer a child, Sonja. It is past time you take on the duties and responsibilities of womanhood." A trace of melancholy entered his voice, and his face took a more somber cast. "Your mother's untimely death has made me all too aware that not even we immortals are guaranteed life eternal. Now, more than ever, I am conscious of the need to promulgate our noble bloodline. Together, you and Nicolae will beget a new generation of pure-blooded vampires."

Sonja recoiled at the thought of bearing Nicolae's children. She burst into tears. "Please, Father! I beg of you, do not make me do this thing!"

Suspicion flared in her father's eyes. "Is there another?" he demanded.

Sonja thought of Lucian. His heroic features shone in marked contrast to Nicolae's ruddy visage. She remembered being cradled safely in the werewolf's mighty arms.

"No," she lied.

Viktor's expression softened. "Forgive me, daughter. I should have known you would never dishonor me so." Crossing the room to join her, he draped a paternal arm over her shoulder. "Surely, you have always known that as an Elder's daughter, it would be your womanly duty to make an advantageous match?" He sighed sadly. "It is a pity that your mother is not alive to counsel you in these matters. I daresay she would do a better job of it than I."

"But . . . must it be Nicolae?"

Her father nodded gravely. "I have given my word to his father." He turned her toward him and wiped a scarlet tear from her cheek. "It may not be so bad as you fear. Perhaps your gentle persuasion can curb his more . . . excessive tendencies. And fatherhood may change him as well. Trust me, my dearest daughter, there is nothing more powerful than a father's love."

Except where a royal alliance is concerned, she thought bitterly. She held her tongue, however, sensing that nothing she could ever say would weaken his resolve.

Whatever shall I do? The thought of surrendering her virtue to Nicolae, of sharing her bed with him for all eternity, made her physically ill. Yet her father's word was law, at least for the next one hundred years. *By the time Amelia rises one century hence, it will be too late to appeal Father's decision. I shall already be wedded to Nicolae—and my happiness doomed forever.*

There was no one she could appeal to.

Save one.

Sunrise was drawing near as Lucian and his fellow servants cleaned up after the banquet. The vampiric nobles, sated on fine food and blood, had returned to their chambers to sleep off their excesses or perhaps indulge in more private pursuits, leaving the industrious lycans to restore the great hall to order.

Tables and benches were carted away until they were required again, clearing the tiled floor of the hall, which was swept clean of the soiled straw. Hungry servants helped themselves to leftover morsels of meat and bone. Trenchers of stale bread, used as plates at the lower tables, were eagerly snatched up, the juicy trenchers being a prized treat now that the bread was liberally soaked with drippings from the vampires' feast. Leyba, working beside Olga and the other scullions, chortled in glee as she came across a forgotten tankard still partly filled with wine. She avidly gulped down the dregs before returning to her labors. Unbound black hair tumbled past her face as the gypsy wench bent to retrieve a gnawed steak bone that Soren's hounds had left behind.

Lucian leaned against a stone pillar, lost in thought. Although nominally in charge of the cleanup, he paid little attention to the bustling activity, so heartsick was he at the news of Sonja's engagement.

He knew it was irrational to despair so. *She and I could have never been together,* he reminded himself. It was inevitable that she would someday wed another pure-blooded vampire—if not Nicolae, then some other highborn member of the coven. *Why, then, should this moment come as such a blow?*

And beyond his own suffering, his heart ached for the princess's own sake, unwillingly given away in marriage to a callous libertine she had every reason to detest. Moreover, in his heart, he knew there was a bond between him and Sonja. He felt it whenever their eyes met. There was a palpable tension in the air each time they were near each other.

But what did that avail him, as long as she was the Elder's daughter and he was but half-human animal? The gulf between them was too vast ever to be bridged, no matter how fervently he might wish it otherwise.

I cannot lose what was never mine.

Bells rang high overhead, warning that the sun had risen once more. Lucian looked up to find himself alone in the empty hall. All evidence of last night's banquet had been carried away. Dying torches sputtered in the sconces. Only the faint aroma of roast meat and cold blood remained in the cool morning air.

But no, Lucian realized. He was not quite alone. A familiar musky scent teased his nose as he heard a pair of bare feet pad across the floor behind him. Lithe arms wrapped around his waist, and an impertinent chin rested upon his shoulder.

"Why so morose, Lucian?" Leyba whispered in his ear. Her hot breath, redolent of leftover wine and blood, warmed his neck. Her full breasts pressed against his back. The smoky odor of the kitchen clung to her rough wool kirtle. "I know just the remedy you need."

Apparently, his weeks away from the castle had not dimmed the scullery maid's ardor—or, more likely, her desire to attach herself to the highest-ranking lycan in the Elder's household. Her busy fingers toyed with the pewter badge on his tunic before descending lower. Sharp teeth nibbled at his ear.

No, he thought, pulling away from her. Unlike the last time Leyba attempted to seduce him, Lucian was not even tempted. How could he sport with another while the shards of his broken heart bled freely within his chest? All he could think of now was Sonja's imploring eyes as she stared at him behind her father's back. She had looked very nearly as forlorn as he felt.

For the same reason?

Not easily discouraged, Leyba held on to him with stubborn determination. Her lips and tongue came at him again, nuzzling his exposed throat, while her fingers tugged at the buckle of his belt. She growled huskily, like a she-wolf in heat.

"Enough!" He shoved her away, forcefully enough that she stumbled backward, almost falling onto her rear. The bitterness in his soul made him speak more harshly than he might elsewise have done. "Find another panting cur to ply your wiles upon. What we had was a youthful folly, nothing more."

Fury flashed in Leyba's dark gypsy eyes. Her fists clenched at her sides. "You arrogant ass! You think my love's not good enough for you?" Her mocking laughter echoed throughout the hall. "I've seen the way you moon over the Elder's daughter, like she would ever have anything to do with your sort. Beneath your fancy airs, you're just a lycan like the rest of us, and don't you forget it! You're nothing but a trained hound performing tricks for your masters!"

Lucian did not argue with Leyba as she stalked angrily out of the hall, glaring back at him over her shoulder. Her dark curls billowed about her like a departing thunderhead.

He knew she spoke nothing but the truth.

Chapter Eleven

CASTLE CORVINUS

*L*ucian tossed and turned on his straw pallet, but sleep would not come. After attending to the feast all night, he should have been exhausted, yet his mind was tormented by the thought of Sonja marrying Nicolae. Jealousy and depression combined to make every moment an ordeal, keeping him from his rest.

"Lucian?"

He opened his eyes to see a shadowy figure creeping toward him. Irritation flared in his heart as, for a moment, he thought that Leyba was making yet another blatant attempt to seduce him. *Will she never leave me alone?* he thought angrily. *What must I do to discourage her?*

His unwanted visitor drew closer, however, and Lucian saw that it was, in fact, another lycan servant, named Grushenka, who worked as a laundress within the castle. Of peasant descent, she was scrawny and towheaded where Leyba was dark and voluptuous.

"Yes," he inquired, sitting up. "What is it?"

Grushenka looked about her nervously, as though to assure herself that no one was watching, then reached beneath her dingy apron to extract a roll of yellow parchment, bound with a gold silk ribbon.

Lucian's heart leaped at the sight of the ribbon. No lycan female ever possessed anything so fine, but Sonja and the other highborn vampire ladies often wore such ribbons in their hair.

Can it be, he wondered, *that the missive comes from the princess herself?*

"Lady Sonja asked me to give this to you," Grushenka whispered, confirming Lucian's wishful supposition. She glanced around furtively once more. "But not when Soren or anyone else might be looking."

Lucian nodded, trying his best to conceal his mounting excitement. "Many thanks, Grushenka," he said sincerely. "I'm sure the princess appreciates your discretion."

As do I, he thought.

The fretful laundress seemed more anxious to conclude her mysterious errand than curious about the contents of the parchment. She slunk back into the corridors outside the murky alcove in which Lucian slept.

He waited until her footsteps had faded away before carefully untying the ribbon, taking pains not to rip the delicate silk. He lifted the ribbon to his nose and inhaled the unforgettable fragrance of Sonja's hair.

Heart pounding, he unfurled the parchment. Inside he found a short message written in an elegant hand that could only belong to the learned princess. Lucian thanked fate that, unlike many of his lycan confreres, he had taught himself to read:

Dearest friend,

Meet me in the castle chapel at the stroke of noon. Pray tell no one of this note.

Your companion in adversity,

S.

Lucian read the brief missive over and over, the tumult in his soul growing by leaps and bounds each time he perused the tantalizing lines. Although he tried to keep a tight rein on his fevered imagination, wild fancies raced through his brain, filling him with both hope and anxiety. *What does this mean?* he wondered fervidly, all thought of sleep forgotten. *Why this secret meeting?*

Rising from his pallet, he hastily dressed and made himself ready to answer Sonja's summons. The bells had only recently tolled eleven, yet he hurried as though his immortality depended on it. He ran a crude bone comb through his black hair and scraped his teeth with a dry twig he kept for that purpose. He told himself that he was merely making himself presentable for the princess; still, he felt like a nervous swain preparing for his first midsummer dance.

Who knows what the lady intends? he thought. *She has seen me kill in her behalf. Perhaps she simply wants me to dispose of her odious fiancé? If so, I will gladly play the assassin for her.*

The halls of the castle were quiet as he made his way through the fortress. Most of the household, lycan servants included, were resting after the exertions of the night before. Lucian encountered only a handful of guards and scullions, none of whom questioned his purpose in strolling through the hushed corridors.

The chapel was located on the uppermost floor of Castle Corvinus. Few ever visited the abandoned chamber of worship; being immortal already, the castle's inhabitants had little interest in the Church's promises of a life to come. Lucian himself could not remember the last time he had climbed the spiral staircase leading to the chapel's entrance.

Sculptures of long-dead saints flanked a pair of sealed wooden doors. Mythical beasts cavorted on the marble archway about the rotting timber doors, which looked as though they had not been repaired in centuries. An empty stoup, which had once held holy water, stood outside the entrance, its sunken basin now as dry as death.

Rusty hinges creaked loudly as Lucian tugged the doors open. He winced at the sound, but the noisy echoes appeared to attract no attention. He reminded himself that Viktor and Soren and the other vampires were all sleeping the day away.

Which made it the perfect time for him and Sonja to meet.

The chapel itself bore ample evidence of disuse and neglect. Dust covered every surface, from the altar itself to the carved wooden icons arrayed within the chancel. A faded tapestry, depicting the fable of the Wolf and the Lamb, covered the stained-glass window behind the altar, making the chamber safe for Sonja. Cobwebs hung like curtains from the ceiling, veiling the crumbling portraits of Christ and his apostles painted on the plastered walls of the chapel. The reek of ancient incense hung in the stagnant air. Rat droppings littered the floor. No chaplain attended the lonely chamber; the coven had no need of one.

Lucian saw at once that Sonja had not yet arrived. His disappointment was eased by the knowledge that he had come early to the . . . dare he call it a rendezvous?

Restless and impatient, he tore down the hanging cobwebs. The musty chapel was not fit to receive a lady such as

Sonja, for whatever purpose. Cleaning the chamber helped to turn his mind away from fruitless speculation, but only to an infinitesimal degree. *What if she does not come?* he worried. *What if her plans were discovered, or she has changed her mind, perhaps come to her senses? What if I never find out what she truly intended?*

At last, the bells tolled noon. Lucian's heart thundered in anticipation. He held his breath until, on the twelfth stroke, the door creaked open enough to allow Sonja to slip into the chapel.

She is here!

She wore the same yellow samite gown she had worn at the feast some hours ago, suggesting that she, too, had found sleep impossible after her father's shocking announcement. Her chestnut eyes were tinged with red, as though she had been weeping. She closed the door behind her and bolted it shut before turning to face Lucian.

"You received my note," she said softly.

"Aye, milady," he answered.

An awkward silence ensued as they stared at each other across the untidy floor of the forgotten chapel. Lucian realized that this was the first time they had been alone together since the day they spent in the crypt beneath the ruined monastery. "It seems we are fated to keep company on holy ground," he said with a lightness he did not feel.

His weak jest elicited a sad smile. She looked about the chapel, her gaze alighting on the portrait of Christ and his disciples. "You look somewhat like him," she commented, pointing out the slender, bearded figure painted on the wall. "Does that make you a wolf in sheep's clothing, I wonder?"

"I am whatever you wish me to be," he told her. She had already seen him in his most bestial state; there was nothing left to hide from her, save the boundless depths of his true feelings. "What do you require, milady?"

Consternation clouded her lovely face. "You were there," she said bitterly. "You heard what my father intends." She shook her head in dismay. "You were the only one I could think to turn to, the only one who—"

A wracking sob swallowed her words. Tears streaming from her eyes, she ran forward and threw her arms around Lucian, holding on to him as for dear life. Her body quaked against his as she wept openly on his shoulder.

He could think of no clever phrases to comfort her. Hesitantly at first, then with greater conviction, he embraced her, offering Sonja whatever strength was his to tender. He gently stroked her hair as he sought to quiet her muffled sobs.

As the moments passed, he grew increasingly aware of her shapely form pressed tightly against him. He caressed her back through the delicate samite, and long-frustrated desires arose within him. Sonja's physical presence affected him as powerfully as a full moon, unleashing emotions and impulses beyond his control. His blood throbbed through his veins until he could resist no longer; his fingers dug into her pliant flesh as he buried his face in the curve of her neck, licking and nuzzling her cool, clear skin.

A gasp burst from her lips, shocking him back to himself. He tore himself away from her throat and stared anxiously into her eyes. Would he see anger there? Fear? Revulsion?

Brown eyes gazed back at him, showing only surprise. "Lucian?"

He could not contain himself. "I love you, milady!" he blurted. "More than you know!"

To his infinite wonder, a look of joy came over the princess's face. A gleaming smile lighted up the murky chapel. "And I you, my dearest friend!"

Lucian could not believe his ears. *Am I dreaming?* he thought deliriously. *Is this truly happening?*

Emboldened by her words and smile, he kissed her ruby lips, which opened invitingly. Honey and coriander sweetened her breath. Passion overcame them both, and they tugged on the lacings of each other's garments, until lustrous silk and coarse brown wool mingled together on the floor of the chapel, forming a bed of sorts upon which they eagerly explored each other's bodies. Lucian peeled one last linen shift from Sonja's head and shoulders and took a moment to savor her naked beauty in all its splendor. Her ivory skin was clear and unblemished. Her perfumed flesh smelled of lavender. Flaxen hair spread out beneath her head like a golden halo.

"Your skin is so warm," she marveled, running her hand across his chest. "Like a blazing hearth on a winter's night."

"And yours is as cool and refreshing as a mountain stream," he told her as he lay down beside her. His hands found her breasts, and he kissed her deeply, reveling in the sensation of touching her inside and out.

He knew that what they were doing was forbidden. That Viktor would surely have him flayed alive or worse if he knew. But Lucian didn't care. All that mattered was that at long last, his beloved Sonja was within his arms.

I would happily trade eternity for this moment.

There, in the moldering sanctity of the old chapel, they made love on the strewn garments. He took her gently, face to face, not roughly in the lycan manner. Her delicate fangs teased his flesh, never quite breaking the skin. In the end, as their conjoined bodies attained the peak of ecstasy, two sets of eyes glowed brightly in the dark.

The bell tolled five times, rousing them from blissful slumber. Sonja sat up in alarm. "I must go!" she exclaimed.

"The others will be rising soon, and I need to be back in my chambers before the sun sets." She hastily gathered up her discarded clothing. "Soren checks on me every evening without fail—to ensure my safety, he says." Frustration entered her voice. "He will do anything to regain my father's favor."

Lucian knew that she was not mistaken. As much as he wanted to hold on to Sonja and never let her go, their safety depended on keeping their tryst a closely guarded secret. He hurriedly helped her dress, even offering her back the golden ribbon she had used to tie up the scroll that had brought him there. "For your hair, milady," he suggested.

Sonja laughed softly. She stopped lacing up the front of her bodice long enough to give him an impish grin. "I should think, friend Lucian, that after what has just transpired between us, you would finally be ready to address me by my name."

He smiled back at her. His blood thrilled at the memory of the intimacies they had so recently enjoyed. "There may be something to what you say . . . Sonja."

"That's much better," she said. She nodded at the strip of golden silk in his hand. "Keep the ribbon. Carry it secretly upon your person, as a token of my undying love."

"I shall treasure it always," he assured her.

Sonja glanced down at her person. A rumpled samite gown had restored her modesty. She made a vain attempt to smooth out the wrinkled fabric with her palms, then slipped her feet into her pointed leather shoes. "Check the door," she whispered.

Lucian crept obediently to the exit. Opening the heavy door just a hair, he peered out into the corridor outside. To his relief, the hall appeared just as unfrequented as before. After all, what business would any vampire or lycan have in visiting the abandoned chapel?

"The way is clear," he told her. "Hurry."

He opened the door wide enough to let her slip past him. "I will follow later," he promised, "so that none will see us together."

"That is wise," she said, lingering on the threshold. Haste was imperative, yet she paused in the doorway, unwilling or unable to depart.

Lucian knew precisely how she felt.

He inhaled deeply of her perfume, than shared one last tender kiss with her before forcing himself to pull free of her lips. "Go now," he urged hoarsely. "For our love's sake."

She nodded, too choked with emotion to speak, and hurried away down the lonely corridor. Lucian watched her go, then stepped back into the chapel and drew the door shut behind him. He felt drained yet exhilarated at the same time.

In her arms, he thought, *I am more than just an animal. With her, I am a man.*

A voice, nagging at the back of his mind, reminded him that nothing had really changed; that Sonja was still engaged to marry Nicolae in some three months' time; that the love of a lycan for a vampire, and of a vampire for a lycan, could never be accepted by the twilight community to which they belonged; and that their present happiness seemed destined to end in tears.

But, for now, Lucian chose not to dwell on such things. It was enough that he and Sonja had finally found each other.

We have already achieved the impossible, he reasoned, *so who can say what the future might hold?*

Chapter Twelve

CASTLE CORVINUS

A furious thunderstorm raged outside the castle. The howling of an icy March wind competed with booming thunderclaps, their tumultuous contest audible even through the thick stone walls and tapestry-covered window of the chapel. A candle, calibrated to mark the passing of the hours, was now less than an inch high, testifying that nightfall was only an hour away.

Lucian sighed. Soon he and Sonja would have to part once more. Though they had been meeting secretly in the old chapel for more than a month, parting before sunset had not become any easier. If anything, it was growing harder and harder to tear himself away from her at the end of each clandestine tryst.

What I wouldn't give to have her with me always!

They held each other beneath a down coverlet Sonja had smuggled into the chapel some weeks ago. Their covert efforts had transformed the decrepit chamber somewhat, making it a warmer and more inviting place. Cushions and candles had been placed around the chapel. Dust, cobwebs, and rat droppings had been swept away. Burning incense combated the musty atmosphere.

Lucian felt as though he had been granted new life as well; the last several weeks had been the happiest of his existence, despite the constant need to conceal their love from the rest of the world.

Sonja shivered beside him. "Are you cold?" he asked, reaching for a fur-trimmed cloak lying across the foot of the coverlet. Only a thin linen shift protected Sonja's upper body from a chilly draft that penetrated the stone walls through cracks in the mortar.

"Nay," she answered, refusing the cloak. Sonja grimaced unhappily. "I only shuddered at the realization that Saint George's Eve is but two months hence."

Lucian's spirits sank at the thought. He and Sonja seldom spoke of her impending arranged marriage to Nicolae, fearing to spoil their precious hours together, but perhaps the time had come; they could not deny the cruel reality of her engagement much longer. "I know," he conceded.

Desperate brown eyes entreated his. "Perhaps we can run away together?"

If only that were possible, he thought. He had considered it, of course, but he feared for Sonja's safety beyond the protection of the coven. "Where could we go?" he asked her glumly. "We would be alone in a world of mortals, like the ones who tried to kill us both at the keep." A vivid memory of Sonja facing death at the hands of an angry mob flashed behind his eyes. "We would have to try to pose as mortals, with the threat of exposure constantly hanging over us." He threw up his hands. "How long could we conceal your aversion to daylight, my monthly transformations?" He paused to let the bitter truth of his words sink in. "Hell, I've barely spoken three words to a mortal in my entire life! How could I possibly hope to pass for one on a daily basis?"

It would only be a matter of time, he thought, *before our true natures were revealed.* He saw them both burning at the stake in the square of some godforsaken mortal hamlet, the flames reducing Sonja's lovely body to ash as surely as a ray of sunshine would. *Do I dare risk Sonja's eternal life, even for the sake of our love?*

"But you told me Brother Ambrose is dead," she protested. "My father killed him before your very eyes."

He shook his head. "I fear the monk was not unique. Believe me when I tell you that the mortal realm remains our enemy." He gestured at a cracked and faded mural on the opposite wall, which depicted writhing sinners cast down into the pits of hell by Satan himself. Bat wings sprouted from the Devil's shoulders, while bloodstained fangs were bared in a malevolent grin. "Do you see? As far as the outside world is concerned, we are all the spawn of Satan, soulless monsters who live only to poison the world with our evil." His voice held not a grain of doubt. "There is no refuge for us there."

Sonja fell silent, unable to dispute his dire assessment of their chances. "Perhaps it will not be so bad," she murmured finally. "Staying here, I mean. We can keep on seeing each other, even after the wedding. 'Tis not uncommon, particularly in politically arranged marriages, for vampire ladies to take lovers, provided they do so discreetly."

But not with lycans, Lucian thought. *Never with my kind.*

"Who knows? Perhaps Nicolae will leave me alone after our wedding night." Sonja's voice faltered, as though she were trying to convince herself and failing. "They say he prefers mortal mistresses to vampire women."

"This is true," Lucian granted, even though he hated the

very idea of sharing Sonja with another man, with Nicolae least of all. But what other choice did they have?

She cuddled closer to him, resting her head on his shoulder. "I suppose you could see it as romantic, in a way," she murmured, still struggling to find a glimmer of light in the darkness ahead. "We'll be like Lancelot and Guinevere or Tristan and Iseult."

"Indeed," he said to comfort her, well familiar with the legendary lovers she spoke of thanks to the performances of various bards and minstrels. Given Sonja's superior education, he knew it was not necessary to point out that both tales ended sadly.

Must our love lead to heartache as well?

A sharp knock at the door jolted them both. "Lady Sonja?" shouted a gruff voice Lucian instantly recognized as belonging to Soren. "Are you in there?" The bolted doors rattled as Soren tried to force his way inside. "Lady Sonja? I must speak to you at once!"

The lovers froze in panic. Lucian shot a glance at the calibrated candle to see if they had lost track of time, but no, the amount of wax remaining indicated that sunset was still nearly an hour away. Soren must have risen early for some reason and come in search of Sonja.

Sonja glanced hesitantly at the doors, clearly uncertain whether to respond to the overseer's hails. *Perhaps if we say nothing,* Lucian thought, *Soren will give up and go away.*

"Lady Sonja!" Soren pounded heavily on the oaken door. "You must answer me. I can see the candlelight through the cracks in the wood. Lady Sonja!"

So much for that idea, Lucian realized. Soren sounded as though he had no intention of leaving until he spoke with Sonja. "Stall him," Lucian whispered as he leaped to his feet and began gathering up his scattered garments and belongings. He moved swiftly but stealthily, trying to make as little noise as possible.

"Your pardon, Soren," Sonja called out. For herself, she snatched up her cloak and hastily wrapped it around her. She drew the fur-trimmed hood over her unbound hair. Her feet slipped into her shoes. "I apologize for the delay. I shall be with you shortly."

Soren rattled the door impatiently. "Please, your ladyship!" he insisted. Did he fear she was being held hostage or mayhap preparing to leap through the stained-glass window? "Unbolt the door!"

Lucian kicked assorted loose articles of clothing behind the marble altar, then ducked behind the tapestry depicting the Wolf and the Lamb. Sonja waited for the hanging fabric to settle, then nervously approached the door. Lucian watched through a minute tear in the tapestry as she unbolted the door. She opened it just enough to reveal Soren's scowling face glaring at her from the corridor outside.

"Patience, good Soren," she said with feigned nonchalance. "How may I assist you?"

"You were not in your bedchamber!" he complained, as though her unexplained absence was a personal affront. "Your father rose early and sent me to summon you, but you were nowhere to be found. I searched everywhere for you, until I found a scullery maid who remembered seeing you climb the stairs to this deserted rat hole." He barged into the chapel despite Sonja's hesitant efforts to keep him outside. Suspicious eyes searched the forgotten chamber, no doubt spotting the cushions and candles arrayed about the room. He sniffed the incense-laden air. "What are you doing here?"

Lucian held his breath behind the tapestry, praying that the clamor of the storm would mask the sound of his racing heartbeat. Judging from the faint illumination coming through the stained-glass windows at his back, the day outside was dark and overcast. *Small wonder Viktor awakened early*, he surmised. *We were careless not to anticipate as much.*

"I find this old chapel to be an ideal place to study and be alone with my thoughts," Sonja explained. She glanced at the ponderous tome lying on the floor by the altar, taking care to hold the front of her cloak tightly shut. "As you know, few visit this particular chamber anymore, so I am seldom interrupted in my studies—at least until now," she added pointedly. "I fear I dozed off while reading, which is why I was slow to respond to your inquiries a few moments ago."

Sonja's lies struck Lucian as plausible enough, but would Soren believe them? What if he insisted on searching the chapel instead? Lucian sweated behind the tapestry, every muscle in his body tensed for action. If forced to it, he would battle Soren with his bare hands and teeth. Without the full moon to transform him, he and Soren would be far too evenly matched to guarantee an easy victory, but Lucian would not surrender Sonja to the mercy of the Council without a fight. *It doesn't matter what happens to me*, he resolved, *but I will not see Sonja punished for loving me.*

Agonizing moments dragged on interminably as Soren mulled over Sonja's words, a dubious expression on his bearded face. Sonja sought to distract him by prattling on as though nothing were amiss. "What say you, Soren? Would not this venerable chapel be an inspired setting for Nicolae and me to exchange our wedding vows? I must remember to suggest as much to my dear father when next we meet to discuss my nuptials."

"This pest hole?" Soren replied. He sneered at the neglected chapel with open disdain. Sonja's query, however, succeeded in reminding him of his original purpose. "Your father awaits," he announced brusquely. "Come with me now."

But Sonja knew better than to face her father wearing only a shift beneath her cloak. "You forget yourself, Soren," she said, asserting her authority. "The daughter of an Elder is not to be ordered about like some common serving wench." She drew herself up majestically, raising her chin high. "Go now. You may tell my father that I shall be with him anon."

Soren's expression darkened. Sonja's dismissive tone obviously nettled him. "But milady—"

"Leave me, knave," Sonja rebuked him, "before I report your insolence to my father."

Soren's fists clenched at his sides, but he wisely held his tongue. "As you wish, milady," he muttered as he turned his back on the altar and stalked out of the chapel. Lucian breathed a sigh of relief as he heard the overseer's heavy tread disappearing down the stairs at the end of the corridor.

Sonja closed the chapel doors behind him, and Lucian slipped out from behind the tapestry. His heart was still pounding from their narrow escape. Sonja rushed into his arms, and he felt her tremble within his embrace. Lightning flashed behind the tapestry.

"I was so frightened," she confessed, resting her head against his chest. "For a few moments there, I was certain we were to be discovered."

"As was I," he told her. "Thank fate for the storm outside." And the incense, too, he realized. Vampire senses were not nearly so acute as those of his own breed, yet Lucian was grateful for the overpowering scents and sounds cloaking his presence. "You did well to drive Soren away before he searched the chapel."

He could not even imagine what the consequences of such a disaster would have been; no pure-blooded vampire princess had ever been caught with a lycan lover in the centuries-old history of the coven. The Covenant spelled death for such a transgression, but surely Viktor would not have his own daughter put to death.

Would he?

It had been a near thing, Lucian realized. He held Sonja tightly within his grasp, as though to protect her from dangers both past and forthcoming. *We must be more careful in the future,* he resolved.

Much more careful.

Now

A.D. 2002

Chapter Thirteen

BUDAPEST

*L*ucian waited for Kraven at their usual meeting place, a dismal alley in one of central Pest's grimier neighborhoods. Darkened warehouses and sweatshops loomed above the empty street. Broken glass and cigarette butts littered the pavement beneath a broken street lamp that the city seemed in no hurry to repair. Graffiti covered the sooty brick walls of the alley, while several meters away, a concrete overpass blocked Lucian's view of the sky.

The cool summer night had lured Lucian out of his armored limo, so he paced outside the car, accompanied by Miklos, his bodyguard on tonight's mission. Ordinarily, Raze joined him on such outings, but his fierce lieutenant was still recovering from the injuries he'd received during the incident at Statue Park. Lucian frowned at the thought of that mysterious attack, which had cost him the lives of two loyal soldiers. That a vampire had also been reportedly killed provided only meager consolation, particularly while the identity of the assailant remained unknown.

I like to know the names of my enemies, he brooded. His brown leather jacket was open in the front, revealing the gleaming pendant resting against his chest.

Sonja's pendant.

He glanced at his wristwatch. It was eleven thirty-five, five minutes after the agreed-upon time for the meeting. *Where the devil is Kraven?* Lucian's fingertips curled inward like claws. Spring-loaded titanium blades hid beneath the sleeves of his jacket. *He should know by now that I don't like to be kept waiting.*

At last, a sleek black limousine pulled into the alley, parking only a few meters away from Lucian's own vehicle. Soren emerged from the driver's seat, automatic pistol in hand. He grunted at Lucian, acknowledging the lycan's presence, and cautiously inspected the alley for any signs of betrayal. Lucian spotted a pair of telltale bulges beneath the shoulders of the former overseer's black suit and guessed that Soren's beloved silver whips were coiled underneath his jacket.

Some things never change, Lucian reflected. The Irish vampire was clean-shaven now, where once he had sported a dense black beard, and his allegiances had shifted dramatically, but Lucian knew that at heart, Soren was still the same sadistic brute he had always been. Lucian's back had not forgotten the excruciating bite of the silver lashes.

Barbed vertebrae tore through his ragged tunic, making ribbons of his hide. Merciless silver burned his skin, even as the whip sliced through his defenseless flesh, paring it to the bone.

Quickly determining that no deadly surprises were in store, Soren opened the passenger door of the limo and gestured for Lucian to step inside. The lycan leader nodded at Miklos, who he knew would keep a close eye on Soren, then slid into the backseat of the vampires' limo and closed the door behind him.

Kraven waited inside the car, stylishly clad in a tailored Armani suit. Expensive rings glittered on his fingers. A golden chain hung about his neck. Kraven had done well for himself since Lucian had first met him more than eight hundred years ago. Now Kraven ruled over Ordoghaz in Viktor's name and claimed credit for "killing" Lucian centuries ago.

This suited Lucian, who had his own reasons for letting Viktor and the other vampires think him dead.

For now.

"What's this all about?" Kraven demanded petulantly. As ever, Kraven attempted to conceal his fear of Lucian behind a show of arrogant bluster and indignation. "Dammit, you know how dangerous it is for us to meet like this! Suppose someone sees us together?"

Lucian ignored Kraven's feeble histrionics. He knew who truly held the power in their alliance, even if Kraven liked to pretend otherwise. "I judged the need to be worth the risk," he stated, resting his back against the cushioned black leather seat. "I assume you know of the incident at Statue Park?"

"Yes, yes," Kraven said impatiently. "Some lunatic hurled grenades at your agents during an arms deal. Selene told me all about it."

Lucian knew that Selene was a female Death Dealer, said to be singularly relentless in her pursuit of lycans; he had yet to meet her, but she had claimed the lives of many of his followers over the years. He looked forward to returning the favor someday soon.

"So?" Kraven whined. "What of it?"

Lucian fixed an intimidating gaze on Kraven, who gulped involuntarily. "I need to know, Kraven, that you had no involvement in this attack."

"What? You think I had something to do with your flunkies getting killed?" Kraven threw up his hands in frustration, all wounded innocence. "You can't blame me if the Death Dealers track down a couple of careless lycans. That's what they do."

"But the Death Dealers came under attack as well," Lucian pointed out. "And at least one vampire was burned alive by an unidentified third party. That is not exactly business as usual." He glanced through the tinted window at Soren, who had long resented the authority of the Death Dealers; there had been bad blood between the ex-overseer and the elite vampire warriors for centuries. "I certainly hope, for your sake, that this was not some ill-advised preemptive strike against your enemies in the coven. The time will come to rid ourselves of Viktor's loyal Death Dealers, but not just yet. I've waited too long for my revenge to risk upsetting everything now, not when we're so close to victory."

A growl entered his voice, and his blood began to boil dangerously at the prospect of his carefully laid schemes going awry at this critical juncture. Amelia would be returning to Europe within a few months to preside over Marcus's Awakening, but if all went according to plan, none of the Elders would live to see the new year. The war was almost over, assuming that he could just keep control of the situation . . . and Kraven.

The cowardly vampire blanched at Lucian's angry snarl. "I swear upon my life," he insisted. "I had nothing to do with that attack! I know as little as you do!"

Could it be he was telling the truth? Lucian was starting to think so. Kraven was nothing if not deceitful, as Lucian knew better than most, but after eight centuries of dealing with the treacherous vampire, Lucian thought he could tell when Kraven was lying shamelessly—and this was not one of those times.

In truth, it is I who usually feeds Kraven his lies.

His mind flashed back to the first time he met the ambitious young vampire, outside the gates of Ordoghaz. In his memory, he heard Kraven's silver crossbow bolt whiz past his head once more. *Who would have ever imagined,* Lucian thought, *that we would end up allies of a sort, if only until my plans are realized? Once the Elders are dead and the Corvinus strain within my grasp, Kraven will be expendable, and Soren as well.*

That glorious night could not come too soon.

But if Kraven was not responsible for the ambush at Statue Park, who was? Lucian was troubled by the notion of a genuine third party intruding into the ancient conflict just as he stood at the brink of his ultimate triumph. It was almost as though, against all reason, Brother Ambrose had risen from the grave after all these centuries, striking out at werewolf and vampire alike, much as he had in days of yore.

Is that what we're dealing with? he wondered. *Not the insane monk per se but his contemporary equivalent? Some sort of self-appointed monster hunter?* Lucian scowled at the thought. The last thing he needed right now was some delusional mortal gumming up the works. *I need to nip this crisis in the bud before it endangers all my plans.*

"Very well," he told Kraven, moderating his tone somewhat. "I believe you when you say this is not your doing. But make no mistake: we must get to the bottom of this mystery as swiftly as possible." He paused to consider his options. "I assume the Death Dealers are investigating the attack?"

Kraven nodded. The color returned to his face as he realized that he had escaped Lucian's wrath. "Of course. Selene is obsessed, as usual, with finding the killer."

"Good," Lucian declared. With luck, this Selene would dispose of the problem for him, but just in case, he needed to be kept in the loop. "You must report their findings to me as soon as they're available. Keep me informed on the progress of the investigation."

In the meantime, he thought, *I can pursue my own avenues of inquiry.* One way or another, the enigmatic killer needed to be eliminated. *I can afford no loose cannons at this point in my long campaign.*

"Yes. Right," Kraven agreed readily. "I'll make sure Selene tells me everything she learns." A worried look came over his face as, now that he was no longer the immediate target of Lucian's suspicions, he began to grasp the larger implications of the situation. "You don't think this could interfere with our plans, do you? What if this assassin knows what we're up to?" Panic kindled in his eyes. "The Council will have my head if they learn that you're still alive and that I've been conspiring with you to depose the Elders!"

Lucian sighed inwardly. He often wished he had chosen a less faint-hearted partner all those centuries ago. This was hardly the first time Kraven's unsteady nerves had required calming.

"I think it highly unlikely," he assured the anxious vampire, "that this wild card is privy to our plans. Chances are, he or she is merely a well-armed human out to rid the world of vampires and werewolves and the like." He chuckled disdainfully, for Kraven's benefit. "You know the type . . . they usually get themselves killed in no time."

Kraven seemed to relax a bit. "You really think so?"

"Of course," Lucian lied. In truth, he would not rest easy

until he had determined the true identity and motives of the Statue Park assailant. "Just keep your wits about you, and everything will proceed as planned."

I hope, he added silently.

Their business concluded, at least as far as he was concerned, Lucian opened the door and stepped back out into the night, where Miklos and Soren continued to glower at each other in stony silence. He stepped toward his own vehicle, then heard Kraven call after him.

"Hold on," the vampire said indignantly. Kraven emerged from the car and crossed the alley. "There's one more thing. Selene knows that your agents have been dealing with Florescu. If I were you, I'd find another supplier."

In fact, Lucian had already deduced as much from the Death Dealers' presence at Statue Park. Still, he was reluctant to break off all contact with Florescu; for better or for worse, the human arms merchant had the best merchandise. *We'll just have to be a lot more careful in our dealings with him.*

He opened his mouth to reply, only to start in surprise as his keen ears detected the muffled report of a silenced rifle. A second later, before Lucian could utter a word of warning, Miklos went down, a bloody hole exploding in the side of his head. Reddish steam issued from the wound, proof that a silver bullet was frying the bodyguard's brain.

Speak of the devil! Lucian thought furiously. He knew at once that their unknown enemy had struck again.

"What the hell?" Kraven exclaimed as Soren grabbed the other vampire's shoulders and shoved him toward their waiting limo. Lucian drew his own weapon, a Glock automatic pistol, from beneath his leather jacket and searched for the source of the fatal shot. A muzzle flared atop the nearby overpass, pinpointing the location of the sniper, and Lucian felt a sudden burning pain in his kneecap. He looked down to see blood streaming down his leg. Silver sizzled inside his knee like molten lava.

Foolishly, he turned to Kraven and Soren for assistance. "Help me!" he called out. "I've been hit!"

The fleeing vampires ignored his pleas. A third shot winged Kraven in the arm, and Soren flung his injured leader into the back of the limo. Without so much as a glance in Lucian's direction, Soren dived behind the wheel of his car. The limo peeled rubber out of the alley, leaving Lucian behind.

Bloodsucking bastards! he thought venomously as he watched Kraven's limousine disappear into the night. Soren had deserted him again, just as he had at the keep eight hundred years ago. Lucian resisted the temptation to waste precious bullets by firing at the retreating vehicle. *They'll pay for this—once the Corvinus strain has made me invincible!*

But first he had to survive the sniper's assault. Gritting his fangs against the pain in his leg, he limped toward his own parked limousine. Instinctively, he tried to transform into a werewolf, but the damnable silver blocked the Change. Given a few minutes to focus his thoughts, he could attempt to expel the bullet from his body through sheer concentration, but time was not on his side; he could hardly expect the sniper to leave him alone while he healed himself. Extracting the bullet would have to wait until he made his escape.

He fired off a round of covering fire at the overpass but had no way of knowing whether any of his wild shots hit home. Spasms of pain shot up and down his injured leg. Crossing the alley felt like hiking over the Carpathians, and he was gasping for breath by the time he grabbed onto the door of the limo, hoping against hope that Miklos had left the keys in the ignition. *I need to get away,* he thought. *Find out who this nameless assassin is.*

A sharp pain jabbed him in the side of the neck. He reached for his throat and yanked a hypodermic dart from his jugular. A foul-smelling green fluid dripped from the hollow silver needle at the tip of the dart. It smelled vaguely like the serum his own kind used to dose newly converted lycans who couldn't yet control their transformations.

I've been tranked, he realized.

The drug took effect immediately. His vision blurred, and his legs grew rubbery. The Glock slipped from his fingers. He sagged against the door of the limo, trying to stay on his feet, but it was too late. Darkness closed in on him like the catacombs beneath the old monastery.

He was unconscious before he hit the ground.

Seated in the backseat of the limo, Kraven whimpered in pain. Blood spilled from his arm, and he pressed down on the wound with his other hand, trying to stanch the flow. "Damnation!" he cursed, even though the silver bullet was hardly likely to kill him. "This hurts like hell!"

"Hold on, regent," Soren urged him from the driver's seat. "There will be painkillers back at the mansion."

"No!" Kraven cried out in alarm. "We can't go back to Ordoghaz, not yet. How the devil will I explain getting shot while meeting with two lycans . . . with Lucian, of all creatures?" Kraven shuddered at the thought; the pain in his arm was nothing to the sufferings he would endure should his collusion with the infamous lycan warrior be exposed. "Head for the nearest safe house!"

Yes, he thought, *that's the right move.* The coven kept a number of safe houses throughout the city, hidden away in various inconspicuous locations. They were mostly used by the Death Dealers for stakeouts and interrogations, but they also provided emergency refuges for any vampires who found themselves stranded in the city too near sunrise. There would be quantities of cloned blood on store and first-aid supplies.

His mind raced frantically, looking for a way to salvage this disaster. *Don't panic,* he ordered himself. *I can still turn this around. Nobody needs to know what I was doing tonight.*

Soren arrived quickly at the closest, most convenient safe house: a broken-down brownstone in a rundown corner of Pest, not far from the city's notorious red-light district. Decades of smog and soot had blackened every centimeter of the building's dingy exterior. Steel-shuttered windows and spray-painted graffiti made it appear the ugly pile of bricks had been deserted for some time. Kraven hoped to hell that Soren had the right address.

After parking the limo at the curb, Soren helped Kraven out of the vehicle. A group of junkies loitered on the steps of the old brownstone, but Soren chased them away with a snarl and a flash of his fangs. Crack vials shattered beneath Soren's boots as he assisted Kraven up the steps and snapped apart the padlock sealing the front door. He held the door open while Kraven staggered inside.

Rats scurried away in a hurry as the two vampires invaded the unlit foyer. Kraven's eyes quickly adjusted to the dark, and he found himself at the foot of a winding series of stairs that led to the upper floors of the building. Trash was strewn about the scuffed vinyl floor of the lobby: protective coloration, disguising the building's true nature.

"The interrogation room is on the sixth floor," Soren informed him. Kraven trusted Soren to know such things, which were quite outside his own interests.

"Of course they are," he said sourly, eyeing the daunting climb ahead. "I don't suppose there's a working elevator?"

"I'm afraid not," Soren said.

Naturally, he groused silently.

Cradling his wounded arm, which had already stopped bleeding, Kraven let Soren help him up the endless stairs. The dilapidated steps creaked alarmingly, and every step sent a fresh jolt of agony through his arm, but at last, they reached the sixth-floor landing. Kraven watched impatiently as Soren shouldered open a door to the left of the staircase. The loyal henchman flicked on a light switch as Kraven stepped through the door.

Fluorescent lights came on, exposing a sparsely furnished room that looked positively spartan compared with Kraven's lush accommodations back at the mansion. Instead of antique beds and sofas, there were only a few sturdy metal chairs and tables, weapon racks on the walls, and several neatly stacked crates of ammunition. Cracked plaster walls were unadorned, save for a single bulletin board bearing the mug shots of various known lycans and their associates. Closed-circuit TV screens monitored the lobby, stairs, and corridor outside. Sealed metal shutters kept out both sunlight and prying eyes. Chains and shackles hung from the ceiling or were affixed to the metal chairs, the better to contain unwilling occupants. The bare wooden floor was speckled with dried lycan blood.

Typical Death Dealer decor, Kraven thought uncharitably. *All business, just like Selene.* He had been trying to entice the gorgeous Death Dealer into his bed for centuries now, but her single-minded fixation on the war had always gotten in the way. *I imagine she'd feel right at home here.*

He planted himself in an uncomfortable steel chair while Soren hustled up some supplies. A large silver refrigerator hummed away in one corner of the room, next to a wooden ammunition crate. Soren yanked open the door of the fridge, exposing several packets of refrigerated blood. He hastily retrieved a couple of packets and handed them over to Kraven. "These will help you to heal," he said.

The translucent plastic packets were cold to the touch. A stamped label on the bags identified them as products of Ziodex Industries, a major biopharmaceuticals firm that just happened to be owned entirely by Viktor and his estate. Ziodex provided the coven with a substantial stream of income, along with copious amounts of cloned human blood.

Kraven tore open the seal on the first bag and gulped down its contents. The refrigerated blood would have been better warm, but this was no time to be a connoisseur. The rich, salty liquid did wonders for his constitution; he could feel the shock and trauma of the gunshot wound ebbing away as the blood restored him. The silver bullet still ached beneath his skin, but it was nothing he couldn't endure for a few minutes more.

At least he could think clearly again.

"We're going to have to burn this shirt," he instructed Soren, "and clean up the backseat of the limo, too." He drained the second bag of blood and gestured for a third; this one he placed against his wounded arm, letting the chill of the blood numb the pain somewhat. "In fact, we should arrange to dispose of the limo as soon as possible. If there's one thing our kind are good at finding, it's bloodstains."

Soren produced a first-aid kit from a storage locker. He used a scalpel to cut away the sleeve of Kraven's Armani jacket, then went to work on the black silk shirt underneath. Kraven winced at the sight of his expensive wardrobe going under the knife but reminded himself that there was plenty more where that came from; one of the perks of running the coven was an almost unlimited clothing allowance.

"Perhaps," Soren suggested, "we ought to tell the Death Dealers something of the attack, so that they are aware that the assassin has acted again."

These raids must have Soren worried, Kraven thought, *if he wants to cooperate with the Death Dealers.* While Viktor and Marcus were entombed and Amelia occupied in America, Kraven had allowed Soren to form his own internal security force, which often butted heads with Kahn and his Death Dealers. Their rivalry was a deep one, which was one of Soren's primary motives in joining Kraven's plot to overthrow the Elders. Kraven had promised to disband the Death Dealers once he took over the coven and established his historic truce with Lucian. *Soren should know better than to invite the Death Dealers' scrutiny, especially now.*

"How am I to explain why our attacker used silver bullets?" Kraven asked him. "And what if the sniper's primary target turns out to be Lucian after all? How to explain our presence at the attack?" He shook his head. "No, it's too risky. There are too many questions we don't want asked. Selene and the others will have to track down this maniac without news of this latest incident."

Fortunately, he had faith in Selene's determination and abilities. Intent on avenging Diego's death, she would not rest until she liquidated the unknown assassin. *Certainly,* he mused, *that woman knows how to hold a grudge. She still hasn't forgiven the lycans for slaughtering her mortal family all those centuries ago.*

Or so she believed. The truth, as Kraven knew full well, was rather more complicated.

"Excuse me, regent," Soren declared. He pressed the tip

of a hypodermic needle against Kraven's bare bicep. "This will help with the pain."

The injection stung momentarily, but Kraven soon felt its analgesic effect. Even still, he flinched as Soren put down the syringe and approached him again with the scalpel. Removing the bullet from his flesh was not going to be pleasant, especially since the open wound had already healed over.

"What became of Lucian, I wonder?" Soren said, perhaps to distract Kraven from the bloody business ahead. "Do you think he survived?"

The suggestion that Lucian might have actually died came as a shock to Kraven. He had been so intent on his own survival that the thought only now occurred to him that, when last seen, Lucian had been left to face the sniper's bullets alone. *Can it be,* he wondered in amazement, *that Lucian is truly dead at last?*

In truth, the prospect of Lucian's bloody demise filled him with mixed feelings. On the one hand, Lucian's support was key to his entire conspiracy against the Elders. It was the lycans who were, with Kraven's covert assistance, to assassinate Amelia upon her return to Budapest, providing Kraven with the opportunity to seize control of the coven while the other Elders still slumbered in their tombs. *And it was to be my groundbreaking peace treaty with Lucian,* he recalled, *that would cement my place as the undisputed ruler of both the Old and New World covens. With Lucian dead, my dreams of supplanting the Elders—and taking Selene as my royal consort—will be much more difficult to attain.*

On the other hand, Kraven had to admit that it would be a relief to be out from beneath Lucian's oppressive shadow after all these years. He had never truly trusted the scheming lycan, who often failed to show Kraven the deference he deserved. *If Lucian is dead,* he realized, *I will no longer have to live in fear of the other vampires discovering that he is still alive.*

Kraven bit down on his lip as Soren's scalpel sliced deeply into his flesh. He tasted his own cold blood upon his tongue.

In theory, of course, Lucian had already "died" centuries ago. *Has this mysterious assassin,* Kraven thought, *done in reality what I only claimed to do?*

Kill Lucian?

Then

A.D. 1202

Chapter Fourteen

CASTLE CORVINUS

*L*ucian hurried down the corridor toward the chapel, glancing back over his shoulder to make certain he was not being followed. Excitement warred with apprehension in his heart and soul as he wondered at the note he had received via Grushenka, summoning him again to the chapel for the first time in weeks. He and Sonja had not dared to meet in their trysting spot since Soren had surprised them there more than a month ago. *Why now?* he pondered. *What can be so urgent?*

He paused before the door of the chapel. Could this be a trap of some kind? No, he reassured himself, he would know Sonja's delicate handwriting anywhere. The note had manifestly come from his beloved. Moreover, it was early morning on a sunny April day. Soren and Viktor would surely be asleep in their respective chambers.

Wouldn't they?

He knocked hesitantly on the door, then quickly slipped inside, closing the door behind him.

"Lucian!"

His heart soared at the sight of Sonja standing before the altar, clad in a sylvan green gown brocaded with velvet vines and leaves. Her turquoise pendant rested atop her breasts. All his fears were momentarily dispelled by the thrill of finding himself alone with his beloved once more. They ran toward each other eagerly, falling into a passionate embrace. Their lips met in joyous reunion, and Lucian lost himself in the heady sensation of kissing Sonja again after weeks of loneliness and deprivation. The familiar taste of coriander and honey stirred his senses, and he wondered how he had ever survived without her.

She alone makes my life worth living.

At length, their lips came apart, and reality intruded upon their idyll. Sonja rested her head on his shoulder, her arms still wrapped tightly around his waist. "Thank fate you came!" she exclaimed. "I've been trying to slip a note to Grushenka for days, but Soren seems to haunt my every movement. I think he'd lock me in my chambers from dawn to dusk if he dared."

Sonja's lament sent a chill down Lucian's spine. How much did Soren suspect? And how far would the ruthless overseer go to regain Viktor's favor?

"What is so urgent?" he asked her. "Not that I do not welcome any opportunity to be in your company."

She gently pulled away from him. A smile played on her features as she took his hand and laid it on her stomach. Lucian stared at her in confusion until, beneath the brocaded silk, he felt life stirring within her belly.

He gazed at her in wonder. "You are with child?"

"Our child," she affirmed, smiling back at him.

Lucian was stunned by her revelation. "But how is it possible?" He could not tear his hand away from the new life quickening within her womb. "A lycan and a vampire . . . ?"

"You and I are both pure-blooded," she observed. "You were born a lycan, and I a vampire. I daresay this rare combination is what allowed us to conceive a child together." A speculative tone entered her voice. "There are vague references in the ancient annals that hint as much—and suggest that such a union might produce a being of extraordinary power."

Lucian marveled at the very idea. *A hybrid of our two races,* he thought. *Half lycan, half vampire.* Who knew what wondrous attributes such a child might possess? *Perhaps enough to change the world. . . .*

Sonja eyed his thoughtful expression. A flicker of concern showed on her face. "Does this news please you, beloved?"

"How can you doubt it?" he answered, rushing to reassure her. Honor and emotion both compelled him to his knees. He knelt before Sonja and took her hand in his. "Dearest Sonja, jewel of my existence, will you do me the incalculable honor of becoming my bride?"

Tears of happiness burst from her eyes. "Of course, dear Lucian, with all my heart!" She glanced about her, an irresistible idea dawning on her jubilant face. "And look, my love, the chapel is already prepared for us."

Like her, Lucian saw no reason for delay. No Elder or Council member would ever sanction their union, so a private ceremony of their very own would have to suffice. He rose to his feet and escorted Sonja to the altar. The fabled Wolf and Lamb looked down on them from the tapestry as they prepared to take their vows. Lucian filled a tarnished brass communion cup from a sack of wine they had hidden away months ago. He lifted the goblet before him as he faced Sonja before the altar.

"I, Lucian, of the lycan breed, swear upon my eternal life

and soul that I will love, honor, and protect you for all time to come. With this wine, I pledge you my everlasting fidelity."

He sipped from the goblet, then passed it to Sonja, who accepted the cup readily.

"I, Sonja, daughter of Viktor and Ilona, likewise swear that I will love, honor, and cherish you for all eternity. With this wine, I declare myself your true and ever-faithful wife."

She sipped from the same cup as he, then placed it reverently upon the altar. Her lovely face beamed radiantly.

It is done, Lucian thought. No rings had been exchanged, no blessings bestowed, yet he had no doubt that his life had been transformed irrevocably. *We need no vaunted authority to sanctify our union; the purity of our love is sacrament enough.*

Now they were truly man and wife.

He took Sonja into his arms again, feeling a profound sense of responsibility toward her and their unborn child. Marriage and maternity, he realized, had forced a momentous decision upon them.

"We must flee this place," he told her. Never mind that he could not allow her to go through the farce of wedding Nicolae a few weeks hence; her pregnancy and the birth of their child would surely expose their affair for all to see. "We must leave the coven forever and never return."

"Yes," Sonja agreed. "I understand." She trembled within his fervent embrace. "But how will we escape my father's guards? You know that he will stop at nothing to capture us both."

Lucian nodded. The risks were great, but they had no other choice. Each passing day increased the odds that Soren or someone else might become aware of Sonja's delicate condition. *We must get far away from Castle Corvinus soon,* he resolved.

But how?

* * *

In his dreams, Soren once again dined at the high table, at Viktor's right hand. Respect and authority were once more accorded him as was his due. He savored his status among the other vampires, which rendered the ignominy of his squalid mortal past of no consequence. He had come a long way since his days as a pitiful Viking slave. . . .

"Master Soren!" A husky voice intruded upon his triumph. An insistent hand nudged his shoulder, rousing him from slumber. He awoke to find himself back on his cot outside the castle's dungeons. Plain linen sheets covered his muscular frame.

A servant wench leaned over him, still tugging on his shoulder. Her coarse wool kirtle and tumbling mane of wild black hair marked her as a lycan even before Soren identified her as Leyba, a wanton scullery maid no better than the rest of her degenerate breed.

He sat up angrily, shoving the wench aside. "Lycan slut!" he cursed her. "How dare you disturb my rest?!" Tossing aside his sheets, he reached for his whips, which hung on a wooden peg next to the dungeon door. Although he was deep underground, he sensed at once that the sun had not yet set. "I'll teach you not to accost your betters!"

"Wait!" Leyba cried out. Sprawled on the dank stone floor, where Soren's blow had deposited her, she held out her hand before her. A shiny golden ribbon was clutched between her fingers. "Don't you want to know what the Lady Sonja is getting up to . . . while you sleep the day away?"

Soren paused at the mention of the princess's name. Forgetting his whips for the moment, he snatched the ribbon from the wench's hand and examined it closely. The gleaming fabric was nothing less than the finest silk, of the sort only the most highborn vampire ladies might possess. It

dawned on him that the Lady Sonja had a gown of much
the same hue.

"Where did you get this?" he demanded.

Leyba smiled slyly, seeing that she had his attention. "Far
be it from me to cast doubt upon the virtue of an Elder's
daughter," she declared. "Let me say only that I found this
keepsake beneath the pallet of a certain lycan whom I know
to be besotted with the princess."

"What?" Soren clenched his fist, crumpling the delicate
ribbon. He had no doubt that the wench was referring to
Lucian, whose untimely rescue of Sonja had led directly to
Soren's own fall from Viktor's favor. *I knew it!* he fumed. His
cold blood heated up as he recalled how Sonja had
brusquely dismissed him when he caught her squirreled
away in that rundown chapel. *I knew the haughty tart was
hiding something.*

Still, caution compelled him to eye Leyba suspiciously.
"How do I know you didn't steal this ribbon yourself?" he
accused her, threatening her with the back of his hand. "If
you're lying to me. . . ."

"I speak the truth, I swear it!" Rising to her feet, she
backed away from his upraised hand. "I would have gone to
Lord Viktor himself, but a lowly servant such as myself cannot hope to have the ear of so exalted a personage. I had
hoped you might convey my dire tidings to the Elder."
Gypsy eyes gleamed craftily. "Did I think wrong?"

Soren would sooner trust the Devil than a lycan bitch,
yet he felt convinced that Leyba was not deceiving him, if
only because her lewd insinuations confirmed his own suspicions that the princess could not be trusted. A rare smile
graced his saturnine features as he saw before him an opportunity to restore himself to Viktor's good graces.

Thrusting the ribbon back at Leyba, he strode forward

and grabbed her roughly by the arm. "Come!" he commanded, all but dragging the wench toward the spiral staircase leading to the castle above. "The Elder must hear of this at once!"

They met in her bedchamber early that afternoon, after Sonja dismissed her various servants and ladies-in-waiting. Their plan, such as it was, was to leave the castle the second the sun disappeared below the horizon, then head for the densest regions of the forest, much as they had during their nocturnal trek to Ordoghaz months ago. Soren would no doubt notice Sonja's absence at once, but with luck, they could elude the inevitable search parties by avoiding the main roads and pathways. Moving quickly, they hoped to reach the ruined village of Strasba before dawn, so that Sonja could take refuge in one of the surviving buildings.

And then what? Lucian fretted. The full moon would rise tonight, giving him the strength to effect their escape, but at some point they would have to try to blend into the mortal world. Sonja's jewelry would pay their way for a time, at least until he could find employment as a mortal. But what trades were available to a lycan retainer who had served the vampires for all his immortal existence?

While Sonja packed the last of her jewelry into a small ivory chest, Lucian took a moment to survey his love's private chambers, which he had never dared to visit before. A wooden canopy bed, hung with curtains, dominated the room. With its feather mattress and pillows, the bed looked far more luxurious than Lucian's own humble straw pallet. Sprigs of lavender were sprinkled atop the bed to sweeten the sheets and keep away fleas. Pine chests held the princess's wardrobe, while sumptuous tapestries, cleaner and in better condition than the one in the chapel, adorned the walls.

His hand delicately swept along the edge of a lacquered cherry vanity, tenderly exploring the combs, hairpins, and perfume bottles arrayed atop the table. Lifting his eyes, he gazed into the brass mirror above the vanity, heedless of the silver beneath the polished glass, and stared thoughtfully at his own reflection.

Hers has always been the life of a princess, he realized, *accustomed to only the finest accommodations and possessions. What can I possibly offer her in comparison?*

"Forgive me," he said, "for forcing you to leave all this comfort and opulence behind."

She closed the lid of her jewelry case. "Do not be foolish, my husband," she assured him. She smiled at him from a few paces away. "I made my choice of my own free will. Happily will I face the world at your side, rather than live without you for one night more."

Her reflection joined his as she slid up next to him, resting the soft curves of her body against his rougher form. Contrary to mortal folklore, her peerless beauty was fully captured by the polished mirror. They kissed, and he felt once more how lucky he was to have found her. *One way or another,* he vowed, *I will carve out a place for us in the outside world.* He pressed his hand against her belly and felt again the cherished life they had created together. *We will live in happiness forever, Sonja, I, and our precious baby. . . .*

Without warning, the locked door burst open. Viktor stormed into the bedchamber, his face a livid mask of rage. Fiery eyes took in the incriminating scene of Lucian and Sonja embracing before the mirror. "What is the meaning of this?!" he roared in fury.

Lucian stepped protectively in front of Sonja as Soren and a pair of armored Death Dealers followed Viktor into the chamber. To his surprise, a familiar female figure squeezed past the guards to reach the Elder's side. "You see!" Leyba yelped, casting an accusing finger at Lucian and Sonja. "It is just as I said." She glared at Lucian, a malevolent smirk on her face. "Your precious daughter entertains a wolf in her boudoir!"

Spiteful bitch! Lucian cursed her. He was dismayed to see Sonja's gold silk ribbon—his fragile token of their love—wrapped around the female lycan's finger. He had noticed earlier that it was missing, but in his excitement and anxiety over Sonja's pregnancy, he had given the matter little thought. *Your petty jealousy has doomed Sonja and me.*

Viktor ignored Leyba's taunts, intent on his disgraced daughter. "How could you do this, sully yourself with an animal?" Rage contorted his patrician features, and he hissed through his fangs. "You have dishonored your noble heritage, as well as your mother's memory!"

"Please, Father!" Sonja begged, holding on to Lucian from behind. "Do not be angry! I love Lucian, truly I do. We are man and wife!"

"What?" Viktor raged. "Have you taken leave of your senses?" He turned to bark at Soren, who stood a few paces behind the irate Elder. "This is your fault! You were supposed to watch over her!"

Soren went visibly pale. "But milord!" he protested, aghast. "I did my bes—"

"Enough!" Viktor silenced the anxious overseer. "I shall deal with you later." He turned back toward Lucian and Sonja, and the unchecked fury on his face gave way to a look of icy resolution. "Take them both," he instructed the guards, "and round up the rest of the filthy lycans."

"No!" Sonja protested, but to no avail. Viktor stepped to one side and let the two Death Dealers surge past him.

Chain mail covered their leather armor. One-handed swords hung at their sides.

"Stand back!" Lucian warned. Without the full moon on his side, he was badly outnumbered, but he would not surrender Sonja without a fight. He drew his wolf's-head dagger from his belt and adopted a defensive stance. He bared his fangs as a growl emerged from his throat. "I've never killed a vampire before, but there's a first time for everything!"

The first Death Dealer—Ulrik by name—lunged at Lucian, grabbing for the lycan's arm. Lucian slashed out with his blade, slicing open the soldier's palm. The scent of spilled blood filled the chamber.

Ulrik backed away warily. Drawing his sword from its scabbard, he exchanged a glance with his fellow soldier, Lazar, who likewise drew his sword. Silver-plated blades caught the candlelight. The guards cautiously advanced toward their intended prisoners, circling Sonja and Lucian as much as the chamber's generous furnishings permitted.

It was best to keep them on the defensive, Lucian strategized. With his free hand, he snatched up a writing quill from the vanity and hurled it like a dart at Ulrik's face. The pointed quill speared the Death Dealer in the eye, and he dropped to his knees, clutching his face in agony. Cold vampire blood seeped between his fingers.

An instant later, before anyone could react to the first soldier's blinding, a glass perfume bottle shattered against Lazar's face. Slivers of broken glass invaded his skin while the oily perfume stung his eyes and cuts.

Take that, churls! Lucian thought triumphantly. He viciously slashed the air with his dagger, and a frightened Leyba ran out of the room. *Never underestimate a lycan in love!*

"Bah," Viktor snarled impatiently. "Must I do everything

myself?" He strode past the stricken guards, menace in his dark eyes.

Lucian readied himself for battle, but the Elder was too swift, too strong. He came at Lucian like a thunderbolt, knocking the dagger from his hand with a single blow, then grabbing Lucian by the throat and lifting him from the floor. Viktor held Lucian at arm's length before him, so that Lucian's feet dangled impotently in the air. He kicked and thrashed in a desperate attempt to free himself from the Elder's iron grasp, tugging on Viktor's clenched fingers with both hands, but he was helpless before the ancient vampire's superior power, like a wolfling cub being carried about in its mother's jaws. Viktor's grip tightened around Lucian's throat so that he could hardly breathe.

"Stop it, Father!" Sonja cried out frantically. She pounded against Viktor's adamantine form with her fists, but she might as well have been hammering on the castle walls itself for all the good it did; the Elder remained unmoved, either physically or emotionally. "Don't hurt him, I beg of you!"

"Soren," Viktor intoned, not even looking in Sonja's direction. He ripped Lucian's pewter badge from his tunic and hurled it angrily across the room. "See to my daughter . . . if you think you can manage that."

"Yes, milord!" Soren hastened to obey. He rushed forward and seized Sonja from behind, clamping her arms to her side. She tried to twist free, but the burly overseer easily overpowered her. Lucian watched in agony as Soren roughly hauled Sonja out of her own bedchamber. No doubt the humiliated brute welcomed the opportunity to abuse the apparent source of his troubles. *Unhand her, you vein-sucking monster!* Lucian thought.

A jabbing pain in his side brought him back to his own predicament. "I've told you before, lycan," Viktor snarled, withdrawing the blade of a silver dagger from between Lucian's ribs. "Keep your eyes to yourself!"

He squeezed more tightly on Lucian's throat, cutting off his air. Lucian gasped like a fish out of water, choking to death within the Elder's grip. He tried to growl in defiance, but all that emerged from his larynx was a pitiful squeak.

Forgive me, Sonja, Lucian thought as all-enveloping darkness encroached on his vision. Viktor's demonic countenance, glaring up at him with malign intensity, was swallowed up in shadow.

I tried to protect you!

Chapter Fifteen

CASTLE CORVINUS

Lucian woke to find himself chained to the cold stone floor of the dungeon. Sputtering torches threw writhing shadows on the moldering limestone walls. Rats chittered in the corners, alarmed by his sudden movements. A blazing brazier failed to dispel the dank, frigid atmosphere of the dungeon. Darkness clustered beneath the high domed ceiling.

In truth, he was amazed to find himself still alive. His bruised throat ached from Viktor's unbreakable stranglehold. Lucian tried to reach up and massage his neck, only to be halted by the shackles around his wrists. The damp floor stones sent a chill through his bones, and he trembled despite himself. Hunger and thirst added to his misery. *How long have I been unconscious?* he wondered. *Is it day or night?* All he could tell for certain was that the full moon had not yet risen.

"Lucian!"

He looked up from the floor to see Sonja only a few yards

away, chained to a great oak column, her arms bound uncomfortably above her head. Her brocade gown hung in tatters on her slender frame. Iron shackles held her fast. Her chestnut eyes were rimmed with red. Crimson tears ran in torrents down her porcelain cheeks. "Thank fate you've awoken!" she exclaimed. "I feared my father had all but killed you!"

"Sonja!" Lucian called out to her. He could not bear to see her mistreated so. Snarling like a mad dog, he tugged uselessly against the unyielding chains. "My love! What have they done to you?"

"Quiet!" Soren emerged from the shadows, silver whip in hand. Vengeful eyes shot daggers at Lucian. "Another word, and you'll taste my whip." He glanced ominously to one side. "And that goes for the rest of you mangy curs!"

Sobs and muttered curses reached Lucian's ears, and he realized that he and Sonja were not the only captives in this forsaken place. Ignoring his sore neck, he peered back over his shoulders and saw, to his dismay, his fellow lycans penned behind the iron bars of a prison cell. The caged servants yelped and whined piteously, despite Soren's warning, and the foul-tempered overseer cracked his whip against the bars of the cell, striking sparks in the murky gloom. Lucian saw that the iron bars were laced with silver alloy, the better to trap the distraught lycans inside. Along with several other mothers, Olga clutched her baby to her chest, trying her best to quiet the frightened infant's cries. Lucian also spotted Grushenka among the prisoners, although Leyba was conspicuously missing.

No! Lucian thought. *Leave them alone!* His heart broke for the other lycans; it was not just that they should suffer for his crime, if crime it was. His anger rose, supplanting any lingering fears for his own safety. Was this how the vampires repaid them, after generations of loyal service?

Measured footsteps approached the dungeon from outside. A reinforced wooden door swung open, admitting Viktor, Nicolae, and various members of the Council. Their luxurious velvet robes contrasted sharply with the dismal surroundings. Viktor's face was frozen in a somber mien, and even Nicolae appeared sobered by the gravity of the situation. Council members murmured darkly among themselves as the regal vampires took their places at the top of a set of low steps leading down to the sunken floor of the dungeon. A large brass disk, emblazoned with ancient runes, was mounted above the arched doorway behind them.

"Father!" Sonja pleaded. "Show mercy, please. We meant no harm!"

Viktor's head turned slowly toward his daughter. His mighty broadsword was sheathed at his side. "You are my only child," he informed her, "and the sole inheritor of my bloodline. Yet you have left me no other choice. You have broken the Covenant. You must be judged."

The Elder's forbidding tone filled Lucian with dread. "Lord Viktor!" he cried out, hoping to strike a bargain with Sonja's father. "I take full responsibility. Do whatever you wish to me, but spare your daughter!"

"Soren!" Viktor barked, not deigning to answer Lucian directly. His lip curled in contempt. "Teach this vile animal a lesson!"

"With pleasure, milord." Soren stepped forward, uncoiling his silver whip. He sneered through his thick black beard. "I should have done this ages ago."

Lucian braced himself for the blow he knew was coming, yet no amount of preparation could have steeled him against the searing pain that raced through his body as the whip viciously lashed his back again and again. The barbed vertebrae tore through his ragged tunic and made ribbons of his hide, burning his skin even as they sliced through his defenseless flesh, paring it to the bone. The pain was unendurable.

Chained to the post only a short distance away, Sonja twisted within her bonds and shouted desperately at her father and his dire companions. "Nooo! Leave him be!" she yelled on Lucian's behalf. "Stop it! Stop!"

But the lashes kept coming. Behind him, over the thunderous cracks of the whip, his lycan brothers and sisters went berserk, enraged to see one of their own kind treated thus. Though caged, they threw themselves against the silver-tainted bars, growling like the untamed beasts within them. Without the moon's liberating glow, they could not shed their human guises, yet they raged like creatures of the wild, rending their crude homespun garments and gnashing their teeth. Angry curses gave way to savage howls and roars as the wronged servants voiced their primeval wrath against their masters.

We will never forget this night, Lucian vowed, even as the merciless whip shredded his flesh anew. At last, he was left gasping on the blood-slick floor. Crimson welts showed through the gaps in his rent tunic.

Soren drew back his lash once more.

"Please, no more!" Sonja begged frantically. "You'll kill him!"

"And what of it?" Viktor glared at her accusingly. "What does this wretched creature mean to you?"

Sonja swallowed hard. "He is my husband . . . and the father of my child." She stared boldly into her father's eyes. "Your grandchild!"

"*What?*" Viktor stiffened in shock. A flicker of trepidation passed across his face, and he reached for the hilt of his sword. "You are with child?" he asked in a horrified tone. "By this animal?"

Scandalized gasps escaped the Council members behind Viktor. Nicolae's jaw dropped in astonishment.

"By my one true love," Sonja asserted defiantly. She seemed to draw strength from the memory of their times together. "Our blessed union has conceived a miracle!"

Viktor struggled to contain himself. "Heresy," he hissed. "*Abomination!*" His face twitched in revulsion before congealing into a grave and rigid expression. When he spoke again, his voice was as hard and unbending as steel. "There can be no forgiveness for what you have done, not even for the daughter of an Elder." His hand came away from his sword. "What I do now, I do for the sake of all our kind."

Turning his back on Sonja, he marched steadfastly toward the arched stone doorway. The other vampires stepped aside to let him pass, then filed out behind him. Their velvet robes rustled like cobwebs as they departed the dungeon, leaving Soren behind to watch over the prisoners. The heavy oaken door slammed shut, trapping Sonja, Lucian, and the lycan captives inside the fetid torture chamber.

Bloodied and exhausted, Lucian lay prostrate upon the floor, which was now sticky with his own lifeblood. *Is this the end?* he wondered, praying that the torment was soon to cease. Perhaps, despite his unforgiving words, Viktor would be content with Lucian's destruction and, upon time and reflection, spare Sonja and the others. Lucian could not imagine that the wrathful Elder could condemn his only daughter forever.

By fate, she is his own flesh and blood!

The scream of protesting metal reverberated nearby, echoing throughout the cavernous chamber. Lifting his eyes, Lucian saw Soren wrestling with a heavy iron wheel mounted on the wall in a shadowy alcove at the far side of the dungeon. Soren's silver whip was draped over his shoulders as the overseer put his back to the task before him. The corroded wheel did not want to move at first, but Soren's determined efforts finally proved enough to crank the wheel in a clockwise direction.

Timeworn metal gears began to squeak and grind in the ceiling overhead. Panic flooded Lucian's face as he guessed what Soren intended. Sonja also grasped what was transpiring. Her wide brown eyes stared into Lucian's, terror-stricken.

Is this what Viktor had decreed for his daughter?

"Please, no," Lucian whispered hoarsely, but the relentless gears kept grinding against each other. Directly above Sonja's head, at the very apex of the domed ceiling, a circular iron hatch slowly dilated. Several yards away, Soren backed deeper into the shelter of the secluded alcove. Lucian saw a glint of sunshine overhead and realized, to his horror, that it was still daylight outside.

The deadly radiance poured through the widening gap, which opened onto a vertical shaft rising the entire height of the castle.

The golden beam fell directly on Sonja, who let out a bloodcurdling scream.

No, not the sun! Not on her! Lucian lunged forward desperately, and the heavy chains snapped taut, holding him back. The iron shackles cut savagely into his flesh, yet he barely noticed the pain. He strained with all his might, working himself into a lather of blood and sweat, but there was not a damned thing he could do to save the woman he loved.

He could do nothing but watch as her pale face blackened and crumbled. Sonja tossed her head from side to side, but she could not escape the unsparing sunlight as it turned her vulnerable flesh to charcoal. Smoke rose from her flaxen hair moments before it burst into flame, turning the shrieking princess into a human torch. Her face contorted in agony, showing her fangs, and her blistering arms twisted helplessly above her head. His beloved bride was being burned at the stake, just as Lucian had always feared.

"Noooo!" he shouted like a madman, his raspy cry of despair joining hers in one final, excruciating moment of communion.

"Sonja!"

Lucian shuddered uncontrollably on the floor of the dungeon, drained of tears and emotion. Hours had passed, and the blood beneath him had long since dried. The killing sun slowly faded from the sky, and the purple glow of twilight shone through the circular hole in the ceiling.

Sonja was dead. All that remained of his beautiful and loving wife was a lifeless, gray statue of charred bone and ash. Her powdery arms were still raised above her, held in place by the unyielding iron shackles. A look of anguished sorrow, for both herself and their unborn child, was baked on the statue's agonized features. Only a single golden shimmer added a touch of color to the bleak gray figure: Sonja's crest-shaped pendant, still clasped around her charcoal throat.

As the last hint of sunlight disappeared from the sky, the prison door slammed open once more. Viktor entered the dungeon, garbed in somber hues of mourning. Long-faced and solemn, he made his way across the chamber to the crumbling effigy that was once his daughter. If the blackened ruin troubled him, his stony face bore no evidence of it.

Ignoring Lucian completely, he reached out and touched

the gilded pendant embedded in Sonja's ashes. His eyes watered briefly, and a look of genuine grief flashed across his face, but it passed quickly as his aristocratic countenance reassumed a cold, distant expression. He plucked the pendant from Sonja's throat, easily snapping the delicate chain, and turned toward Lucian at last. Icy disdain and hatred smoldered in his eyes.

His callous inhumanity inflamed Lucian, who matched the Elder's baleful gaze with a red-hot look of his own. His blood surged volcanically within his veins. "You heartless monster!"

He pounced at Viktor like the wolf he was, but the stubborn chains jerked him back once more. Viktor nodded at Soren, who emerged from the safety of his alcove now that the sun had set. The sadistic overseer fell upon Lucian at once, bludgeoning his lacerated body with devastating kicks and blows. Soren's fists and boots crashed against Lucian like a rain of meteors until his battered form dropped back onto the damp stone floor, panting and gasping.

But though his body lay defeated, Lucian's unquenchable fury still burned like the eternal fires of hell. "I'll kill you," he croaked through broken and swollen lips. "I'll make you pay for her life, you bloodsucking devil!"

Viktor stepped forward and grabbed Lucian's long hair. He savagely yanked the prisoner's head back so that he could stare into Lucian's pulped and bloody face. Viktor's own features wrinkled in disgust.

"For you, death will come slowly. I can promise you that." A cruel smile revealed his heinous intentions. "Forget the whip," he instructed Soren. "Fetch me my knives."

At that moment, through the opening in the ceiling, the full moon slid into view from behind a bank of billowing clouds. The bright lunar orb shone down on Lucian.

For once, he readily surrendered to the Change. His blood-streaked eyes turned cobalt blue, and a bitter laugh escaped his lips. Renewed strength flooded his exhausted sinews as his body gained size and weight in the space of a heartbeat. His bloodstained tunic and leggings came apart at the seams, and coarse black fur sprouted from his hide, hiding the ugly welt marks on his back. His hearing and sense of smell heightened immeasurably, so that he could practically taste the alarm in Viktor's blood as the haughty Elder suddenly grasped his mistake.

You should never have let the moonlight find me, Lucian thought vindictively. *Now the tables are turned.*

The metamorphosis took place in an instant, and it was as a complete werewolf that Lucian lunged once more at his nemesis. This time, the iron chains snapped before his inhuman strength, and he leaped at Viktor, his outstretched claws preceding him. With a single swipe of his shaggy arm, he snatched the gilded pendant from Viktor's grasp.

The Elder recoiled from the werewolf's claws, stumbling backward across the dungeon. He bumped into the iron bars of the nearby cell, provoking a ferocious roar from within. The bestial noise alerted him to danger, and he threw himself away from the cell only seconds before a hairy arm clawed at him through the tightly spaced metal bars.

Viktor whirled around, stunned to discover that every one of the lycan prisoners had become a fully transformed werewolf. The cramped cell was now packed with growling, snapping monsters, trying like hell to chew their way through the confining iron bars. The musky scent of a score of fur-covered werewolves filled the dank, unwholesome atmosphere of the torture chamber.

While Viktor blinked in surprise, Soren charged at Lucian from across the room. Broken chains dangled from the werewolf's wrists like decorative streamers, and he spun about with preternatural speed, sending the heavy chains slicing through the air at the oncoming vampire. The chains gave Soren a taste of his own medicine as they smacked loudly against the overseer's midsection, shattering his ribs.

An almost-human smile distorted Lucian's wolfen snout. It felt good to be at the other end of the whip.

Heated shouts came from outside the crypt. Lucian moved to throw the heavy wooden doors shut, but he was too late: a squad of Death Dealers, led by Nicolae, poured into the chamber, clutching silver-plated swords and pikes. "Get him!" Viktor shouted to his soldiers. "Kill that treacherous cur!"

There were too many of them, Lucian realized. Even in wolfen form, he could not stand against so many foes, not while his bestial allies still struggled to free themselves from their hateful cell. His eyes searched desperately for an escape route, coming to rest on a narrow window recessed in a dark alcove more than twenty feet above the floor. *That will do!* he thought gratefully.

It was a long way up, but his powerful hind legs were sufficient to the task; exploding into motion, he landed in a single pounce on the narrow stone ledge beneath the alcove. Mercifully, the upper reaches of the dungeon were built directly into the castle's outer walls, so that the outside world beckoned no more than ten feet below him. The open forest called out from the bottom of a rocky slope.

For a moment, he lingered within the deep limestone shelf, silhouetted against the moonlight sky beyond. He looked back at Sonja's charred remains and clutched her tiny pendant as if it were the most valuable treasure on earth.

Then he turned his murderous gaze upon Viktor himself, as the tyrannical Elder quivered with anger and frustration on the floor of the prison. *Someday,* Lucian vowed, *you will pay for what you have done to my princess and my species.*

Crossbows laden with silver bolts aimed upward at Lucian, and he realized he could tarry no longer. Turning his back on the dungeon below, he dove through the open window. The warm April wind blew against his face, ruffling his fur, as he fell through the air toward the ground below.

He hit the slope on all fours, then sprang up on two legs, standing as a man did despite the hairy pelt covering his body. He howled triumphantly at the savior moon even as angry cries and tumult erupted from behind the grim gray walls of Castle Corvinus.

Behind Lucian, the sinister fortress loomed ominously amidst the craggy Carpathian Mountains; before him, an impenetrable forest of dense pines held out the promise of safety and freedom. He loped full tilt toward the sheltering woods.

The night was broken by the heated cries and pounding footsteps of a brigade of Death Dealers stampeding out through the castle's gate. The irate vampire warriors chased after him, hurling threats, curses, and unheeded commands at his fleeing back. Chain mail rattled loudly amid the towering pines. Silver crossbow bolts whistled through the air, coming to rest in the trunk of a bushy fir tree only inches from the werewolf's head.

He ran from his determined pursuers as fast as his furry legs could carry him. Clutching Sonja's precious pendant in his hairy paw, he escaped madly from his tragic past into an unglimpsed future.

Mark my words, Viktor, he thought vengefully. *You have not heard the last of me.*

This means war!

*   *   *

Viktor stood on the parapet as his Death Dealers scoured the darkened forest below. Torches glowed like fireflies throughout the misty woods surrounding the castle. A full moon lit up the sky above Viktor, mocking his carelessness.

He found himself wishing that Sonja had died at the keep along with her mother. Better that she had perished then, an innocent victim of a mortal mob, than let herself be seduced by an unclean animal. *At least then I would not have been forced to end her life myself!*

Grief for his lost daughter tore at his heart, but he took comfort from the knowledge that he had made the only decision possible under the circumstances. The abomination the lycan had planted in Sonja's womb had been a threat to the coven's very future. There had been no choice but to destroy it utterly.

But, oh, the price he had paid!

Bootsteps sounded on the wall walk. Viktor looked away from the forest to see Soren approach him. The overseer held an upraised torch, and his leather boots were splattered with mud and fallen pine needles.

"Well?" Viktor demanded.

Soren shook his head. "The werewolf continues to elude us. We will search the woods until dawn, but he is a crafty beast. He knows how to hide his trail!"

Viktor scowled, remembering how, in happier times, Lucian had distinguished himself as a tracker of his own kind. Now, it seemed, those very skills were being used against them.

The Devil take me for a fool if I ever trust a lycan again!

Thoughts of missed opportunities tormented him. *I should have realized something was amiss,* he mused, *when Sonja was so appalled at the prospect of marrying Nicolae.* His fists clenched at his sides. *Had she already succumbed to the*

*beast's seductive wiles by then, or might I have still had a chance
to turn her from that fatal course?*

He would never know.

Another set of footsteps approached him, from the opposite end of the parapet. Irritation flared within his heart as
he saw that it was the dark-haired lycan wench who had
first informed Soren of his daughter's misdeeds. The worth-
less scullion crept toward him, Sonja's damning ribbon still
clutched between her grimy fingers.

"Yes?" he asked impatiently, already regretting that he
had not consigned this particular bitch to the dungeon
along with the rest of her filthy breed. "What do you want?"

"Nothing but what I deserve, Elder." She grinned
wolfishly at him, her bright eyes gleaming in the moonlight.
"Has Leyba not done well? Did I not speak the truth?" She
extended an open palm before him. "How might I be rewarded for my great service?"

The trull's naked greed infuriated him. "You dare to approach me now—and expect to profit from my daughter's
ruin?" He snatched the blazing torch from Soren's grip and
thrust it at Leyba, setting fire to the wench's hair and clothing. "Here's your reward, she-beast! Burn as she burned!"

Leyba let out an agonized howl as her squalid hide went
up in flames. Her raucous caterwauling assailed his ears,
and he grabbed her with both hands. Heedless of the fire
consuming her flesh, he lifted her high above his head. In
his mind's eye, he saw Sonja—his precious Sonja!—burning
as well. His daughter's dying screams echoed within his
skull, in concert with the high-pitched keening of the lycan
bitch who had betrayed her.

Viktor flung Leyba from the parapet with all his strength.
The blazing figure arced across the sky like a falling star be-

fore crashing to earth somewhere within the shrouded forest below. Her final cries were lost to the night.

The Elder sagged against the battlements, exhausted more from emotion than from exertion. *If only I could cast away my painful memories so easily,* he lamented, feeling the loss of his daughter like a stake to his heart. *First my wife, now my Sonja . . . I am bereft of family and affection.*

"Well done, milord," Soren said gruffly. "The bitch had it coming."

Viktor shot Soren a murderous glare. "Be thankful I do not set you to the torch as well!" he snarled. "I have not forgotten your many failures where my late daughter is concerned."

Soren staggered backward, taken aback by the Elder's savage rebuke. "But milord . . . !"

"Silence!" Viktor ordered sharply. "If you are wise, you will not try my patience further."

He turned away from the crestfallen overseer and stared darkly out over the parapet. Alas, Leyba's death had not eased his pain or quelled his all-consuming anger. Killing the female meant nothing; it was the male, Lucian, who had brought this catastrophe down upon him.

I will not rest, Viktor vowed, *until the lycan who despoiled my daughter is dead . . . even if I have to exterminate his entire loathsome species!*

Now

A.D. 2002

Chapter Sixteen

BUDAPEST

*B*uilt by the Turks during the sixteenth century, the Petofi Baths were one of the oldest and most prestigious of the city's famed thermal baths. In theory, the bathhouse closed to the public at dusk, but tonight the interior lights still could be seen through the frosted glass dome above the main pool. A gleaming black limousine was parked in front of the building, while the front entrance was guarded by a pair of unsmiling thugs packing suspicious bulges beneath their leather jackets.

Selene perched atop the central cupola, unseen by the human guards below. She had easily gained access to the roof of the bathhouse by scaling one of the adjacent buildings and stealthily dropping onto the large glass dome. Sneaking past mortals was simplicity itself compared with stalking lycans; for once, she didn't have to worry about her scent giving her away.

I could get used to this, she thought. *Too bad I'm only interested in killing lycans.*

Using a glass cutter, she quietly removed a small, round segment of the dome and peered through the peephole at the scene below.

The steaming octagonal pool glowed green in the dimly lit bath. Green marble columns supported the dome. Rose-colored granite walls, dating back to the glory days of the Ottoman Empire, surrounded the pool, and arched door-ways led to the attached locker rooms, sauna, and side pools. Selene could feel the heat from the sulfurous waters rising through the hole in the ceiling.

Leonid Florescu lounged within the heated pool, having booked the historical baths for his exclusive use this evening. A young blond woman, whom Selene assumed to be his mistress, shared the bath with the notorious arms dealer. A floating chessboard bobbed atop the water be-tween them. An open bottle of plum brandy rested on the tiles at the edge of the pool, next to a plate of *fatányéros*. A pair of additional bodyguards stood watch over the cham-ber's exits and entrances. Given Florescu's profession, Selene had to assume that the guards were well armed.

Selene drew her eye away from the peephole, satisfied with what she had seen. Her intel regarding Florescu's whereabouts had proven correct. Now all she had to do was pry some more information straight from the horse's mouth. She had questions that demanded answers, questions that she hoped would lead her one step closer to finding Diego's killer.

An exploding grenade, sending her comrade's body flying. An armored figure spraying fiery death from a flamethrower. Diego's body burning up before her eyes, his dying screams ringing in her ears. . . .

Selene shook her head to clear her mind of the painful memories. A look of grim resolution hardened on her face as she stood atop the dome and drew a pair of twin Berettas. Her long leather trench coat flapped in the breeze. Her dark brown hair blew across her face.

Aiming downward at the frosted glass beneath her boots, she squeezed the triggers of her weapons.

The graceful dome shattered before the hail of bullets. Selene dropped toward the bath below, preceded by a shower of broken glass.

She kept firing as she fell, taking out both bodyguards even as she plummeted feet-first toward the luminous green water. The guards died reaching for their guns, their bodies dropping onto the tiled corridor surrounding the bath. Florescu's blond mistress screamed in fright.

Selene hit the center of the pool with a splash. Ignoring the stifling heat of the water, she quickly holstered her drenched handguns and palmed a pair of shining silver throwing stars. Her boots struck the floor of the bath, and she sprang upward, breaking through the steaming surface of the water, *shuriken* in hand.

Drawn by the commotion, the two guards from outside came running into the bath chamber. Selene's throwing stars spun threw the air, catching each of the two men in the throat. Bright arterial blood spurted through their fingertips as the wounded gunmen clutched at their necks, slicing their palms and fingers on the razor-sharp points of the *shuriken*. Their bodies quickly joined their associates' on the soggy tiles. Streams of blood flowed across the floor of the bathhouse into the pool itself, creating crimson swirls in the choppy green water.

As a rule, Selene went out of her way to avoid harming humans, whom she regarded as noncombatants in her eternal war against the lycans. These particular humans, however, were not exactly innocent bystanders. *If Florescu and his goons choose to involve themselves in our war,* she decided, *then they had better be prepared to suffer the consequences.*

Despite her scruples, the sight and smell of so much spilled blood tantalized Selene. She licked her lips involuntarily, resisting the temptation to dip her finger into the crimson swirls and give it a lick. It had been a long time since she'd tasted fresh human blood, as opposed to the cloned variety.

Instead, focusing her mind on her mission, she waded forcefully toward Florescu, who was backed up against the edge of the pool, his eyes wide with alarm. Her waterlogged coat and leathers dragged on her, but Selene did not let the added weight slow her down. Her dramatic entrance, she observed, had capsized the floating chess set. Pawns, rooks, and other pieces drifted like flotsam in the agitated water. Florescu's mistress opened her mouth to scream again, but Selene shot her a warning look.

"Don't even think about it."

The blonde clammed up fast, and Selene turned her full attention to Florescu, who looked properly cowed. His parboiled complexion paled to a slightly less vivid shade of scarlet. "Who are you?" he asked tremulously. "What do you want?"

Selene saw no reason not to reveal her true nature. Her eyes assumed an azure glow, and she flashed her fangs at the sweating arms dealer. The crimson nectar spreading through the pool, impossible to ignore by one of her kind, made it all too easy to assume the visage of a bloodthirsty undead.

Just give me an excuse to bite you, Leonid. You look like you have plenty of blood to spare.

Her scare tactics had the desired effect; Florescu gasped out loud and crossed himself. *Scratch a sophisticated mortal urbanite,* she thought, *and you'll usually find a superstitious peasant underneath.*

Good. That just makes my job simpler.

"I want answers," she told him. "About the attack at Statue Park—and the person responsible."

Once she'd gotten over the shock of Diego's death, it hadn't taken her long to put the pieces together. The faceless killer at the park had been equipped with state-of-the-art military body armor, plus silver hand grenades just like the Death Dealers used. And where did she and her comrades get most of their ordnance?

She had remembered, too, how eager Florescu had been to exit the park that evening, not even bothering to take the time to count his money. Perhaps because he knew of the bloodbath in store?

"I don't know anything about that!" he protested. His jowly face was slick with perspiration. "That had nothing to do with me."

Selene wasn't buying it. She grabbed onto Florescu's scalp and shoved his head beneath the hot, sulfurous waters. She counted slowly to ten, then waited for the first rush of bubbles to rise past his submerged face, before yanking his head out of the pool. Red-tinted water streamed down his face and sluiced from his nose and mouth. He gasped raggedly for breath.

"Try again," she suggested.

"I told you!" he sputtered. "I don't know anything!"

"Wrong answer."

She pushed his head back under the water. *This is taking too long,* she thought impatiently. Despite the thick stone walls of the ancient bathhouse, it was only a matter of time before someone reported the gunfire. The blonde whimpered loudly a few feet away, and Selene briefly considered knocking her unconscious. *Just my luck, she'd probably drown.*

Selene counted to twenty this time, then brought Florescu up for air again. Was it just wishful thinking, or was he starting to look a bit blue beneath his flushed red skin? "Had enough?" she asked harshly, treating him to another glimpse of her ivory fangs. "Tell me about that bastard in the armor."

Tears flowed from his eyes, merging with the bloody water running down his face. "I had no choice!" he sobbed pitifully. He was breathing so hard Selene feared he might have a heart attack. "She made me tell her about the meeting. She would have killed me otherwise!"

Selene let go of Florescu's scalp. Her eerie blue eyes widened.

She?

Then

A.D. 1202

Chapter Seventeen

CARPATHIAN MOUNTAINS

*T*he day was waning fast as Lucian tracked through the verdant forest on foot. Soon he would have to seek shelter for the night, unless he found what he was looking for. He trudged through the clotted underbrush, far from any mortal paths, as he traversed a wooded valley lying deep between the spurs of the jagged, snow-topped mountains.

Nearly a month had passed since his escape from Castle Corvinus, yet Lucian knew that Viktor and his Death Dealers would still be looking for him. For safety's sake, he had taken to traveling by day while hiding at night.

Has it truly been almost a month? he thought, his throat tightening. The pain of Sonja's death was still fresh within him, tearing at his heart and soul. He could still hear her agonized cries, smell her soft and supple flesh burning in the sunlight, along with the precious child she carried within her. The ghastly memories haunted him day and night, as did hopeless fantasies of the life they might have had together, a life that he would never know. *Sometimes it feels as though I lost her mere hours ago.*

That first night, he had taken refuge in the charred ruins of Strasba, abandoned after the vampires set fire to the village two months ago. Human tears had streamed down a wolfen muzzle as he'd whimpered in pain and despair, mourning the loss of his one true love. He had not even been able to howl his grief to the moon, lest his heartsick keening bring his undead enemies down on him. That hellish night had been the longest in his entire immortal existence.

The next day, he had rooted through the blackened timbers in search of provisions. Most of the villagers' earthly possessions had been destroyed in the fire, but Lucian had managed to salvage a decent steel knife and a quantity of gold and copper coins. Ironically, it was the modest stone chapel, Brother Ambrose's final sanctuary, that had provided the richest pickings: there he found the greatest store of currency, as well as fresh garments to clothe his nakedness. A hooded cloak concealed his face, while a monk's black robe hid the telltale brand on his arm. Sandaled feet trod softly on the mossy forest floor.

Most nights he spent at mortal inns, posing as a wandering pilgrim, which was true enough in a way. He had found to his relief that his disguise, complete with a cross and rosary beads, helped blind humans to his true nature. Apparently, they could not imagine that any werewolf or vampire would willingly don the trappings of their faith.

In this way, he had eluded the Death Dealers for weeks, but Lucian had more than mere survival on his mind. Revenge was his abiding obsession now, not just against Viktor but against every arrogant vampire who had ever lorded over a lycan. He could not believe that he had ever admired, let alone envied, his former masters. He saw now that the vampires' elegant veneer of culture and civilization masked a cold-blooded barbarity more heinous than that of the most savage lycan.

They are all bloodsucking parasites who deserve to be put to the sword! Except for Sonja, of course.

He gently touched her gilded pendant, which now occupied a permanent place around his own neck. He tried to remember her as she had been—loving, beautiful—rather than as the lifeless pile of cinders she had become. *I shall never forget you, my love,* he silently vowed, *or the happiness we once shared.*

A happiness that Viktor had destroyed without mercy.

If Lucian had his way, the vampires would pay for Sonja's unforgivable murder, but he knew that a lone wolf would not be enough to overthrow Viktor and his undead ilk.

I need an army.

Hence today's hunting expedition, deep into the primeval heart of the rugged wilderness.

Lucian had been tracking this lycan pack for days. Travelers' tales, recounted nightly in inns and alehouses, spoke of a plague of supernatural beasts that had been preying on neighboring livestock—and the occasional careless mortal—for months now, most often on the nights of the full moon. From the humans' horrified descriptions of the mangled remains left behind by the monsters, Lucian recognized the handiwork of his renegade kinsmen.

Better, he mused, *that such ferocity be turned against the vampires instead. They should be our true prey, now and for all time.*

His eyes probed the dense brush and bracken before him. Broken branches and half-buried droppings kept him on the correct path through the closely packed oaks and beeches. The heavy canopy overhead cast the forest floor into shadow, but Lucian's expert gaze had no trouble following the lycans' trail. Their spoor was obvious to one who knew where to look.

He glanced upward through the interlaced tree branches to see the sun sinking slowly toward the west. *The moon will be full tonight,* he recalled. *If they're smart, the vampires will stay safely behind their castle walls.*

Twilight's crimson radiance was painting the distant mountaintops red by the time Lucian's ears detected the clamor of raucous voices and laughter. He cautiously circled to the right in order to stay downwind; there was no point in alerting the noisy celebrants until he was ready to make his entrance.

He expected he would need every advantage he could get.

Creeping stealthily through the woods, he spied ragged figures cavorting around a smoldering campfire. A wedge-shaped clearing, nestled at the base of a rocky cliff, played host to a throng of unruly men and women clad in crudely stitched furs and tattered rags.

Success! He had found the marauders he sought.

The feral lycans looked indistinguishable from any other pack of wild renegades. Dirty, ill groomed, and obstreperous, they reminded Lucian of that final hunt with Lady Ilona and her Death Dealers, when he'd led the vampires straight to the outlaws' camp. Guilt stabbed him as he recalled the vital part he had played in enslaving his lycan brothers and sisters.

Never again! he swore. *Henceforth, I will fight only to free my kind from the vampires' yoke.*

Drawing courage from his conviction, he strode boldly into the primitive camp, inwardly lamenting the ease with which he did so. Had none of these ruffians ever heard of lookouts or sentries?

"Greetings, my esteemed relations!" He threw back his hood and raised empty palms to show that he was unarmed. "A prodigal son desires your hospitality and attention."

His unexpected appearance provoked an uproar among the pack. Wild-eyed lycans, already excited by the imminent return of the full moon, halted their revels to stare suspiciously at the new arrival. Lucian soon found himself surrounded by hostile faces and curious fingers. Strangers tugged on his cloak and robe, perhaps fancying how the sturdy garments would fit upon their ill-clad frames.

"Is he mortal?" an eager voice asked. "Meat for the taking?"

"I don't think so," another lycan answered, with more than a hint of disappointment in her voice. She sniffed his hands and neck. "He smells wolfen, like one of us!"

A scruffy and undisciplined lot, Lucian assessed the welcome party coolly, *but they will have to do—for a start.* "I assure you, my friends, that I am quite as lycan as yourselves." His eyes searched the faces around him, looking for the stamp of authority, while doing his best to ignore the noisome odor of their unwashed bodies. "Where is your leader? We must have words."

A tremendous roar drew Lucian's attention to an imposing figure standing atop a dark outcropping of rock. He saw a muscular, broad-chested male lycan with a mane of silvery white hair. A shaggy sheepskin cloak was draped over the man's powerful shoulders like the mantle of a king.

"I, Sandor, am leader here," the man declared, his arms crossed over his hairy chest. Sharply pointed canines jutted up from beneath his lower lip. "What do you want of me?"

The man's imperious attitude reminded Lucian unpleasantly of Viktor and his fellow Elders. "Come closer, and we shall speak," he said defiantly. *I've played the dutiful servant long enough,* Lucian thought; the day was long past when he would willingly kowtow to anyone, vampire or lycan. "If you dare."

Sandor scowled at Lucian's impertinence but was not about to refuse a challenge in front of his subordinates. He bounded off the weathered stone outcropping, covering the distance between them in a single leap. The lycans surrounding Lucian parted to let their ruler approach the newcomer. Lucian could not help noticing that Sandor was at least a head taller than him and outweighed him considerably as well.

And that was before the Change. . . .

Sandor eyed Lucian's robes and rosary with derision. "You've come to the wrong place, Brother," he mocked. "We need no priest!"

The other lycans laughed like hyenas at their leader's jest, but Lucian took their jeers in stride. He stripped off his robe and cloak, revealing a brown wool tunic and hose. A plain steel dagger was tucked beneath a leather belt. "I am neither monk nor priest," he stated. "Indeed, I come bearing tidings of war, not peace."

"War?" Sandor repeated in confusion. He thrust his head forward, until his protruding fangs were only inches from Lucian's face. "Who the hell are you? You smell like a lycan, but you talk like a fucking blood!"

"My name is Lucian," he said, seeing no need to mince words. "I intend to lead this pack against our great enemy, the vampires. You can step aside and aid me in this endeavor . . . or you can be destroyed." He drew his dagger from his belt and tossed it carelessly onto the grassy sward at the base of the cliff. "The choice is yours."

Sandor's face flushed with rage. "You challenge me, little wolfling?" he bellowed, spraying Lucian's face with saliva. The hairs on his brawny body bristled, and his dark eyes took on a bluish hue. He stepped backward and shrugged off his sheepskin cloak. Cobalt eyes glanced at the darkening sky, where the full moon would shortly rise. "I don't even need to Change to break you like a twig!"

"We shall see," Lucian said. Conscious of the moon's approach, he kicked off his sandals and hastily stripped to the skin. Although raised as a servant, he knew enough of the customs of wild lycans to be confident that the other lycans would not come to Sandor's defense; a pack leader had to meet such challenges single-handed. "I would prefer not to kill you. The vampires are our true enemies, not each other. But I will do whatever is necessary to take command of this pack."

"The only thing you're going to do is die!"

Without further ado, Sandor charged at Lucian. The massive lycan slammed into Lucian at the same moment that the moon showed itself above the treetops, transforming them both in mid-struggle. Sprouting claws raked across Lucian's torso even as his rib cage expanded to meet the blow. His own claws extended from his fingertips, slashing at Sandor's protruding snout and leaving bloody gouges across the larger werewolf's muzzle. Sandor's spreading fur was silvery in color, in contrast to Lucian's dark black pelt. Foam dripped from the dueling werewolves' jaws and their titanic roars and growls echoed against the smooth black face of the cliff at the far side of the clearing. Patches of torn fur went flying into the shadows as the enormous beasts snapped and clawed at each other. Bright red blood sprayed like mist.

The lambent moon transformed their audience as well,

changing the ragtag band of lycans into a pack of frenzied werewolves. Shouted whoops and cheers of encouragement gave way to an ear-splitting chorus of savage howls.

Sandor was even stronger than he looked. A backhanded swipe of the silver werewolf's arm sent Lucian flying backward into the trunk of a towering oak. He hit the tree with bone-jarring force, leaving him momentarily dazed. The moonlit clearing swam before his eyes.

I need a change of strategy, he realized. *Now.*

Sandor came at him again, racing across the grass on all fours. Bloody fangs gleamed within his gaping jaws.

To buy himself time, Lucian turned and clambered up the side of the oak. His claws found purchase in the bark, and he scaled the tree at a feverish pace, anxious to place a margin of safety between himself and the great silver werewolf, if only for a moment.

Frustrated by his foe's retreat, Sandor reared up at the base of the ancient oak and roared in fury. He grabbed hold of the tree trunk with his powerful forelimbs and shook the tree with all his might. His volcanic blue eyes locked onto Lucian's, daring the smaller werewolf to abandon his perch atop the tree.

The wolf in Lucian wanted to answer Sandor's fierce growls with tooth and claw, pouncing back down into the fight, but Lucian knew he had to curb his more bestial instincts if he wanted to triumph over the indomitable pack leader, who had no doubt survived many a challenge to his reign. Sandor was strong, but, like most lycans, he relied entirely on brute strength and ferocity.

I, on the other hand, have my intellect.

Lucian's shrewd blue eyes surveyed the field of battle, looking for a way to turn the terrain to his advantage. His gaze fell on the vertical face of the granite cliff, and an idea occurred to him. *I need to have this wolf at my mercy, not the other way around. . . .*

An impatient Sandor began climbing the tree toward Lucian. With a parting growl in Sandor's direction, Lucian leaped from the treetop to the clearing below, forcing startled werewolves to dive out of the way of his plummeting form. He landed nimbly on the grass, then turned to roar defiantly back at Sandor, who was halfway up the tree before discovering that his prey had returned to the ground. He barked indignantly.

As his plan depended on Sandor chasing after him, Lucian took a moment to taunt the silver-haired werewolf. He barked contemptuously at Sandor, slashing at the empty air with his claws. The outraged pack leader responded to the bait by hurling himself from the leafy oak onto the ground after Lucian. The impact of his landing rocked the floor of the clearing, and his thunderous roar drowned out the howling of the wolfen spectators.

That's it, Lucian encouraged him. *Don't let me get away.*

The wind whipped through Lucian's sable fur as he ran full tilt toward the looming cliffside. He felt Sandor's hot breath on his back and heard the silver werewolf's massive paws crashing through the grass and brush behind him. Sandor was faster than he looked as well; Lucian knew he had only seconds to spare before the bloodthirsty beast brought him down.

The stark gray cliff seemed to come rushing toward him, blocking his escape. At the last minute, however, Lucian's paws pushed off from the ground, and he ran up the face of the cliff before flipping over in the air and landing squarely on Sandor's back.

Four sets of claws dug into the silver wolf's leathery hide, holding fast despite Sandor's increasingly frantic efforts to dislodge him. Sandor flailed wildly with his forelimbs but found it difficult to grab onto the snarling creature on his back. He spun about on his hind legs in a useless attempt to get at the smaller werewolf.

Time to end this, Lucian thought. Safely clear of Sandor's snapping jaws, he sank his own fangs into the silver werewolf's neck. Hot blood gushed past his teeth as he tore out his opponent's throat.

A crimson fountain spurted from the beast's severed jugular. Sandor's roar fell silent, and he toppled face-first toward the ground. Lucian jumped free of his falling foe and watched in silence as the werewolf's body twitched spasmodically on the grass. Taking no chances, he took hold of Sandor's huge head with his forepaws and then twisted the werewolf's neck until he heard bone crack.

Lucian stood panting above a furry silver carcass, while the other werewolves looked on in cowed silence. His victory brought with it a twinge of regret. *If fate is kind,* he thought, *Sandor will be the first and only lycan to die at my hands.*

Still, he was alive, and the pack was his. Surrendering to the moment, Lucian threw back his head and howled triumphantly at the moon. Hesitantly at first, then with greater enthusiasm, his fellow werewolves joined in. Their fierce, primeval music rang out across the forest, surely sending a chill through any mortal close enough to hear the inhuman symphony.

A smile curled back Lucian's wolfen lips. These baying beasts would be the nucleus of his new army . . . an army that would liberate their oppressed species—and wipe the hated vampires from the face of the earth.

Chapter Eighteen

CARPATHIAN MOUNTAINS

*T*he afternoon sun was streaming through the branches overhead as Lucian led the pack toward their target. The lycans moved stealthily through the pine woods, making as little noise as possible, the better to catch the enemy unaware.

Lucian paused at the top of a rocky slope. He signaled his troops to stay back while he surveyed the scene. He was thankful there was no moon for the lycans to howl at; his strategy depended on the element of surprise.

This raid, he thought, *shall be our baptism of fire.*

The silver mine occupied a wide gorge at the foot of the hill. Sturdy timbers framed the entrance to the mine, which was dug into the side of a craggy mountain at the northern end of the gorge. Stone barracks had been erected to house the miners, along with a company of mercenaries hired to guard the site. A muscle-powered windlass served to pull the heavy chain that drew cartloads of raw ore up from the mine's subterranean depths. Wagons drawn by enormous draft horses waited to haul the ore to the smelter in a small village farther on down the mountain. Sweaty miners emerged as well, bearing buckets of silty water that needed to be cleared out of the mines in order for them to continue the back-breaking work of extracting the precious element from the earth. Armed guards watched over miners and metal alike.

So this is where the goddamn silver comes from, Lucian thought bitterly. His back remembered the scalding bite of Soren's silver whips, reminding him of the importance of today's raid.

Silver was the vampires' greatest weapon against those of his kind, so Lucian had resolved to begin his campaign by seizing control of the very silver mine that provided Viktor with much of his wealth and arms. For better or for worse, Hungary and the Carpathians contained many of the richest silver deposits in Europe, making the hated metal all too readily available to the coven and its merciless Death Dealers.

But not for much longer.

For obvious reasons, the vampires could not employ their lycan slaves to extract the silver, so the coven had hired skilled human laborers, mostly imported from Germany, to work the mines under the protection of the equally mortal mercenaries. The guards wore padded leather armor supplemented by steel gauntlets and kettle helmets. Lucian watched as a trio of bored soldiers leaned on their pikes, exchanging bawdy jokes as the straining miners toiled beneath the blazing sun.

"They don't look too tough to me," a raspy voice whispered in his ear. Lucian did not need to turn around to know that the voice belonged to Josef, his chief lieutenant. "How many of them did you say there are?"

Discovering the balding, one-eyed lycan among the pack had been an unexpected boon. A veteran soldier, short but stocky, Josef had fought valiantly in the Crusades before surviving the bite of a Turkish werewolf. By his own account, the newly converted lycan had then made his way back to Europe from the Holy Land because he preferred the taste of "decent Christian flesh." For himself, Lucian was simply grateful to find a wild lycan who had a solid grasp of military tactics and discipline. *Would that I had a hundred score more of him!*

"About twenty soldiers," Lucian estimated, based on days and nights of furtive observation. Only six guards or so were on duty at the moment, but Lucian knew that more mercenaries were on call in the barracks. "Plus maybe sixty or seventy miners."

His own army numbered fifty-five. More than enough, he judged, to deal with a gang of unsuspecting mortals.

Even without the aid of the moon.

"Fucking sunshine," Josef grumbled, raising a hand to shield his remaining eye from the glare. A brown goatskin eye patch covered the ugly cavity where his other eye had once lodged, the victim of a Saracen arrow back when the crusader was still mortal.

Lucian knew that the doughty ex-soldier was not the only member of his pack who found it disconcerting to be abroad by daylight. Although the sun was not lethal to them, as it was to their undead foes, lycans—like wolves—were instinctively nocturnal. It had required considerable effort on Lucian's part to persuade his newly acquired army to attack the mines well before sunset.

"That sunshine is our best defense," he reminded Josef. "How else are we to avoid engaging the vampires directly?" Lucian was not ready to take on the Death Dealers just yet.

When that dreaded battle comes, it will be at a time and place of my own choosing.

He watched as another load of raw ore was dragged out of the mine. To his slight surprise, the all-too-familiar gleam of silver was nowhere to be seen; instead, the jagged chunks piled high in the cart were bluish gray in color, being an impure amalgam of the silver with lead and minerals. Apparently, the silver took on its characteristic hue and luster only after it had been smelted and refined.

The thought occurred to Lucian that perhaps, after he had seized control of the mine, he should use the precious metal to finance his war against the vampires, which would involve finding humans to work the mine for him. For the moment, however, it would suffice simply to cut the coven off from its supply of the deadly element.

"Ready the spears and arrows," he instructed Josef. "We attack on my command."

His lieutenant slunk back into the woods to gather the troops. Within minutes, the advance guard of Lucian's army joined him at the top of the slope, just within the concealing foliage. Crude wooden spears and tightly drawn bows were directed at the unwary guards below. Josef himself drew back the string of a powerful longbow.

I do this in your name, Sonja, my love . . . and in vengeance for our unborn child. "Now!" Lucian commanded. "Let your weapons fly!"

Spears and arrows whistled through the air, raining down on the startled soldiers and whatever luckless miners happened to be aboveground at the moment. Sharpened spear tips and arrowheads pierced mortal flesh, eliciting screams of pain and anger from the ambushed men. Bleeding bodies crashed to the ground, while others clutched at wounded limbs and torsos.

But the battle had only just begun. "Onward!" Lucian
ollered to his blood-crazed warriors. "Fight like wolves!"

The lycan horde streamed down the hillside, howling
ke ravenous beasts. Handmade shields and bucklers de-
·nded their immortal flesh, while they flaunted an eclectic
ssortment of weaponry looted from various ill-starred mor-
·l wayfarers: swords, pikes, maces, sickles, scythes, and
·tchforks. Cobalt eyes gleamed in the sunlight. Yellow
·ngs showed between open jaws as they whooped and
·outed their atavistic war cries. Lingering behind at the top
·f the hill, Josef continued to pick off human targets with
·is longbow, making Lucian wish that there had been time
·nough to tutor more of the primitive lycans in the finer
·oints of archery.

Perhaps next time, he considered, observing the battle
·om atop the slope. The prospect of bringing down a com-
·any of Death Dealers beneath a hail of arrows appealed to
·im. *If the mortals could kill so many vampires at the keep,
·uld not a legion of lycans fare even better?*

Aroused by the agitated cries of their comrades and the feral
·owling of the invaders, more soldiers came running out of the
·arracks, only to find themselves confronted by an oncoming
··alanche of wild-eyed barbarians. Swearing profanely, they
·ised their weapons to meet the yowling berserkers.

Crossbow bolts flew at the lycan charge, only to be
·locked by thick oaken shields. A few stray quarrels found
·eshier targets, but the steel-tipped bolts had little effect on
·e immortal attackers. A single bolt struck Josef in the ribs,
·ut the squat lycan simply yanked the offending missile
·om his body and fired back at the mortals with his long-
·ow, his very next shot spearing a human mercenary be-
·ween the eyes. "Hah!" he laughed robustly. "Not bad for a
·ne-eyed archer!"

Lucian glanced at the useless quarrel lying at his lieutenant's feet. Unlike Death Dealers, these mortal soldiers were not equipped with silver weapons, only ordinary steel and iron. After all, the Elders had doubtlessly reasoned, what would renegade lycans want with silver?

A critical mistake on their part, Lucian gloated, *or so I intend to prove.*

He watched intently as his forces engaged the enemy at the bottom of the gorge. A terrified-looking sentry charged at a frothing lycan with his pike, but the inhuman warrior grabbed the mortal's spear with both hands and easily wrenched it from the grasp of the stunned guard. Tossing the pike carelessly to one side, the same lycan seized the disarmed human and lifted him high above his head before hurling the guard into a crowd of onrushing soldiers, knocking them all from their feet. More lycans fell upon the downed mortals like wolves upon a fallen stag. Geysers of blood erupted from beneath the huddle, drenching the frenzied lycans in scarlet.

Similar dramas played out up and down the length of the gorge. Faster, stronger, and most definitely more ferocious than the overmatched mortals, the lycan army slaughtered its terrified foes at will, although not without suffering the occasional loss; Lucian watched with dismay as a lucky sword blow removed the head of an inattentive lycan named Fritz. The victorious human did not have long to savor his kill, however; within moments, a pack of vengeful lycans tore him apart, limb by limb.

The conflict was brief, bloody, and one-sided. Shaken by the grisly massacre ensuing all around them, the last few mortals threw down their weapons and pleaded frantically for their lives. "Spare us!" they cried, falling onto their knees and clasping their hands before them. "For the love of God, have mercy!"

Lucian chose to grant their pleas, at least for the time being. "Enough!" he shouted, cupping his hands over his mouth in order to be heard over the uproar. "Stand down, my valiant war wolves. The day is ours!"

In truth, halting the bloodshed was easier said than done. Ultimately, he and Josef were forced to descend to the floor of the gorge themselves and physically tear a few of their more maddened brethren away from the defenseless mortals. Finally, Lucian managed to make his wishes clear . . . even if Josef had to crack a few heads together first.

They're savage fighters, Lucian thought of his newfound army, *but they're still short of discipline. I shall have to remedy that situation if we are ever to have a chance at defeating the vampires themselves.*

The surviving guards were rounded up on Lucian's orders. Stripped of their weapons and armor, the trembling soldiers knelt on the rocky floor of the gorge, surrounded by a throng of jubilant lycans, many of whom licked their lips in anticipation of succulent mortal meat. A handful of hapless miners, who had taken cover behind the wagons and barracks during the battle, were made to join the vanquished mercenaries.

"Remember," Lucian ordered loudly, before anyone's appetites got the better of him, "one bite only for each man. I want them infected, not eaten!" Reinforcements were needed for his army—an opportunity to recruit another experienced soldier or two was too good to waste. Even if only a single mercenary survived being bitten, that would still add to the forces at his disposal.

I am offering them a better bargain than their kind have ever offered ours, he observed to himself. *The fortunate among them will become immortal. The rest will simply end their brief mortal existence a few years earlier than expected.*

And as for the miners? Well, they would be working the mines on Lucian's behalf from now on.

Disappointed moans erupted from the throats of the hungry lycans at Lucian's decree. "My orders are final," he asserted, heading off any possible insurrection in advance. "But help yourself to whatever else you find in the mortals' barracks. Take everything: food, clothing, coins, and drink. If I know mortals, there are certain to be stores of wine and ale just waiting to be quaffed!"

As he expected, eager lycans rushed off to loot the humans' quarters. Others rummaged among the captured armor and weapons, claiming the best pieces for themselves. Greed triumphed over bloodlust, except for a handful of particularly savage lycans whose hungry eyes remained fixed on the mortal captives. "Just one bite," Lucian stressed again, before nodding at them to proceed.

Voracious lycans lunged forward, sinking their fangs into the defenseless flesh of the mercenaries, who shrieked in pain and horror as bloody chunks were ripped from their bodies. Lucian heard a few of the other lycans wagering on which mortals would die and which, if any, would become lycans. Within seconds, the betting became quite heated.

"The ones who die?" a cunning young lycan called out. "Can we eat them after they're dead?"

Lucian shrugged his shoulders. "Why not?"

In the long run, he intended to break his followers of their reckless taste for human flesh, if only to avoid provoking mortal reprisals. *One war at a time,* he thought; he had no desire to battle the mortals and vampires both. Although he had turned his back on the Covenant, he still agreed with the Elders that feeding on humans was too dangerous a pastime to risk. Still, he was not ready to impose such a stringent prohibition on his feral subordinates just yet. *I need a victory or two under my belt before I can command that degree of authority.*

Blood spurting from their wounds, the bitten humans collapsed onto the ground, many already going into convulsions as the lycan venom coursed through their veins. Brother Ambrose's ugly death passed through Lucian's mind as he kept a close eye on the proceedings, ready to discourage any of his followers from making a feast of a potential new pack member.

"What about the mortals still down in the mines?" Josef asked him. He tilted his head toward the gaping black entrance of the mine. "I don't think they'll be coming out of their own free will, not after all this clamor up above."

True enough, Lucian conceded. He imagined dozens of terrified miners cowering in the depths of the mine. For a moment, he considered simply walling up the entrance to the mine and letting the trapped humans starve to death in the dark. But no, that would be a considerable waste of meat and manpower, not to mention brutally inhumane. *Better to give them a chance at life,* he reasoned, *provided they are willing to work just as diligently for their new masters.*

"The battle is not quite over," he announced to every lycan within earshot. "More mortals await below the earth, although I doubt they shall put up much resistance." He drew his sword and advanced toward the opaque mine entrance. "Let us herd them up into the light."

To his surprise, none of his warriors fell in behind him. Even Josef remained immobile, seemingly unwilling to follow Lucian into the murky hole in the mountainside.

"Well?" Lucian demanded of them impatiently. "What is it?"

Josef shuffled his feet, declining to meet his commander's

eyes. "The silver, sir," he said sheepishly. "Surely you can't expect any sane lycan to venture into that cursed pit? With all that silver everywhere?"

The man has a point, Lucian realized. He could hardly blame his troops for not wanting to descend into the heart of a silver mine. Indeed, upon reflection, the very thought of being surrounded on all sides by the unmined element made his skin crawl. In his memory, Soren's whips flayed his back anew.

"Very well," he declared. "I shall clear out this rat hole myself." Such a display of unwavering courage was sure to solidify his standing as pack leader. Besides, he figured he was more than a match for a crew of petrified miners. "Josef, watch over our prisoners until I return."

He found a working oil lamp among the captured mining supplies and lit its wick before stepping beneath the timber supports of the mine entrance. Sword in hand, he entered the darkness.

The shaft descended into the mountain at a steep incline, and he quickly left the last glimmer of sunlight behind. Wooden columns supported the dripping limestone ceiling, which was far too low for Lucian's comfort. The endless procession of ore-laden carts had carved deep ruts in the rocky floor of the tunnel. The air was stuffy and full of dust, so Lucian paused long enough to tie a rag across his nose and mouth in order to avoid inhaling any floating particles of silver.

The temperature rose dramatically the deeper he descended, and Lucian was soon soaked with sweat. Perspiration dripped into his eyes, but he was unable to wipe it away without dropping either his sword or his lamp. Groundwater seeped from the porous rock walls, explaining the need for the miners' many buckets. The brackish-smelling liquid trickled down the floor of the shaft, making it more slippery than Lucian would have liked. Noxious underground vapors assailed his nose and lungs even through the rag, along with the reek of countless sweaty human bodies. Rats scurried away from Lucian into narrow side passages and drainage tunnels. Their beady eyes gleamed in the lamplight.

Thank fate the vampires never forced us lycans to labor in these infernal pits, he thought, seeing for the first time a positive aspect to their hereditary aversion to silver. *How can these mortal wretches endure such hellish conditions?*

At first, there was little silver to contend with, the upper portion of the mine having been already denuded of the toxic metal; yet the farther he descended into the lower reaches, the more he became uncomfortably aware of the thick veins of raw silver running through the chipped and chiseled rock all around him. Black and bluish-gray ore, occasionally tinged with green, permeated the walls, floor, and ceiling, only rarely betraying a hint of silver's metallic luster. Quartz crystals glittered like diamonds amid the dull black ore, along with bright flecks of iron and copper.

The presence of so much silver made him feel distinctly queasy. He carefully stuck to the center of the tunnel, doing his best to avoid contact with the walls. If not for the thick leather soles of his boots, he suspected, walking down the shaft would be akin to treading over hot coals.

Am I mad to venture thus? he asked himself. *Perhaps this was not my wisest decision.*

He was almost ready to abandon his original purpose when he heard the muffled sound of hushed human voices directly ahead. Peering past the glow of his own lamp, he saw a flickering radiance at the bottom of the shaft.

He quickened his pace, coming at last to the deepest

level of the mine, some one hundred feet below the mountain. Here the narrow shaft opened up onto a cavernous gallery, hollowed out by the miners' strenuous exertions. Wooden pillars supported the ceiling. Oil lamps rested on rocky shelves, throwing shadows onto the damp stone walls, as well as onto a large iron cart half filled with freshly excavated ore. The makings of a bonfire—sticks, kindling, and so on—had been piled up against one wall of the cavern, preparatory to setting a blaze to weaken a particularly stubborn vein of ore. Cold water would be dashed on the wall after the fire had heated it, causing the solid rock to crack and crumble.

Lucian spotted the remaining miners. At least two dozen men huddled at the far end of the chamber, gripping their picks and shovels defensively. Accustomed to laboring in the purgatorial heat of the mines, the men wore only linen breeches cut off at mid-thigh. Their sweaty flesh was pale from lack of sunlight, so that they almost resembled the vampires who employed them. Powdered stone clung to their faces and bodies, all but masking their individual features. They eyed Lucian warily as he entered the gallery. German curses and exclamations met his arrival.

"Greetings," he said before they could work up the nerve to attack him. His voice was muffled only slightly by the rag across his mouth. "My name is Lucian, and this mine now belongs to me. Lest you consider turning your picks and hammers against me, let me inform you that my forces now control your only means of escape from this pit. Unless you surrender at once, none of you will ever see daylight again."

He paused to let his words sink in. Their stricken expressions were truly pitiful, and Lucian experienced a moment of sympathy for the unfortunate humans, even though he knew that, as mortals, they would gladly put every lycan and vampire to death if they could. *They should be grateful that I am giving them the opportunity to serve us,* he reflected. *If lycans could mine silver for our coffers, there would be no need for these mortals at all.*

His eyes searched their grimy faces, looking for some clue to their intentions. Oddly enough, many of them kept glancing upward nervously. Lucian finally looked up as well—just in time to see an enraged male vampire skittering across the ceiling toward him!

Clad in a sooty black doublet and hose, the bloodsucker traversed the roof of the mine like a great black spider. Azure eyes glared at Lucian as the vampire realized the lycan had spied him. Hissing loudly, he launched himself at Lucian, who dived to one side to avoid the plummeting vampire.

Damnation! he cursed himself, realizing that he still had much to learn as a warrior and commander. *I should have guessed there might be a vampiric overseer lurking in these sunless depths!*

The vampire landed nimbly on his feet only a few yards away. Lucian recognized him now as Zoltan, an undead nobleman who had visited Castle Corvinus on occasion. His dark brown hair was pulled away from his face and tied in a knot at the base of his neck. A drooping brown mustache framed a mouthful of ivory fangs. Virulent blue eyes glowed in the dark.

"Well, well, a lycan in a silver mine." Unlike his human work crew, the cold-blooded vampire seemed unaffected by the oppressive heat of the underground chamber. Not a drop of sweat showed on his chalky white brow. "Now I've seen everything!"

"Times are changing," Lucian informed him, brandishing his bloodstained sword. He wished that he could change, but without a full moon to awaken his inner wolf, he was trapped in human guise. "Your days are numbered."

"I think not," Zoltan answered. Without warning, he dipped his claws into the half-filled cart and snatched up a heavy lump of raw ore. The vampire hurled it at Lucian with preternatural strength.

The lumpen missile slammed into Lucian's gut, knocking the breath from him. He doubled over in pain. His lamp went flying from his fingers, creating a fiery arc that exploded onto the rocky floor only a few feet away from the piled kindling. Burning oil spread through the cracks and crevices running along the bottom of the carved-out gallery.

Clenching his teeth against pain and nausea, Lucian charged at Zoltan with his sword in a desperate attempt to drive the vampire away from the cartload of ore. But Zoltan dodged his sword thrust and grabbed Lucian's other arm, using it to swing Lucian face-first into the wall. The impact jarred his senses, even as the silver embedded in the rock scalded his skin.

Taking advantage of the titanic clash between the vampire and the lycan, the fearful miners ran madly for the exit. Their racing feet pounded up the slanted shaft as they abandoned the spacious gallery to the dueling immortals.

"You should never have come down here, lycan!" Zoltan hissed as he came up behind Lucian and twisted his sword arm behind his back until the blade dropped from his fingers. Lucian struggled to avert his face from the noxious silver, but Zoltan mercilessly pressed Lucian's profile against a wide vein of blue-gray ore. Steam rose toward the ceiling as the entire left side of Lucian's face blistered and burned.

He fought to free himself from Zoltan's hold, but the vampire was too strong. Out of the corner of his eye, Lucian spotted one of the gallery's many wooden support pillars standing less than a foot away. In desperation, he kicked out at the vertical timber, knocking it loose.

The effect was immediate. The limestone ceiling groaned as though dying. Dust and fragments of rock began to rain down on the floor. Rats squealed in panic and scurried to escape. A largish chunk of ore hit Zoltan in the head, forcing him to release his grip on Lucian. He staggered backward, clutching his bleeding skull.

"Brainless lycan!" he ranted. He stared in horror at the crumbling ceiling. "What have you done?"

Lucian instantly realized the vampire's dire predicament. Whereas he had a chance to escape the collapsing mine, provided he moved swiftly enough, the vampire had nowhere to run—except into the glaring daylight.

What's more, Lucian now saw that the burning oil had set the miners' bonfire ablaze. Flames crackled at the rear of the mine, filling the gallery with thick black smoke.

Time to make a run for it. Yet, before he could reach the exit shaft, Zoltan leaped to block his path. "You're not going anywhere, you lycan trash!" the vampire snarled, clutching a miner's discarded metal pick. "We'll perish together if need be."

Lucian had no intention of spending eternity beside the charred skeleton of a vein-sucking vampire. Darting behind the heavy iron cart, he grabbed onto the edge of it with both hands and shoved it forward with all his strength. Iron wheels rolled along the ruts in the floor, zooming toward Zoltan like a battering ram. Legs pumping, Lucian ran the ore-filled cart right over the startled vampire, hearing Zoltan's bones crunch beneath the weight of the combined silver and iron. His own boots trampled the vampire's pulped remains for good measure.

Is he dead? There was no time to find out. With a tremendous roar, the roof of the cavern came crashing down behind Lucian. Dust and debris came flying out of the gallery into the shaft beyond.

Letting go of the cart, Lucian squeezed past the heavy transport and bolted up the inclined shaft as fast as his legs would carry him. Halfway up, he encountered Josef running toward him. The one-eyed lycan had a worried expression on his face and his longbow in one hand. "Sounded like you needed help!" he gasped by way of explanation.

Not anymore, Lucian thought. "Run!" he commanded, hearing the tunnel collapse behind him. "Run for your life!"

Sunlight beckoned, and moments later, they burst from the mine into the gorge. A dense cloud of poisonous dust exploded out of the tunnel in their wake, accompanied by a thunderous rumbling that took several minutes to die down. Lycans stared, bloody jaws agape, at the noise and spectacle of the cave-in. Some cheered to hear the lethal silver buried beneath tons of falling rubble.

Lucian dropped to his knees, panting with exhaustion. Despite his fatigue, he felt exhilarated as well. Not only had he survived, but he had killed his first vampire.

Now the war has truly begun. . . .

Chapter Nineteen

CASTLE CORVINUS

Courtiers and Death Dealers crowded the throne room as Viktor sat in judgment on the accused lycan. The Elder spotted a scattering of lycan servants present as well, busying themselves at their diverse tasks while slyly eavesdropping on the fate of their wretched sister.

Duplicitous vermin! Viktor thought, seated on his ebony throne. A dark burgundy robe enfolded him, like the wings of a slumbering bat. *I should have had them all exterminated weeks ago, no matter what the Council advised.*

A bedraggled female lycan crouched on the floor before him. Silver-alloy manacles clamped down on her wrists and ankles. Greasy yellow hair fell across her face, obscuring her features. A coarse woolen kirtle hung in tatters upon her emaciated frame. Scars, welts, and bruises showed through the ragged garment, testifying to the thoroughness of Soren's interrogation. She sobbed and muttered to herself, as though driven half mad by her ordeal.

Viktor felt no sympathy for her. "Well?" he demanded of Soren. "What did you learn from this lycan slut?"

The dour overseer stood behind his prisoner, his beloved whips draped over his shoulders. "This animal, known to her bestial comrades as Grushenka, denied any knowledge of your daughter's . . . indiscretions. But when put to the question, she confessed to passing notes from the princess to a certain lycan, making possible their assignations."

Viktor winced inwardly to hear his daughter's shame spoken of openly in his own court, but there had been from the beginning no possibility of concealing the scandal, not when Sonja's crimes had demanded the lawful execution of a princess of the blood. Such a momentous event could not be papered over by any transparent tissue of lies. He could only hope that time would someday wipe away all record of his dear Sonja's disgrace.

Would that my own memories could be expunged as well!

"Forgive me, Elder!" the manacled wretch cried out hysterically, apparently aware of her jeopardy despite her addled wits. "I knew not what the letters meant. I meant only to obey my mistress, as was proper!"

Viktor ignored the lycan's fruitless rantings. He could barely bring himself to look upon the filthy wench, knowing that the ignorant animal had contributed to his daughter's demise.

If only I had Lucian in chains in her place!

"She is to be shown no mercy," he decreed. "Make an example of her. I want her drawn and quartered in the courtyard this very night." A crescent moon guaranteed there would be no encore of Lucian's galling escape. "See to it that her fellow servants are made to witness her punishment, so that they may see for themselves the dire consequences of such treachery."

"Nooo!" the condemned bitch keened in alarm, until Soren knocked her senseless with the back of his hand. Excited murmurs arose from the assembled courtiers and their ladies, titillated by the notion of the gory spectacle ahead. Viktor could not remember the last time a lycan had been put to death in such a public and elaborate manner.

Perhaps that is where our error lies, he speculated. *We have grown too soft in our treatment of their kind.*

He watched in stony silence as Soren's minions dragged the lycan away to await her fate. He rose from his throne, intending to sequester himself in his private chambers until it was time for the lycan's execution. He was in no mood to conduct any further business this night.

As he stepped down from the dais, however, he was approached by Nicolae. The pure-blooded heir was resplendent in a red velvet doublet and fawn-colored hose. "Pardon me, Lord Viktor, but might Soren and I have a word with you in private?" The Irish overseer stood silently at the prince's side. "It concerns the lycan situation."

Viktor scowled. *What new way have these vermin found to plague me?* Morbid curiosity, along with the courtesy due an Elder's offspring, compelled him to nod in assent. "Very well," he declared. "Let us retire to my solar."

He turned to address a nearby Death Dealer, who was hovering near the throne hoping to overhear what the Elder had to say. "Kraven," Viktor said curtly. "Attend us."

"Yes, my lord!" Kraven replied eagerly, joining the other vampires as they exited the throne room and strode down a short corridor to the thick oak door that guarded Viktor's private sanctum. The Elder drew open the door and beckoned Nicolae and Soren to step inside. Kraven hastened to accompany them, but Viktor extended a restraining arm. He brushed past Kraven to enter the solar himself, leaving the bewildered Death Dealer outside in the hall.

"Watch the door," Viktor instructed Kraven brusquely. "See to it that we are not disturbed."

The frustrated Englishman tried in vain to hide his disappointment, much to Viktor's private amusement. "Yes, my lord," he said sourly. "I live to serve."

Viktor chuckled quietly to himself as he shut the door in Kraven's face. The young vampire's naked ambition was positively comical. Kraven might well prove to be a useful underling, but Viktor was not about to make him privy to all his secrets just yet. *Perhaps later,* he mused, *after Kraven has proven himself to be as discreet as he is power-hungry.*

A yearning for fresh human blood came over Viktor, and he felt an almost overpowering urge to glut his thirst on some insignificant mortal victims, if only to relieve the unbearable sorrow and anger that had weighed down his soul ever since Sonja's tragic fall from grace. His bloodthirsty imagination pictured a terrified peasant maiden squirming helplessly within his grasp, crying out in vain as his avid fangs pierced her throat. He could practically taste her warm blood on his tongue, so much richer and more intoxicating than the tepid cattle blood the Covenant compelled him to subsist on.

It has been too long, he reflected, *since I have indulged myself thus.* Such nocturnal sorties were his secret vice, known only to his most trusted subordinates. *I must go hunting again soon, once this business with the lycans is concluded. Who knows?* he thought. *Perhaps I will bring Kraven along to clean up afterward. . . .*

For now, however, Nicolae and Soren awaited his attention. He turned away from the door and sat down on a high-backed wooden chair facing the two men, who remained respectfully on their feet. "So," he said gravely, "what about the lycans?"

"Another new volunteer to see you," Josef announced heartily as he stuck his head through the doorway. He gave Lucian a lascivious wink. "This one says she knows you of old."

Lucian looked up from his work. Parchments bearing sketches of the mining camp's new defenses were strewn atop a long oak table that had once belonged to Zoltan before Lucian took the late vampire's quarters for his own. Carved out of the very face of the mountain, from solid rock mercifully devoid of silver, the cavelike chamber had provided Zoltan with a private sanctuary safely cut off from the sun. Oil lamps gave Lucian enough illumination to work by, while an expensive Persian carpet, imported from the Holy Land, covered the hard stone floor.

She? Lucian thought, puzzled. He had no idea whom Josef might be referring to—until the one-eyed Crusader stepped aside to admit a redhaired female clutching a naked infant against her bosom. "Olga," he blurted in surprise.

"Shall I leave you alone?" Josef asked with a grin.

Lucian shook his head. "That won't be necessary." Stepping away from the table, he addressed the woman directly. "Greetings, Olga. I must admit, I never expected to see you or your child again." He gestured toward a bench against a rocky gray wall. "Please, seat yourself."

She remained standing, however, staring warily at Lucian as though she suspected a trick of some sort. Her closed expression betrayed little hint of what she was thinking. Mud and grass stains streaked her clothing, evidence of a long, hard journey from Castle Corvinus. Her baby, whose name Lucian knew to be Ferenz, sucked his thumb contentedly, oblivious to the tension in the room.

"So," she said at last. "It is true what they say. You still live—and wage war against the bloods."

Lucian heard skepticism in her voice. A pang of guilt tweaked his conscience as he eyed the M-shaped brand on little Ferenz's bicep. He knew that Olga bore a similar brand on her own flesh—and that he had helped put it there.

"If you doubt me," he asked her, "then why have you come?"

She was hardly the first to find him here. As word of his escape from the vampires' dungeon spread, lycans from all over had sought him out to join his crusade. But never before had one of these new arrivals had so much reason to hate Lucian instead.

The former renegade thought long and hard before answering. "I saw you whipped in the dungeons," she reminded him. Her voice was cold and flat, as though all emotion had been beaten out of her by the harsh rigors of life at the castle. "When the first few lashes drew screams from your lips, I rejoiced, glad that you were finally learning what it truly meant to be a slave to the bloods. But as the whipping went on, with each new lash stripping the flesh from your back, I suffered with you, realizing that you were still one of us after all. Then, when you rose up in defiance, striking out at the Elder himself, I rejoiced once more, but this time because I saw a werewolf stand up to a vampire— and live to tell of it. And that gave me hope that someday the rest of us might be free as well."

Lucian felt himself deeply moved by the woman's testimony. For the first time, he fully grasped that there was perhaps more at stake in this campaign than his own personal revenge against Viktor. For countless generations, the vampires had oppressed his species, condemning him and Olga and all their kind to never-ending servitude and dooming

onja simply because she, unlike the rest of the vampires,
ared to treat a lycan as her equal.

No more, he vowed.

"I give you my word," he assured Olga. "I shall devote
my life to destroying the vampires, even if it takes more than
thousand years."

She nodded, accepting his promise. "Then Ferenz and I
re where we belong."

The baby squirmed in her arms and started to cry. She
ugged her bodice off one shoulder and offered Ferenz her
xposed breast. The brand on her upper arm was plainly
isible as the babe suckled happily at his mother's teat.

Lucian contemplated the tender scene, and the reality of
onja's death tore at him anew. If not for Viktor's implacable
ustice," he might have watched Sonja nurse their own
hild thus, but such an idyllic moment was never to be his.
onja's father had seen to that.

Watching little Ferenz feed, he could not help wondering
hat his own son or daughter might have become. Sonja
ad believed that their child, the halfbreed offspring of
ure-blooded vampire and lycan, would possess extraordi-
ary attributes. Was that what had alarmed Viktor so much
at he had put his own daughter to death? Did he fear the
nknown power of such a hybrid?

It was something worth thinking about.

Nicolae stepped forward to address the seated Elder. "I'm
raid, my lord, that there is increased unrest among the ser-
ant population. Many of the household lycans, including
my brightest and most able manservant, appear to have de-
cted from the castle altogether, while those who remain
row ever more truculent and uncooperative."

"It's true," Soren confirmed, frowning beneath his beard.

His whips still bore evidence of Grushenka's blood. "Th
stinking curs have gotten goddamn insolent ever since
that night with Lucian."

"You mean the night my daughter died?" Viktor sa
caustically, subjecting Soren to a withering glare. He ha
still not forgiven the careless overseer for letting Sonja fa
under that lycan's spell. *All this might have been avoided,* h
brooded, *if only Soren had warned me in time. I might ha
been able to save Sonja from herself!*

"Just so," Nicolae agreed, diplomatically inserting himse
between Soren and the aggrieved Elder. "Why, just la
night, a lycan server deliberately spilled wine over my ne
satin doublet and displayed a singular lack of contritio
when I upbraided her as she deserved."

Viktor's churning anger erupted to the surface. "Did I n
intend to have every one of the vile beasts put to death aft
Lucian escaped? Yet you and the other Council membe
urged me to reconsider. It was too 'drastic' a step, you sai
not wanting to do without your precious lycan servants
His voice trembled with emotion. "It was not your wife
daughter who lost their lives thanks to these animals' u
controllable appetites!"

"No one is more conscious of your dreadful losses tha
I," Nicolae assured him. "Still, one rebellious troublemake
no matter how abhorrent his transgressions, should n
cause us to reject in haste the venerable institution of lyca
slavery." He spoke in a measured and reasonable tone. "W
have benefited from their servitude for many centuries no
Let us not proceed rashly."

Viktor reluctantly saw some merit in the prince's arg
ment. Who would guard their fortresses by daylight if n
the lycans? "What do you suggest?"

"The problem, simply stated, is Lucian." Nicolae spat o

e name, as though it were a curse. "His escape and his
ccess to date at eluding our justice have made him some-
ing of a hero to his fellow lycans. The rumor among the
rvants is that Lucian is even now raising an army to op-
)se the coven and that lycans from all over are flocking to
s banner." He rolled his eyes. "A ridiculous notion, of
)urse. Doubtless, he is actually lying low in some de-
orable hiding place, terrified of being recaptured, but our
edulous vassals imagine him as some sort of lycanthropic
)artacus, destined to lead them all to moonlit glory."

Soren snarled at the very idea. "I'll show them glory," he
uttered, fondling the handle of a whip, "right before I strip
e flesh from their bones!"

"But first we must dispose of Lucian," Nicolae insisted.
He is the figurehead of this incipient rebellion. Crush him,
nd the other lycans will remember their place." A cruel
nile lifted his lips, offering a glimpse of his fangs. "Sparta-
is was crucified, as you'll recall, and the Roman Empire
ndured another four hundred years. As immortals, I expect
e can count on an even longer reign—but only if Lucian is
ut down like a rabid dog."

Easier said than done, Viktor thought. He lived for the day
ucian was in his power once more, but trying to find a sin-
e lycan in the wilderness was like searching for virgin
ood at a brothel. *How can we hope to lay hands on him
;ain?*

A knock at the door interrupted the meeting. The door
vung open hesitantly, and Kraven stuck his head into the
)om. "Excuse me, milord," he began.

"I told you we were not to be disturbed!" Viktor snapped
ritably. *Can I depend on no one this miserable century?* At
mes, he wished that he had never been Awakened.

"Forgive me, Lord Viktor," Kraven persisted, "but you

must hear this." He pushed the door open farther, reveali
an undead messenger whose leathers were splattered wi
mud and dust, as though from a frenzied ride. A rusty ir
bucket was clutched to his chest.

The urgency in Kraven's tone, along with the dishevel
appearance of the messenger, caught Viktor's attention. I
knew before hearing another word that something w
badly amiss.

"What is it?" he asked.

The messenger staggered forward, visibly short of breat
Sweat plastered his dusty hair to his brow. "Dreadful new
milord. The mines at Mount Vrolok have been seized
bandits. Lycans, no less!"

"*What?*" Viktor rose from his chair in shock and indigr
tion. "How can this be?"

"I do not know, Elder," the messenger replied. "When
ore arrived at the smelter, the foreman sent one of his a
prentices to investigate. He found the mines themselves
the hands of a sizable band of rogue lycans, who tortur
him severely before setting him free with a message from t
bandits' leader—the lycan criminal known as Lucian."

Lucian!

Viktor's nails dug into his palms, drawing blood, as
struggled to contain his fearsome wrath. He shot Nicolae
meaningful glance. Perhaps the rumors of Lucian's ret
army were not so baseless after all.

"What of Zoltan?" he inquired. The undead administr
tor in charge of the mining operation was a cousin of so
to the late Ilona, only a few generations removed from t
bloodline of Viktor's own beloved wife. "What news
him?"

The messenger swallowed hard before stepping forwa
and offering Viktor the bucket he held before him. "This L

cian instructed the apprentice that these . . . remains . . . be
delivered to you personally."

The Elder accepted the bucket. He feared he already
knew what it contained.

Inside were the fragments of a shattered skull. Fangs jut-
ed from a piece of a broken jawbone, suggesting that the
bones had once belonged to a living vampire.

"We believe that to be Zoltan," the messenger reported
unnecessarily.

Viktor seethed with impotent fury. He looked about for
something to vent his anger on and spied Soren standing
glumly a few feet away. "Damn you, you incompetent Irishman!" He lashed out at the overseer, not caring who heard
him. "If you had kept a closer eye on my daughter, as you
were sworn to do, none of this would be happening! By the
dark gods, we should have left you to rot with your Viking
masters!"

Soren opened his mouth to protest, but Nicolae inter-
vened once more. "Wait, milord. Distressing as this news is,
there may be, if you'll pardon the jest, a *silver* lining to the
present crisis." He smiled shrewdly. "At least, now we know
where Lucian is to be found."

Quite right, Viktor realized. Disciplining Soren could
wait; Lucian was the true wellspring of all this turmoil and
tragedy.

"Our moment has come, then," he declared, baring his
fangs in anticipation of the decisive battle ahead. "You
wanted Lucian crushed, Nicolae? Very well, let us spare no
expense or effort to do so." He drew his mighty broadsword
from its scabbard and raised it before him like a scepter.
"This sorry state of affairs has dragged on long enough. We
will answer this outrage with an overwhelming show of
force—the only language these mongrels understand!"

Chapter Twenty

CARPATHIAN MOUNTAINS

*L*ucian felt a storm coming on. Dark clouds rolled acros the night sky, obscuring the stars, while the very air seeme to be holding its breath in anticipation of a violent distu bance in the atmosphere. He watched the sky with a wo ried expression, acutely aware that it was the first night the new moon, when all lycans were at their weakest. *If were Viktor,* he brooded darkly, *now is when I would attack.*

He had been anticipating a vampiric assault for days no ever since he'd sent Zoltan's skull back to the castle pieces. Viktor would surely attempt to retake the mines, b when?

Lucian stood atop the shingled roof of the soldier's ba racks, which his own followers had appropriated for the use. The displaced miners, whom Lucian had conscripted reexcavate the collapsed mine shafts, had been forced sleep outside upon the ground or else within the silve laden depths of the mine itself, where the other lycans st refused to venture.

From his perch atop the barracks, Lucian surveyed the camp's newly erected defenses. A wooden palisade, stretching across the width of the gorge, blocked the sandy road leading up to the mine. Additional timbers had been driven into the ground along the sides of the gorge, their sharpened tips tilted upward at the rocky slopes leading to the forest above. In theory, the pointed stakes would impale anyone who attempted to charge down the hill as he and his lycan warriors had recently done.

Lucian drew comfort from the mine's imposing fortifications. *At least we're ready for Viktor and his troops.*

I hope.

"Lucian!" a lookout posted on the palisade called out to him. The lycan sentry waved his torch to catch his leader's attention. "Something's happening on the road!"

I knew it! Lucian thought, cursing beneath his breath. Viktor was not going to let this moonless night go to waste.

He leaped from the slate rooftop to a narrow walk running just below the top of the palisade. The sentry, whose name was Odon, hurried to meet him. A dented kettle helmet, looted from one of the mine's former guards, protected the lycan's skull. "Look!" he said, pointing south. "There's something moving up ahead."

"Where?" Lucian asked anxiously. He peered out over the pointed tips of the fence, his eyes probing the darkened road descending from the gorge. The dark clouds overhead made the night even blacker than usual, and at first, he could see nothing; slowly, however, he began to discern vague shapes rolling up the road toward them. He glimpsed the outline of a large wooden structure, some eight hundred feet down the road. He heard the creaks and groans of heavy machinery.

The truth hit him with the force of, well, a catapult.

"Watch out!" he cried, even as the first missile can arcing through the sky at them. A whistling noise fille the air as a large chunk of solid rock hurtled toward t palisade.

Lucian leaped to the ground in time, but Odon was n so fortunate. The speeding rock slammed into the uprig timbers beneath him. Stripped pine trunks shattered, ar Odon went flying from the walkway, crashing down on the stony ground amid an explosion of wooden debris.

More boulders followed, quickly reducing the palisade splinters. A few of the missiles overshot the demolished fc tifications, raining down on the mining camp itself. Missil smashed through the slate roof of the barracks, elicitin screams of shock and injury from the lycans housed withi Lucian watched in horror as a load of flaming coals crashe down from the sky. A red-hot lump struck a fleeing lycan the back, knocking him to the ground. Flames leaped from his hair and clothing.

"To arms!" Lucian shouted, trying to rally his follower but all was pandemonium. Panicked lycans ran about confusion, seeking shelter from the terror that fell from t sky. "Gather 'round me!" he cried, drawing a double-edg sword from his belt. "We must make ready to defend ou selves!"

At that moment, the storm broke, adding to the chad Lightning streaked across the sky, followed almost immed ately by a booming crack of thunder. Rain poured from t sky, dousing the blazing coals and soaking everything el: A howling wind blew against Lucian, carrying away his u gent commands.

Then a new noise joined the clamor. It sounded at fi like thunder—before growing loud enough to be recogniz as the sound of pounding hooves, racing up the gorge toward the camp.

No! Lucian thought. *Not now, not like this!*

A legion of mounted Death Dealers came charging out of the night. Silver glinted on the hooves and armor of the galloping warhorses, as well as on the spikes jutting from the horses' gleaming steel headpieces. Undead cavalrymen, wearing crimson surcoats over their mail and leather armor, held their swords and spears aloft as their fearsome mounts easily hurdled the splintered remains of the palisade before chasing after the terrified lycans.

"Death to the lycan scum!"

The hateful cry went up from the Death Dealers as they hacked and stabbed at the disorganized lycans, trampling the bleeding bodies under the argent hooves of their armored destriers. Olga, cradling baby Ferenz in her arms, tried and failed to outrace a mounted vampire who pursued her relentlessly past the shattered barracks. Leaning from his saddle, the Death Dealer caught her in the back of the head with a silver-studded mace, and her brains burst from her shattered skull. Her long red hair turned a brighter shade of crimson.

Grief and guilt stabbed Lucian's heart as he saw the vampire's armored steed ride roughshod over Olga's fallen body, silencing the heart-rending cries of little Ferenz. *She trusted me, and I failed her,* Lucian thought in despair. If there was indeed an afterlife for those of their breed, he prayed that mother and child were now reunited somewhere far beyond the cruel inequities of this world.

But not every lycan fled before the enemy's advance; a few fought back furiously. Crossbows, captured from the mine's previous defenders, fired at the vampires and their steeds, while unarmed lycans pounced at the Death Dealers, sometimes managing to unseat the mounted warriors. Alas, these valiant defenders were all too soon cut down by the flashing swords of Viktor's troops.

The rout reminded Lucian of countless other raids against unwary lycans, many of which he had participated in himself, but this time he was on the receiving end of the Death Dealers' lethal attentions. *We were not ready,* he realized. *I launched my campaign too soon.*

"There you are, you bastard!" a familiar voice shouted at Lucian. It was Ulrik, the Death Dealer he'd wounded in Sonja's bedchamber the night they were exposed. The furious vampire turned his horse and galloped toward Lucian, raising his sword above his head. "Your head is mine!"

But Lucian ducked beneath the swinging blade, then sprang onto the horse's back behind Ulrik. He clamped his legs onto the destrier's flanks and grabbed the vampire's shoulder. Ironically, the warrior's crimson surcoat protected Lucian's palm from the silver chain mail beneath the heavy fabric. Before Ulrik could react, Lucian drew his sword across the Death Dealer's throat, slicing it through. Cold vampire blood sprayed onto the gleaming steel crinet protecting the horse's upper neck and mane. Ulrik clutched at his throat, but blood continued to spurt through the fingers of his metal gauntlet.

My head was not for you to claim, Lucian thought triumphantly as he shoved the dying vampire off his saddle into the mud below. Alarmed, Ulrik's steed reared up onto its hind legs, throwing Lucian free of his precarious perch on the animal's back.

He hit the ground hard, only a few paces away from where Ulrik lay, gasping out his last breaths. The agitated warhorse spun about and tried to trample Lucian with its silver-shod hooves, as though to avenge its fallen rider.

Lucian rolled away from the crashing hooves. Jumping to his feet, he let out a bloodcurdling roar and jabbed at the horse's exposed flesh with the point of his sword. The injuries he inflicted were minor but proved sufficient to chase the riderless warhorse away.

He had slain yet another vampire, but the battle was far from over. "Stand fast!" he urged the pack, brandishing his bloody sword, but to no avail; without the moon to embolden them, the routed lycans stampeded past him, almost carrying him along in their headlong flight. He felt like a salmon fighting its way upstream.

Fear-crazed lycans, desperate to escape the vampire cavalry, squeezed past the sharpened stakes facing the sides of the gorge, scrambling up the rocky slopes despite the torrents of rain streaming down the hillside. Unable to gain purchase on the slippery incline, many of the distraught men and women slid back down the hill onto the waiting stakes. The agonized screams of impaled lycans added to the deafening clamor.

A tremendous burst of lightning illuminated the sky, briefly turning night into day, and Lucian spotted Viktor astride his coal-black charger. The scalloped batwings on his helmet were silhouetted against the flashing clouds as the Elder withdrew his gigantic broadsword from the back of a skewered lycan. His cold blue eyes met Lucian's across the field of battle.

"Defiler!" he shouted over the thunder.

"Murderer!" Lucian accused him back.

Digging his spurs into Hades' flanks, Viktor barreled down on Lucian. The silver horn on the horse's brow aimed straight for the lycan's chest, while the Elder's gore-stained sword was raised and ready. Lucian hesitated, uncertain whether he could outrun the charging warhorse. He raised his own sword, eager to avenge Sonja despite the odds against him.

The golden sunbeam fell directly on Sonja . . . her pale face blackened and crumbled . . .

Before he could engage her murderous father in battle, however, a steel-tipped arrow came whizzing out of nowhere to strike Viktor in the side, knocking the Elder from his saddle. Caught by surprise, Lucian turned to see Josef standing several yards away, his great yew bow in hand.

"Are you mad?" the grizzled soldier exclaimed. He reached back to draw another arrow from his quiver. "That bastard would have run you down!"

He opened his mouth to chastise Lucian further, only to stiffen in shock as the silver horn of another warhorse stabbed him from behind, the point of the horn erupting from his chest. Blood gushed from Josef's mouth. His bow slipped from his fingers, landing in the mud at his feet. The armored destrier reared upward, flinging the lycan's body into the air.

Lucian was shocked by the speed and suddenness of his lieutenant's demise. To think that the doughty soldier had survived the Crusades, only to perish so abruptly

Farewell, my friend. Your sacrifice shall not be in vain.

Turning back toward Viktor, Lucian saw the undead overlord rising to his feet amid the turmoil of the massacre. Mud covered the Elder's crimson surcoat, concealing the rampant dragon embroidered thereon. Sword in hand, Viktor glared at Lucian through the jumble of fleeing and fighting figures. "I am coming for you, lycan!" he promised. "My daughter's honor will be avenged!"

You, avenge Sonja? The father who ordered her execution? The Elder's misplaced wrath infuriated Lucian. If not for you,

Sonja and I could have lived in happiness for all eternity, with our child at our side!

Every primitive instinct in his body urged him to stay and fight, to exact justice for his martyred love, yet reason counseled otherwise. He remembered Viktor's overpowering strength from their confrontation in Sonja's bedchamber; in single combat, he wouldn't stand a chance against the powerful Elder.

His instinct for survival won out.

Lucian turned and ran.

Thunder rumbled in the distance, making Kraven thankful that he had not accompanied Viktor and the other Death Dealers on tonight's assault on the captured silver mines. Immortality, as far as he was concerned, was too short to spend wet and shivering in the cold, slogging through the mud in heavy armor, just for the chance to get yourself killed by some upstart lycan. He was quite content to stay snugly indoors tonight, watching over the castle in Viktor's absence.

The same could not be said for Soren, who clearly resented being left behind once again. The bearded overseer sat glumly at a trencher table in the great hall, nursing his grievances as he stared sullenly in the direction of the far-off storm. His silver whips lay idle on the table.

Kraven, who had been raised on palace intrigues in the court of King Henry I, saw an opportunity. *A disgruntled subject can be a useful pawn,* he observed.

"Come, let us share a drink," he said heartily, sitting down opposite Soren. He placed a flagon of mulled blood and a pair of leather tankards on the table between them. "What's the point of living forever if we don't enjoy the finer things in life?"

Like power, he thought.

Soren grunted but poured himself a tankard of blood. His scowling face remained as morose as before. Clearly, it was going to take more than just a shared drink to get the Irish vampire talking.

"I have been thinking," Kraven began, glancing around to confirm that no one else was listening. He and Soren appeared to have the hall to themselves for the moment. "There is a distinct drawback to serving the Elders. Do you know what that is?"

"Their fucking ingratitude?" Soren muttered.

Kraven silently congratulated himself on drawing a response out of the taciturn overseer. "No, it's that, as immortals, they need never surrender their power to those who come after them. No matter how far you or I may rise—or fall—in their esteem, they shall always be there, retaining ultimate power to themselves."

Indeed, he reflected, *what use is ambition when the throne itself remains forever out of reach?* It had become very clear to him over the past few months that, no matter how obsequiously he catered to Viktor, the tyrannical Elder was always going to treat him as nothing more than a vassal. *I did not become a Death Dealer, risking mortal injury for the sake of social advancement, just to spend eternity sniffing at the very threshold of absolute power and luxury.*

"You spoke of ingratitude?" he prompted.

"Aye," Soren grumbled. "I have served the coven faithfully for nearly four centuries, keeping the lycan rabble in their place, and yet I am cast down—and all because some wanton trollop lets a lycan get into her skirts." He took a swig from his tankard, then wiped his mouth on his sleeve. "Is it my fault that the Elder's daughter was a whore?"

"Certainly not," Kraven agreed readily. "Anyone can see

that you have been sorely ill used." He leaned forward, his voice acquiring a conspiratorial tone. "Mayhap we can help each other improve our respective lots."

Soren lifted his baleful gaze from his drink. He regarded Kraven with cautious interest. "How so?"

"Who can say?" Kraven said with a shrug. "I have no firm plan as yet, but I daresay a propitious opportunity will arise in time. After all, we're just as immortal as the Elders are." He smiled slyly. "What's more, if we're smart and patient enough, we might even outlive them."

Raising their tankards, the two vampires toasted their alliance.

Viktor's threats pursued Lucian across the blood-drenched mining camp. "Run for your life, you cowardly animal!" the Elder railed, hacking and slashing at every ill-starred lycan who came between him and his quarry. "There is no escape for you!"

The driving rain pelted Lucian's face as he bolted for freedom. *Forgive me, Sonja,* he entreated her spirit, ashamed that he lacked the brute strength to avenge his bride's murder. *If only there were some arcane elixir that would give me the might to stand against an Elder,* he yearned, *but such potions are merely the stuff of legend.*

He raced for the entrance to the mine. At his order, the captured miners had reexcavated the shaft, converting an old drainage tunnel into an emergency escape route that was perhaps his only hope of surviving this hellish night. Seeing the entrance ahead of him, he darted into the inky blackness of the mine. The screams of dying lycans followed him.

Rainwater ran down the inclined tunnel, turning the floor of the shaft into a shallow river. Maintaining his balance was difficult; Lucian slipped on the treacherous rock and reached out to steady himself. His palm sizzled as it came into contact with a vein of silver ore, and he yanked his hand back, cursing at the pain. He stumbled on down the tunnel.

Without a torch or lantern, he was forced to navigate the Stygian darkness of the mine by memory. Several tons of solid limestone muffled the thunder booming outside, which grew fainter the deeper he descended beneath the earth. Mercifully, the wails of his butchered followers faded as well. The rush of water cascading past his ankles drowned out whatever bootsteps might be following in his wake, yet he knew that Viktor could not be far behind. *In his own twisted fashion,* Lucian acknowledged, *the Elder is no less intent on avenging Sonja's death than I.*

At last, he came to an intersection, where a narrow side tunnel diverged from the main shaft. This was the escape passage he had been looking for, which led to a separate exit on the eastern face of the mountain. Lucian took a sharp right turn at the crossing, clambering over a pile of waste rock at the opening of the old drainage tunnel.

He hurried faster down the slender shaft, no longer worried about losing his way in the dark. His boots sliced through the silty water flowing past his ankles. Hope bloomed in his heart; perhaps he was going to live through this night after all. He grinned wolfishly as he imagined Viktor's frustration once he realized that a mere lycan had eluded his "justice" yet again. *Never underestimate the craftiness of a wolf,* he gloated, *especially one hungry for revenge.*

The light of an upraised lantern, lying directly in his path, crushed Lucian's hopes in an instant. He skidded to a halt at the sight of an armored figure standing just before

he exit he sought. A crack of lightning revealed none other
han Nicolae himself, holding up the lantern in one bejew-
:led hand and a bloodstained sword in the other. The bod-
es of mutilated lycans lay sprawled on the tunnel floor
>ehind him, half submerged beneath the departing rainwa-
er; apparently, Lucian had not been the only lycan to retreat
nto the mines.

"Speak of the devil." The vampire prince chortled. "If it
sn't the nefarious beast himself." He tilted his head back at
he bloody carcasses behind him. "How fortunate for me
hat I spied these miscreants fleeing this furtive little back
:ntrance of yours, but then, it wasn't entirely luck; I rather
;uspected that you'd have just such a bolt hole."

Lucian had no desire to bandy words with Nicolae. He
leard heavy boots splashing through the tunnels behind
iim and realized there was no way to go but forward.
'Stand aside!" he said, raising his sword. "I'll not be undone
>y the likes of you!"

"Arrogant pup!" Nicolae laughed sardonically. "Why, I
vas mastering the fine art of swordplay while you were still
:mptying the chamber pots of your betters!" He lifted the
antern higher, granting Lucian a better look at his sneering
:ountenance. "Come, lycan, see how a pureblood fights!"

Your blood's no purer than mine, Lucian thought angrily,
onging to slice Nicolae's smirk from his face. Baring his
angs, he ran at the Elder's son, swinging his sword.

Nicolae expertly parried Lucian's slashing blade. Sparks
lew in the darkness as steel met steel. Lucian thrust again,
>ut Nicolae blocked the blow without even letting go of his
antern. "Is that the best you can do, lycan?" the vampire
aunted. "No wonder your kind is destined to do our bid-
ling until the end of time. You're nothing but a pack of ig-
orant beasts!"

"Better than a clutch of soulless parasites!" Lucian snarled back. "Sucking the life from everything you touch! His blood boiled in his veins. "Sonja was the only one among you with a beating heart!"

Despite his fury, though, Lucian quickly realized that Nicolae was simply playing with him. He thrust, feinted and parried, yet the vampire's blade drove Lucian steadily back up the drainage tunnel. Vampire boots and voices echoed from elsewhere in the mine; Lucian knew that it was only a matter of minutes before the sound of their clanging swords attracted Viktor and the other Death Dealers.

He was running out of time.

Nicolae appeared to reach the same conclusion. "Time to end this," he announced, disarming Lucian with an elegant flick of his sword. Lucian's iron blade landed with a splash on the floor, disappearing beneath the bloody slurry sluicing down from the upper reaches of the mine.

Thunder boomed overhead as Nicolae prodded Lucian with the point of his silver blade, poking the unarmed lycan in the chest. Lucian clamped his fangs together, unwilling to give Marcus's heir the satisfaction of hearing him whimper in pain. *If only the moon were shining brightly,* he seethed, *I'd tear this preening vampire apart with my claws and teeth!*

"Viktor would prefer to butcher you himself," Nicolae explained calmly, "but surely I will be forgiven for striking out at the very beast who ravished my own dear betrothed." He winked salaciously. "Tell me, before I slice you to ribbons, was the lovely Sonja as knowledgeable in bed as she was in matters of art and philosophy? A pity I never had a chance to find out for myself!"

An uncontrollable rage suffused every atom of Lucian's being. *How dare this bloodsucking sybarite defile Sonja's memory?* Nicolae's obscene innuendos provoked Lucian even nore than the silver sword's point jabbing into his chest. Ie opened his jaws to roar in defiance—and was startled to eel bone and muscle begin to shift beneath his skin.

What is this? he thought in amazement. It was impossi-le—the moon was dark—yet he felt the first inklings of the Change coming on.

Every hair on his body bristled and began to grow. His ngers and toes curled into claws. His spine stretched be-eath his rain-soaked tunic. Bones twisted and ground gainst each other. Blood pounded in his temples.

Yes! he thought fervently. The pain was worse than usual, s though his flesh were being forced into a new shape gainst its own inclinations, yet Lucian refused to surrender. hrough sheer force of will, he pushed the Change onward. *hat's it!* he urged his inner wolf, as it snapped and clawed at e weak human frame confining it. *Break loose! Break free! For Sonja!*

"Alas, I'm afraid Viktor will have to settle for your head n a pike," Nicolae declared, too enraptured by the sound f his own voice to pay heed to the warning signs of his foe's ccelerating metamorphosis. "No doubt, he will want to dis-lay it prominently back at the castle, perhaps in the center f the courtyard for all to see. *That* should bring the rest of our uncouth breed to heel . . . wait! What's happening?"

His inattention cost him dearly. One final convulsion cked Lucian's body. Then, for the first time in the annals of e immortals, a werewolf roared into existence without the oon to call it forth. The nightmarish form of an immense ack beast filled the narrow confines of the exit shaft.

"No!" Nicolae blurted, eyes wide with shock. His lantern ipped from his fingers, crashing down into the running ater. "This cannot be!"

A shaggy arm swiped at the prince, knocking his silver

sword away. A second blow sliced through Nicolae's mai
shirt as if it were made of gauze. Daggerlike claws opene
up the vampire's gut, spilling his chilly entrails out onto th
floor of the tunnel. Gore turned the flowing water incarna
dine.

You never knew Sonja as I did, the werewolf thought vin
dictively. He lunged forward, crushing Nicolae's skull be
tween his powerful jaws. He would have liked to hav
stayed and dismembered the prince at leisure, but his tufte
ears heard the sound of at least a half-dozen Death Dealer
splashing down the side tunnel toward him, the irate Elde
among them.

"Out of my way!" Viktor bellowed impatiently. "The beas
is mine!"

Not tonight, Lucian decided. Even in his wolfen form, h
was not ready to take on Viktor in single combat. As muc
as he hated to abandon the fray, and the army he had unwit
tingly led to the slaughter, he could not deny the irrefutabl
fact that tonight's battle was already lost. There was nothin
to be gained by dying along with the rest of the pack; onl
by escaping now could he hope to carry on his crusad
against Viktor and his bloodthirsty parasites. *Better to aveng
my followers later than die with them now.*

Dropping onto all fours, he bounded out of the min
shaft and made for the forest below. Wind, rain, thunde
and lightning spurred him onward, along with the tantaliz
ing hope that someday Viktor would know what it was lik
to flee for his life. *Now that the moon no longer holds sway ove
me, anything is possible.*

Despite tonight's grievous defeat, he vowed to continu
his war against Viktor and the other vampires. *Somewher*

he mused, *there must be a way to match the staggering power of the Elders, some secret hidden away in the very origins of our respective races.*

I shall attain that power, he resolved, *no matter how many centuries it takes.*

My war has only just begun.

Now

A.D. 2002

Chapter Twenty-one

OUTSIDE BUDAPEST

$\mathcal{T}$he chains tugged on his wrists, and at first, Lucian thought himself back in Viktor's dungeon, a scene he often returned to in nightmares. Then his head cleared, and he realized that he was indeed manacled but somewhere else entirely.

Where am I? he thought groggily. The last thing he remembered was receiving a tranquilizer dart in his neck, back in that dismal alley in Pest. Now he found himself chained to a cold stone wall, lacking both his brown leather jacket and the spring-loaded wrist blades that were ordinarily hidden beneath his sleeves. He looked around and found himself staring at a pillar of dusty brown skulls.

It took him a second to recognize where he was. *The crypt beneath the old monastery where Sonja and I sought refuge from the mob.*

Eight centuries had wrought surprising changes in the underground mausoleum. Although human bones still decorated the limestone walls and the vaulted ceiling, modern technology now existed side-by-side with the morbid relics.

Electric lights had replaced the candles in the skeletal chandelier, while the wall directly opposite him was covered with what appeared to be a sophisticated high-tech surveillance system. Closed-circuit TV screens offered multiple views of the monastery above, which apparently had been converted into a private residence sometime over the centuries. A computerized control panel, full of blinking lights and switches, was built into the wall beneath the security monitors. A grotesque archway, constructed entirely of human skulls, led to another branch of catacombs, tantalizing him with the prospect of escape. Gypsy music played softly in the background.

A figure sat at the control panel, his or her back turned to Lucian. Kevlar body armor shielded the figure from the neck down. A visored steel helmet rested on the control panel next to the armored stranger. A pistol was holstered at the figure's waist. Close-cropped black hair covered the back of the stranger's head.

Is this the mystery sniper, Lucian wondered, *or simply a soldier in my enigmatic foe's employ?* He yanked experimentally on his manacles, but the silver-alloy chains refused to budge; clearly, they were designed with immortal strength in mind. *Perhaps if I change?* A bloody bandage covered his injured knee, but he no longer felt the silver bullet burning within his leg. *Apparently, my unknown captor wants me alive, at least for the time being.*

The rattle of the chains attracted the attention of the figure at the control panel. "Ah, awake at last, are we?" said a sultry voice Lucian had not heard for nearly a millennium. "It's about time. I was starting to fear that I had overestimated the dosage required to knock you out."

A stainless-steel desk chair spun around, revealing the

face of his captor. Lucian recognized the sly, exotic features at once.

"Leyba!" he gasped.

"Hello, Lucian," she said with an evil grin. Malice gleamed in her dark eyes. "Long time no see."

Lucian was stunned by this unexpected reunion. "But . . . I thought you dead!" Although he had not personally witnessed the scullery wench's fiery demise, he had soon learned of it from the various castle servants who had joined his ranks in the early days of the war. "Viktor killed you, eight hundred years ago!"

"It took me almost that long to recover," Leyba said venomously. "I landed in a lake located deep in the woods beyond the castle, but even still, every bone in my body was broken, my flesh and organs singed to a crisp." She shuddered at the memory, and her wicked grin faded. "The only thing that kept me alive was the thought of having you at my mercy, just as I do now."

She drew the pistol from her holsters. A Walther P-88, from the looks of it. "And by the way, don't even think about Changing." The muzzle of the Walther flared, and silver agony exploded in Lucian's right leg. "I removed my earlier bullet so that you wouldn't die on me, but another nine millimeters of silver should keep you in human form for the time being." She shrugged beneath the matte-black Kevlar armor. "I suppose I could have just dosed you again, but where's the fun in that?"

Lucian grimaced in pain as blood streamed down his leg, irrigating the floor of the medieval ossuary. Hatred ignited within him, especially as he recalled how the jealous Leyba had betrayed him and Sonja to Viktor, but he struggled to control his temper for the sake of the war. He could not afford to provoke Leyba now, not when he was so close to destroying the vampires once and for all.

There will be time enough to deal with Leyba later, he reasoned, *after Viktor and the Elders are no more. But first I have to keep this psychotic female from killing me!*

"I am not your enemy, Leyba."

Her bitter laughter implied otherwise. "And who started this goddamn war of yours? I was the first casualty, but I was hardly the last. How many lycans have died because you couldn't keep your grubby paws off that perfumed vampire princess?"

It took all of Lucian's self-control to overlook his captor's caustic dismissal of Sonja. *You are not fit to utter her name,* he thought angrily but held his tongue. "This is Viktor's war, not mine!"

"Maybe that's what you tell yourself," she countered, "but I know better. None of this would have happened if you hadn't rejected me in favor of the Elder's slut of a daughter. Thanks to you, I was burnt alive—and our species has been hunted to the brink of extinction!" She rose from her chair and crossed the vault to confront Lucian face-to-face. "I've waited generations for my revenge. Imagine my disappointment when I first heard that Kraven had killed you. Deep down inside, though, I knew you were still alive. I've been shadowing the vampires for years, hoping they would lead me to you, but you've kept out of sight for far too long." A scowl gave way to a smirk. "I figured that attack at Statue Park might lure you out of hiding."

"Very clever," Lucian conceded. Perhaps if he appealed to her sense of racial solidarity? "You're still a lycan, Leyba, as am I. Trust me when I tell you that this war is far from over. The time of Viktor's Awakening draws near. If we work together, we can destroy the vampires once and for all."

"Shut up!" she snapped. "I don't care about your fucking war. A plague on both your houses!" She smiled mirthlessly. "You see, I'm no longer the ignorant scullion you remember. I've acquired a degree of culture and learning over the centuries, just like your precious Sonja."

You'll never be her equal, Lucian thought. A growl escaped his lips. *My Sonja had a kind and loving heart, with malice toward none. You're still the same spiteful bitch you always were.*

"Besides," Leyba taunted him, "you're a fine one to speak to me as one lycan to another, allying yourself with the likes of Kraven and Soren." Her voice dripped with contempt. "What's your game now, Lucian? Are you trying to get back in the vampires' favor again, just as you were back in the old days? You were never happy being a lycan like the rest of us. You always wanted to be one of the bloods instead." She spat in his face. "No wonder you chose a vampire mistress over your own kind."

Insanity twisted the woman's Gypsy features, and Lucian realized there was no reasoning with her; Leyba's maniacal hatred ran too deep. He dared not tell her about the plot to assassinate the Elders, let alone the top-secret scheme that not even Kraven knew, a scheme born of the science of the last few centuries: to transform himself into an all-powerful hybrid of vampire and werewolf . . . like the unborn child Viktor had destroyed so many centuries ago.

Thanks to Leyba's treachery.

"It was you who betrayed me," he accused her. His memory supplied the vile image of Sonja's golden ribbon gripped in Leyba's thieving hand. "You exposed us to Viktor—and were fool enough to expect a vampire's gratitude. Don't blame me for your downfall, Leyba. You brought your misfortunes on yourself." He glared at her with undisguised revulsion. "I only wish that Viktor had done a better job of killing you."

The Walther struck Lucian across the face, hard enough to rattle his teeth. "Go to hell, you blood-loving bastard! Before I'm done with you, you'll admit your guilt. You'll beg me for forgiveness, even if I have to skin you alive with red-hot silver!"

I'll be damned before I beg you for anything, Lucian thought defiantly. He tried to change, but, as Leyba had predicted, the silver bullet in his leg kept his inner wolf at bay. If he concentrated hard enough, he might be able to expel the bullet from his flesh, but what was to stop Leyba from shooting him again once she saw what he was doing? Best to keep that trick in reserve, he calculated, in the unlikely event that the vengeful bitch ever gave him a chance to recover from the torture to come.

Leyba walked across the vault to an upright metal cabinet. She opened its door, revealing a well-supplied weapons locker, including several machine guns and a flamethrower. A drawer slid out from one side of the locker, and she extracted a gleaming straight razor. She held the razor up beneath the bony chandelier, so that its silver gleam caught the light. Insulated gauntlets protected her own flesh from the toxic metal.

Another memory came back to Lucian with excruciating clarity: using Kraven's knife to slice Viktor's brand from his own arm, so that Kraven could offer the bloody fragment of skin as proof of Lucian's "death." For all Lucian knew, the grisly trophy was still buried away somewhere in the coven's archives. He only remembered how painful it had been, flaying his upper arm with the sharpened edge of a silver blade. *It looks as though I'm about to relive that experience, and then some.*

His chief regret, as he braced himself for the ordeal ahead, was that he might not live to see his plans against the

Elders come to fruition. He would have to hope that Raze would carry on in his stead and bring the vampires' despotic reign to its long-awaited end. *One way or another,* Lucian vowed, *my will shall be done.*

Leyba faced him once more. "Miss me?" she taunted with a hint of her once-brazen lewdness. She pressed the flat of the blade against Lucian's cheek and smiled malevolently as his skin sizzled at its touch. She sliced open his shirt with the tip of the razor, leaving a thin red line down his chest. Her eyes widened at the sight of Sonja's pendant, and her lips peeled back, baring her fangs. "Time to exact my pound of flesh," she announced, "plus eight hundred years of interest . . ."

A sudden explosion rocked the subterranean crypt. Dust and gravel rained down from the ceiling. Moldering skulls and clavicles crashed onto the floor. An ear-piercing alarm echoed through the gloomy catacombs.

Leyba stepped back from Lucian, surprise and confusion written all over her face.

"What the fuck?" she exclaimed.

Selene moved like a shadow through the darkened monastery, which, until recently, had served as Leonid Florescu's country estate. According to Florescu, the refurbished medieval edifice had been claimed by the same deranged female lycan who had terrified the human arms dealer into assisting her in her guerrilla warfare against both the coven and her own kind. "She wants revenge on you all," Florescu had reported.

Revenge for what? Selene wondered. Allegedly, the lycan called herself Leyba, but Florescu had professed to know nothing more about her motives or origins. Given just how scared he'd seemed of Selene herself, the ruthless Death

Dealer was inclined to believe him. *I should have known Diego's killer would turn out to be lycan,* she thought icily. *Sounds as if I'm dealing with a rabid bitch here.*

She checked the door of the refectory for booby traps, eased it open, then gestured for the rest of her team to follow her. Mason and Yoshio stealthily emerged from the rear of the chapter house, their matching black trench coats marking them as Death Dealers as surely as their grim, implacable expressions. They held their submachine guns, loaded with silver ammunition, at the ready as they crept after Selene, who was armed with her trusty Berettas. Her brown eyes probed the unlit chamber before her.

So far, so good, she thought. According to Florescu, who, along with his mistress, was now being kept on ice at a safe house in the city, the nerve center of the estate's security system was located in a subterranean crypt under the adjacent chapel. Selene was taking an indirect route toward the entrance to the catacombs in hopes of avoiding detection, while the other strike team went for the direct approach. With any luck, they'd catch the murderous lycan between them.

She produced a miniature walkie-talkie from within the folds of her trench coat. "Selene to Kahn," she whispered into the receiver. "We've entered the building through the chapter house and are now proceeding east via the refectory."

"*Roger that, Selene,*" a voice answered through the walkie-talkie. She recognized the familiar Cockney accent of the veteran weapons master, who was leading a team consisting of himself, Nathaniel, and Rani. "*We're in position outside the main entrance to the chapel. Let us know when you need a big, noisy distraction.*"

"You'll be the first to know," she promised him. The plan

ıs for Selene's team to attempt a covert infiltration of the
mer monastery before Kahn and his people unleashed a
-frontal assault. *Let's hope I run into this Leyba bitch first,*
ene thought as Diego's dying screams echoed in her
mory. *I want to put this mad dog down myself.*

The refectory, where the long-dead brothers of Saint
lpurga had once taken their meals, had been converted
o a lavish dining room, with a polished mahogany table
ıg enough to seat a small army. Clearly, black-market
ns dealing paid well these days, especially when one was
plying both sides of a twilight war that had been going
for centuries. Selene made a mental note to remind
aven of Florescu's double dealing before they let the ne-
ious mortal free again.

Skirting the edges of the elongated dining table, they
de their way across the refectory toward the cloisters be-
ıd. Selene hung back to watch their rear as her fellow
ath Dealers approached the oak door at the far end of the
ıing room. A pinprick of ruby light caught her eye a mi-
second before she identified it as a laser beam.

"Watch out!" she hissed.

Too late. Yoshio's shoulder broke the beam, triggering an
omated security response. Ultraviolet lights flared to life
ive them, blinding the Death Dealers instantly. "Shit!" Se-
e cursed as her skin began to burn. Although not as
ıal as genuine sunlight, the UV radiation still hurt like
Devil. Somebody (Florescu? Leyba?) had obviously been
rried about vampires.

Selene dropped to the floor and rolled beneath the table,
ting a couple centimeters of solid mahogany between
self and the UV lights in the ceiling. She threw her arm
oss her eyes, which were already squeezed tightly shut.

A pair of boots bumped against her head. She heard a

muttered curse and realized that Mason had sought shelter
under the table as well.

But what about Yoshio?

The other Death Dealer cried out in pain as the radiation
seared his face and hands. Boots pounded against the floor,
racing madly away from the burning light. Selene heard
Yoshio bolt for the door at the far end of the refectory.
"Wait!" she called out. "It might be rigged!"

The doorknob clicked open, and the subsequent explosion confirmed Selene's worst suspicions. She flattened herself against the floor as shrapnel slammed into the walls and
furniture. Smoke and dust suffused the air, along with the
acrid aroma of gelignite. "Yoshio!" she shouted, coughing on
the harsh black fumes. Her ears rang from the explosion.
"Talk to me, Yoshio!"

Only the sound of falling debris answered her.

"I think he's gone," Mason said, echoing her own thought.

Selene seethed in frustration. First Diego, now Yoshio.
Two Death Dealers down, and the lycan murderess remained at large. *Not for much longer,* she vowed.

"What about you?" she asked Mason.

"I'm all right," the American vampire answered. "I took a
couple pieces of shrapnel, in the back and in my hip, but
nothing a little blood can't fix." A sharp intake of breath belied his flippant tone. "Mind you, I can't actually see what
my wounds look like, what with the blinding light and all."

Perversely, the blast that had apparently killed their comrade had left the infernal UV lights intact. Determined to do
something about that, Selene rolled onto her back and fired
blindly upward with her Berettas, targeting the lamps with
more guesswork than precision.

Silver slugs tore through the mahogany tabletop and
slammed into the ceiling. Lightbulbs exploded amid

)wer of sparks, and blessed darkness descended on the
ing room once more. Selene opened her eyes. She looked
vard the fatal doorway.

Yoshio's gory remains were splattered all over the walls
l ceiling, beyond all hope of regeneration. His subma-
ne gun was a heap of twisted metal lying in a puddle of
od and fallen plaster. The gruesome scene only made her
re determined to liquidate the lycan responsible for this
ocity. There would be time enough to mourn Yoshio later.
st, Leyba had to die.

Reloading her Berettas, Selene crawled from beneath the
llet-riddled table and checked on Mason. There were
t-aid supplies back in their van, she knew, and a refriger-
r filled with packets of cloned blood. "What do you
d?" she asked him urgently.

"Don't worry about me," he insisted. Vengeful blue eyes
wed from a face burnt red by the brutal UV rays; her own
e and hands felt just as raw. "I'll be okay. Go get that
king animal!"

A quick inspection confirmed that Mason's injuries were
re superficial than life-threatening. She breathed a sigh of
ef, and not just because her fellow soldier was likely to
over; the last thing she wanted to do right now was give
rba a chance to get away.

"Stay here," she instructed Mason. She stripped off her
g black coat and laid it like a blanket over her wounded
nrade. The coat's flapping tail would only be a liability if
encountered any more laser beams. She retrieved the
kie-talkie from inside the coat and was not surprised to
l Kahn anxious for a report in the wake of the explosion.
Selene quickly updated him on the situation, including
hio's death. "I can use that distraction now."

"Understood," Kahn said grimly. *"Be careful."*

"You, too," she replied, signing off.

A few moments later, the sound of gunfire issued fro[m] the other side of the monastery, where Kahn and his tea[m] launched their assault on the chapel itself. *So much for su[b]tlety,* Selene thought; all hope of taking Leyba unaware ha[s] gone up in smoke the minute Yoshio triggered that fir[e] alarm. *She knows we're here.*

Taking care not to step on any of Yoshio's splattered r[e]mains, she raised her guns and warily moved through t[he] exploded doorway.

"Goddamn bloods!" Leyba snarled. "They're crawling o[ut] of the woodwork like cockroaches!"

She stared furiously at the mounted security monitor[s.] Ghostly figures in long black coats swarmed across t[he] screens. Lucian flashed back to another squadron of va[m]pire warriors, ransacking a defenseless peasant village, a[nd] marveled at how little things had changed over the ce[n]turies. "Looks like you've got company," he taunted Leyb[a.] "Perhaps we have a common enemy after all?"

"Don't get any ideas," she warned him, not looking aw[ay] from the banks of closed-circuit TV screens. Having s[i]lenced the alarms, her fingers now feverishly worked t[he] controls of the security system. "This place belongs [to] Leonid Florescu now," she informed him. "You know, yo[ur] friend the arms dealer? I can fight off a battalion if I ha[ve] to."

As nearly as Lucian could tell, there were at least tw[o] teams of Death Dealers converging on the chapel. [He] watched as one team, led by a black vampire with a shav[ed] head, stormed down the central nave of the old chur[ch] only to be driven back by a ferocious hail of gunfire comi[ng] from somewhere behind the altar. Lucian's brow wrinkled

onfusion. Who was firing at the Death Dealers? Was Leyba
ot working alone?

"A T-two remote-controlled weapons platform," the one-
me Gypsy wench bragged as if reading his thoughts.
Courtesy of the U.S. military, by way of the black market."
he operated the mechanism by means of a joystick at-
ched to the control panel. "All strictly state-of-the-art."

On the screen, the chapel's invaders retreated behind the
st row of pews and began firing back at the altar with pis-
ls and submachine guns. Elsewhere, on another monitor,
noke and dust obscured the image from a once palatial
ning room. Leyba peered intently at the murky screen,
hich suddenly went black entirely. "Son of a bitch!" she
vore.

Lucian wondered about the camera at the other end of
e darkened monitor. Damaged by the explosion—or shot
it by an eagled-eyed vampire?

More important, he observed that the Death Dealers' at-
ck had definitely served to divert Leyba's attention from
ician himself. Indeed, so intent was she on defending
r sanctuary that she hadn't even noticed that the explo-
ons above had begun to weaken the ancient limestone
ill behind him. He tugged quietly at his manacles, feel-
g the silver-alloy chains give a little. He was still not
ite strong enough to tear the manacles loose from the
ill, not with this wretched silver bullet in his leg, but
rhaps he could remedy that situation, now that Leyba
is distracted.

He closed his eyes and concentrated, doing his best to
ut out the din of warfare raging above, as well as Leyba's
gry curses. He focused all his willpower on the caustic
mp of silver burning within his flesh, poisoning the very
sues surrounding it. Straining muscles rippled along his

leg, while the tendons in his neck stood out tautly, like stee
cables. Blood pounded in his temples. A tremor rocked hi
leg, making it difficult to keep standing. His jaws clenche
as tightly as his fists. *Out!* he commanded. *Out!*

It had taken him centuries to master this trick, but a
last, a slick, bloody wad of metal oozed out of the festerin
bullet wound. The pulped silver slug slid down his leg ont
the floor, the muted clink of its landing completely lost i
the roar of the gunfire.

That's better. Lucian opened his eyes, which were now
brilliant cobalt blue. He stretched his fingers and felt lor
yellow claws extend from his cuticles. He licked his lip.
even as his jaws protruded from his face.

Let Leyba concentrate on her undead intruders, he though
at least until I complete the Change.

Selene's skintight leathers gleamed like liquid obsidian a
she stepped out of the refectory into the moonlight. Cov
ered walkways or cloisters surrounded a square courtyar
boasting an ornate marble fountain that Selene suspecte
was a fairly recent addition to the former monastery. Acros
the courtyard, at the far end of the cloister before her, tł
old dormitory ran from north to south, connecting to tł
chapel and bell tower on the left. Selene eyed the tower wit
interest, an idea forming in her mind.

The moon was only a quarter full, but Selene knew th
was no guarantee that she wouldn't encounter a fully tran
formed werewolf before the night was out. Too many lycar
were able to transform at will these days; she had to assun
that Leyba was one of them.

She stepped cautiously beneath the shade of the covere
walkway, only to hear the whir of electronic machine
coming to life in the center of the courtyard. Instinctive

e leaped upward, clinging to the cloister's overhanging
iling with her hands and boots.

And just in time, too. A remote-operated machine gun
se from beneath the marble fountain and began strafing
e cloister beneath her. Selene flattened herself against the
onework as powdered stone went flying beneath the re-
ntless automatic weapons fire.

This place has too many bloody deathtraps, she thought irri-
bly, uncertain whether to blame Florescu's paranoia or
yba's. She guessed that she had inadvertently trod upon a
essure-sensitive tile in the walkway below. *Very well. I
n't make that mistake again.*

Hanging upside down from the ceiling, she crawled above
e booby-trapped cloister until she came to the western wall
the dormitory, which had reputedly been converted into
ites of guest rooms. What kinds of snares and pitfalls, she
ondered, awaited within the long rectangular building?

She decided not to risk it.

Swinging up from beneath the covered walkway, Selene
nded nimbly on the shingled roof of the dormitory. To her
t, several meters away, the bell tower rose at least two sto-
s above the roof of the chapel. Judging from the explosive
cket emanating from the chapel itself, she guessed that a
ated firefight was going on inside the old medieval abbey.

She unclipped her walkie-talkie and checked in with
hn. "What's your status?" she asked.

"Stalled for the moment," he reported. She could barely
ar him over the roaring gunfire in the background. *"She's
 us pinned down behind the pews with multiple remote-
trolled weapons platforms."* She heard an edge of frustra-
n in his voice. *"We could try to blow them out of the water
h our grenades, but that might collapse the stairways to the
acombs themselves."*

"Well, hold off bringing the whole place down for a fe
more minutes." She glanced again at the looming bell tow
"I have an idea."

Selene scurried along the roof of the dormitory to th
northern face of the tower. She quickly scaled the weathere
stone spire, grateful to discover that there seemed to be le
security outside the estate's buildings than within. Reachir
the top of the tower, she squeezed through a narrow wir
dow into the belfry itself. Fresh alarms sounded, but Seler
didn't care; if all went as planned, she wouldn't be stickir
around.

A single cast-iron bell, the size of a pup tent, hung from
sturdy oaken crossbeam. Selene hurried forward and plac
a small explosive charge where the bell was connected
the beam. She set the timer for less than fifteen second
then ducked beneath the lip of the bell and yanked the cla
per free before wrapping herself inside the curved met
surface. *This is either brilliant or utterly suicidal.*

She wouldn't have to wait long to find out.

Five, four, three, two. . . .

The charge went off, blasting the massive bell loose fro
its moorings. Selene closed her eyes and gritted her fangs
the bell plummeted down the length of the tower, taki
her with it. Bullets and shrapnel ricocheted off the iron ex
rior of the bell as the accelerating object set off four stori
worth of concealed deathtraps, but the dense metal casi
protected Selene from harm, even as a roaring wind bl
against her face and hair. She fought back an urge to shri
as the floor of the chapel seemed to rush up at her with te
rifying speed.

Going down, she thought. *Next stop: the catacombs.*

The bottom of the bell slammed into the floor below
and kept on going, smashing through crumbling stone a

tiles until it came to rest with a bone-jarring impact, at least one story below the chapel.

Selene dropped from the side of the bell onto a pebbly limestone floor. Her head was ringing, and every bone was vibrating like a tuning fork, but she appeared to be more or less intact. She checked her guns and was relieved to find them both still holstered to her hips. A rare smile graced her lips as she realized that her ridiculous stratagem had succeeded.

Ready or not, Leyba, here I come.

Lucian could not hold back a triumphant howl as he burst from his chains. Seated at her control panel, Leyba spun around in surprise to see a huge black werewolf lunging at her. She grabbed for her gun, but not quickly enough; Lucian knocked the Walther from her hand with one swipe of his enormous paw.

Viktor chained me, too, he reminded her silently. *You should have remembered how that turned out.*

Leyba staggered backward. She snatched her bulletproof helmet from the counter and hastily placed it over her head. She faced the werewolf across the bone-littered floor of the crypt.

Her Kevlar armor, Lucian realized, presented Leyba with a double-edged sword. On the one hand, the high-tech body armor provided her with a degree of protection against his fangs and claws; on the other, it prevented her from making the Change herself.

Hatred blazed in Lucian's cobalt eyes. Sonja's pendant gleamed on his furry chest. He was considering his options when a tremendous impact rocked the catacombs, as though an asteroid had suddenly crashed to earth several meters away. Centuries-old skulls toppled from their perches. The bony chandelier plunged to the floor, the electric lights shattering in an explosion of glass and sparks. Only the phosphor glow of the security monitors lit the crypt, casting flickering shadows on the werewolf and his foe.

Out of the corner of his eye, he spied dust falling from the ceiling of the catacombs leading away from the crypt. The entire tunnel appeared in imminent danger of collapse, taking with it his best chance to get away from both Leyba and the invading Death Dealers.

Time to exercise the better part of valor, he concluded. As much as he longed to test his claws against Leyba's armor, he could not risk falling into the hands of the Death Dealers again, not when he was so close to gaining his ultimate revenge. *Destroying Viktor takes priority; Leyba is just a petty irritant by comparison.*

Turning his back on the vengeful Gypsy, he dropped onto all fours and raced toward the crumbling catacomb. The very walls seemed to rumble angrily around him as he bolted into the beckoning tunnel, putting as much distance as possible between himself and Leyba's losing battle against the determined Death Dealers.

The skull archway collapsed behind him, cutting off Leyba's only escape route. As his powerful legs carried him into the future, he could not help reflecting on the irony that in the end, he owed his life and freedom to his greatest enemies.

Selene took a moment to catch her breath, then lifted the lip of the iron bell and crawled out from beneath its protective shell. As hoped, she found herself in a musty catacomb, somewhere beneath the ancient chapel. Glancing upward, she saw a jagged hole in the floor above her. The rat-a-tat of nonstop gunfire descended through the gap, and she surmised that Kahn and his team were still trying to shoot their way past Leyba's automated defenses.

Good, she thought; that meant she had the murderous lycan all to herself. All lycans were her enemy, of course, but this hunt had become more personal than most. She owed Leyba for her comrades' deaths.

She rose to her feet and brushed the dust and powdered stone from her leathers. In theory, Florescu's underground command center was directly ahead. A flickering artificial glow, coming from farther down the tunnel, seemed to confirm that assessment. The unmistakable growl of a ravening werewolf sent adrenaline racing through her veins, and she hurried down the subterranean corridor, past carved stone niches holding rotting human skeletons. Her faithful Berettas rested impatiently within her grip.

The eerie radiance, which she soon identified as the light from one or more television or computer monitors, grew brighter as she approached a stone archway that seemed to open up onto a larger chamber beyond. She slowed her pace and approached more cautiously, wary of an ambush.

In the dim lighting, however, she never noticed the desiccated human rib, which snapped beneath the sole of her boot with a sound like a rifle shot.

Shit!

An armored figure stepped into view. Selene caught a whiff of burning petrol and threw herself backward only seconds before a stream of bright orange flames erupted from the nozzle of an all-too-familiar flamethrower.

She instantly flashed back to that awful night in Statue Park, when she had been forced to run for her life, leaving the burning corpse of another vampire behind.

Not this time, she vowed. She had planned ahead for this reunion.

Holstering her right Beretta, she drew a silver throwing star from her belt and hurled it with surgical precision. The spinning *shuriken* zipped past the flames and sliced through the fuel line linking the nozzle of the flamethrower to the metal tank mounted on Leyba's back.

A startled cry emerged from the lycan's helmet as the flamethrower's fiery tongue sputtered out. Fuel sprayed from the ruptured line, dousing Leyba with gasoline, which streamed down the matte-black surface of her armor to pool at her feet. "Dammit!" the lycan cursed.

But Selene wasn't done yet. Just as she had prepared, she flung a small plastic capsule at Leyba's helmet. It exploded on impact, smearing thick black paint across the lycan's bulletproof visor, effectively blinding her.

Leyba angrily ripped the helmet from her shoulders. Feral blue eyes glared at Selene with murder on her mind.

Selene stared at the face of Diego's killer. She had never seen this woman before, not even in the coven's comprehensive files on all known lycans.

"Who are you?" she demanded, aiming her Beretta at the woman's forehead. Part of her wanted to execute Leyba on the spot, in payment for the lives of Diego and Yoshio and the Elders knew who else, but first she wanted some answers. "What's behind this insane vendetta of yours?"

"Wouldn't you like to know, blood?" Leyba snapped, tempting fate and testing Selene's patience. "Maybe I just don't like immortals."

Keeping one eye on the petrol-soaked lycan, Selene scanned the dimly lit crypt. Shattered restraints occupied one corner of the vault, while the debris-covered floor also bore the bloody imprint of a lycan paw. She remembered the feral growl she had heard only minutes ago and looked in vain for a lurking werewolf. A heap of ancient skulls was piled high in front of what looked as if it might have been another set of catacombs. A squashed silver bullet rested on the floor, not far from the broken steel fetters.

What kind of party did I just interrupt? Selene wondered dubiously. *Is there more to this story than just one crazed lycan bitch?*

Before she could interrogate Leyba further, another burst of gunfire sounded overhead. Glancing up at the monitors, she saw that Kahn and the others had finally managed to shoot apart the chapel's automated weapons systems. Her fellow Death Dealers advanced toward the rear of the chapel, looking for the entrance to the catacombs. Selene hoped she hadn't complicated their search too much by dropping a jumbo iron bell through the back of the church.

Leyba's own eyes followed her gaze. A bitter expression came over her face as she saw the other Death Dealers making their way toward her underground lair. She eyed Selene strangely. "Your eyes look like hers, you know . . ."

Whose? Selene blinked in confusion.

"Filthy vampire whore!" Leyba snarled, overcome by a sudden uncontrollable rage. Her face began to change, the nostrils flaring, jagged fangs erupting from beneath her lips. Half wolf, half woman, she charged at Selene as though determined to claim one last victim before meeting her inevitable end. Her cropped black hair turned into a wild mane. Froth bubbled from her snapping jaws.

Selene's first shot ignited the petrol covering Leyba's armor. Flames raced up the lycan's body, setting her sable tresses ablaze. She howled in agony, sounding far less human than Diego had when he went up in flames. Selene stepped backward to avoid the thrashing figure, then emptied the rest of the silver magazine into Leyba's skull, just for good measure.

The burning lycan dropped to the floor of the demolished crypt, her lifeless form joining the scattered bones of generations of long-dead monks. It was, Selene decided, a more dignified death than she deserved.

She heard bootsteps rapidly descending a staircase somewhere behind her. "Selene!" Kahn shouted. "Where are you?"

"Over here," she called back.

Lowering her gun, Selene waited for Kahn and his team to catch up with her. Soon they would be able to retrieve Mason and return to the mansion, where she would be able to report to Kraven that yet another homicidal lycan had been exterminated.

Mission accomplished, she thought, yet a few lingering questions remained. Walking away from the smoldering corpse, she picked up the squashed silver bullet she had spotted earlier. Slick with lycan blood, it still felt warm to the touch. *Where did this come from?* she asked herself. *And whose bloody pawprint is there on the floor?*

She wondered if she would ever know what had really happened here.

Epilogue

Epilogue

had leaned over the computer. It was then turned... when it was... Indicated that at the center... and when there was nothing... taken... and her eye was rest...

I am pleased to see you back in business, Leonid," Lucian ...d with a sly smile. "I understand you recently ran afoul of ...ew of my, er, competitors."

Florescu swallowed hard. "That's nothing you gentlemen ...ed to worry about," the florid arms dealer insisted. "Just a ...ght misunderstanding."

With Statue Park compromised, the meet was taking ...ce in the bowels of a long-forgotten bomb shelter deep ...neath the city's subway tunnels. Water dripped from the ...ling, nurturing the mold growing over the concrete walls ...d cracked cement floor. Raze stood behind Lucian, ...tching over his leader.

"Of course," Lucian reassured Florescu, amused by the ...man's attempt to dismiss his recent involvement with ...th the Death Dealers and Leyba. He had no doubt that the ...mpires had sternly warned Florescu against selling any ...re arms to their enemies, yet if there was one thing Lu-

cian had learned over the centuries, it was that human
avarice was almost as undying as the Elders themselves.

*War makes strange bedfellows, just as some might say that
strange bedfellows can often start a war.* He, for one, was per
fectly willing to keep dealing with Florescu, provided th
human could provide the lycans with the weapons the
needed to defeat their immortal foes. *I have taken many risk
and endured many ordeals to come this far, but all my sacrifice
will have been worth it when Viktor lies dead at my feet—an
my dear wife and child are avenged at long last.*

"What do you have for us today, my friend?"

"Something I think you will be very interested in," Flo
rescu replied with a gleam in his eye. He was clearly happie
talking shop than reviewing his recent misadventures
"Something completely new."

He snapped his fingers, and one of his thuggish subordi
nates handed him a black leather briefcase. Florescu opene
the case to reveal several rounds of glowing blue ammuni
tion. Each cartridge seemed infused with encapsulated sun
light.

"Experimental tracer rounds," the human announce
proudly, "newly developed by the American military and al
ready available on the black market—for very special cus
tomers."

Ultraviolet ammunition, Lucian realized. His eyes lit up a
he grasped the possibilities. *Daylight harnessed as a weapon.*

"Well?" Florescu asked. "Are you interested?"

Acknowledgments

My second excursion into the *Underworld* proved just as enjoyable as the first, thanks to the gracious efforts and assistance of the many people involved in the project. My thanks go to my editors past and present at Pocket Books, John Ordover and Ed Schlesinger; to the good folks at Sony, including Grace Ressler and Cindy Irwin; and to my agent, Russell Galen. And special thanks go to screenwriter Danny McBride, who generously allowed me to pick his brain regarding obscure points of *Underworld* lore.

Finally, as ever, thanks to Karen, Alex, Churchill, Henry, and Sophie. Just because.

About the Author

A lifelong fan of vampires and werewolves, Greg Cox wro[te] the official novelization of the first *Underworld* movie. [He] has also written numerous books and short stories set in t[he] universes of such popular series as *Star Trek, Daredev[il], X-Men, Roswell, Iron Man,* and *Xena: Warrior Princess.* Rece[nt] horror fiction can be found in the anthologies *Buffy [the] Vampire Slayer: Tales of the Slayer,* Volumes Two and Four.

He lives in Oxford, Pennsylvania.